HARD TO KILL

A JANE SMITH THRILLER

JAMES Patterson

AND MIKE Lupica

LITTLE, BROWN AND COMPANY

LARGE PRINT EDITION

Little, Brown and Company
Hachette Book Group
1290 Avenue of the Americas, New York, NY 10104
littlebrown.com

First Edition: September 2024

Little, Brown and Company is a division of Hachette Book Group, Inc. The Little, Brown name and logo are trademarks of Hachette Book Group, Inc.

The publisher is not responsible for websites (or their content) that are not owned by the publisher.

The Hachette Speakers Bureau provides a wide range of authors for speaking events. To find out more, go to hachettespeakersbureau.com or email hachettespeakers@hbgusa.com.

Little, Brown and Company books may be purchased in bulk for business, educational, or promotional use. For information, please contact your local bookseller or the Hachette Book Group Special Markets Department at special.markets@hbgusa.com.

ISBN 9780316569910 (hc) / 9780316579476 (large print) / 9780316582407 (Walmart edition)

LCCN is available at the Library of Congress

Printing 1, 2024

LSC-C

Printed in the United States of America

HARD TO
K LL

A JANE SMITH THRILLER

ONE

JIMMY CUNNIFF CALLS TO tell me to get dressed, we're taking a ride.

"Am I allowed to ask where we're going?"

"To check in on an old friend."

"Am I allowed to ask which one?"

He tells me. And I tell him I'll be ready when he gets to my house.

Now we're standing at the top of steps leading up and into a courthouse, a new one for us, the Nassau County Courthouse in Mineola.

Rob Jacobson, my former client, one I recently got acquitted of a triple homicide in Suffolk County, is about to turn himself in one county over. On another triple homicide. Like Jimmy always says: You can't make this shit up.

"Apparently he's gonna tour," Jimmy says. "Like the Ice Capades."

"Ice Capades ended years ago."

"I was making a larger point," he says.

"You often are."

Jimmy is my investigator, wing man, best friend, former hot-ticket NYPD detective. His divorce from the cops wasn't pretty. But then neither were my divorces from husbands one and two.

"Here he comes," I say.

"It's a perp walk," Jimmy says. "Not a red carpet."

With plenty of time to spare, it got out, the way everything gets out in the modern world, that Jacobson and his new lawyer, Howie "the Horse" Friedlander, were going to do it this way, here at the courthouse. Jacobson's renting a house not far from mine in Amagansett, between East Hampton and Montauk. Having him led out of a residence in handcuffs was not the optic Howie or Rob wanted, as if any good optics could come from a moment like this.

The crowd today isn't the size that we routinely got during trial in Riverhead. A trial that ended, thanks to Jimmy and me, in Jacobson's acquittal. But now, in what felt like a blink, he has been charged with murdering another father, wife, teenage daughter. It was the Gates family last time. This time the Carsons of Garden City.

"He says he was set up," I tell Jimmy Cunniff.

"Set up again? For three more murders? What are the odds?"

"He's either a psychopath or the unluckiest SOB on the face of the earth."

"I'll take psychopath for two hundred, Alex," Jimmy says.

"Alex Trebek is dead."

"So are all those people."

Howie Friedlander is walking next to Rob. Howie got his nickname because he's about the size of a jockey. A case like this is the kind of ride lawyers like Howie and me look for their whole lives but hardly ever get.

All Howie has to do is what I did:

Win.

Rob Jacobson's trying to look as sure of himself as ever, the cameras back on him, at the center of his own three-ring circus all over again.

It's been a few months since I've seen the aging frat boy. He seems a lot older and the thousand-dollar suit he's wearing hangs on him a little bit.

But there's a deeper difference in him today. Maybe his old friends in the media can't see it. But I can.

In his eyes, mostly.

"He's scared this time," I say to Jimmy.

"You mean he wasn't scared last time of living out his days in a federal prison?"

"Last time he had us," I say.

Jacobson is doing something he never used to do on his way into the courthouse in Riverhead: ignoring the questions being shouted at him, from both sides of the railings.

He only stops when he sees Jimmy and me.

As soon as he does, he taps Howie on the shoulder and holds up a finger, telling him to wait.

Then walks right over to me, ignoring Jimmy.

"Janie," he says, suddenly back into character and back in charge of things. "You shouldn't have."

"You're right. I shouldn't have."

"Come on. Admit that you've missed me."

I make a gesture that takes in the whole scene.

"What I don't miss is all this."

"You sure?" he says.

"Like they say, Rob. Another fine mess."

"I'm innocent."

"Tell it to your new judge."

Before I can step back, he is leaning close to me. "We need to talk."

Howie Friedlander wants to hear what's being said, so he steps in, puts a hand on Jacobson's arm, and gently pulls him toward the courthouse doors.

"We need to get this over with," Howie says.

I watch as the doors open and two cops who could double as bouncers step outside. One of them is carrying handcuffs, which means shit is about to get very real for Rob Jacobson.

Again.

Before they put the cuffs on him, he turns around and looks back, his eyes suddenly pleading with me. Not even trying to hide how scared he is, Jacobson puts one of his free hands—while they still *are* free—to his ear and mouths as if into a phone: *Call me.*

Then, as if he's silently shouting at me, he mouths one last word:

Please.

Then the cuffs go on him and the doors open back up and he's gone.

Jimmy sees me staring in Jacobson's direction. Maybe he can see in my eyes that I didn't just tell Jacobson the whole truth. I don't miss scenes like this, that *is* the truth. But I do want to be inside the courthouse, breathing that air again, instead of being out here, like I'm on the sidelines at the big game.

"Why do you look like you've got a hook in your mouth?" Jimmy asks.

"Probably because I do."

TWO

IT DOESN'T TAKE LONG for my friends in the media to move right in on me after Jacobson is inside the courthouse.

"Let's get out of here," Jimmy says as he sees them coming.

I grin at him. "And why would we want to do something like that?"

It's worth pointing out here that for me to get more face time on cable news than I did during Jacobson's first trial I'd have to be involved in a juicy sex scandal.

I wish.

From behind one of the cameras I hear, "Do you think he's going to get away with it again, Jane?"

"Are you implying that he got away with something when I was the one representing him?"

"Just asking you what you think."

"The jury spoke," I say. "Almost as eloquently as I so often did during that trial."

It gets a laugh.

I put up my hands in mock surrender now.

"Ladies and gentlemen, pay close attention, because you may never again hear these words from me, at least not consecutively: No comment."

But it's as if at least one of them has read my mind about being here.

"Come on. Don't you wish it was you perp-walking right alongside him?"

"No."

Yes.

"Tell the truth, Jane."

"You can't handle the truth," I growl.

It gets another decent laugh, if only from fans of *A Few Good Men*. I tell them not to forget to tip their waiters, and Jimmy and I start walking down the steps.

We're only halfway down to the street when I see a guy in a hoodie staring up at me from the sidewalk, about fifty yards away. Giving me—in words that Jimmy taught me from his cop days—the hard eye.

Jimmy is still walking, not realizing right away that I've stopped, as the guy in the hoodie extends his arm, cocks his thumb and index finger of his hand, makes a shooting motion.

Then he's around the corner and gone.

Now Jimmy stops.

"You look like you saw a ghost," he says.

"I did."

"Ghost got a name?"

"Yeah. Nick Morelli."

A star witness in Rob Jacobson's first trial until the Coast Guard found his fishing boat out on the water near Montauk without him in it.

"He's dead," Jimmy says.

I'm still staring at where he'd been on the sidewalk.

"Or not."

THREE

"YOU'RE BEING WAY TOO quiet," Jimmy says as we're getting off the Northern State and onto the Long Island Expressway.

"I'm thinking."

"You generally do most of your thinking out loud, you don't mind me saying."

"What if it was Morelli I just saw?" I ask. "And if he's been in hiding, why did he make a point of making sure I saw *him*?"

Nick Morelli had once dated Laurel Gates, the teenage daughter of Mitch and Kathy Gates, all three of whom Jacobson had been charged with murdering. He'd testified about seeing Jacobson making out with Laurel Gates across the street from the Stephen Talkhouse in Amagansett the summer she died.

The day after Morelli testified, he'd disappeared.

Body never found.

Jimmy says it's still an open case with the East Hampton Police. Being Jimmy, he checks from time to time, but they keep telling him there has been no evidence—credit card or bank statements or sightings—that Morelli is still walking among us.

"There was a time when we thought Jacobson might have had Morelli killed, remember?" I say to Jimmy. "Just because Morelli wasn't going to do our guy much good alive."

"Stop me if you've heard this one before," Jimmy says. "But our *guy* said he didn't do that, either."

We drive in silence for a few miles before Jimmy suddenly bangs his hands hard on the steering wheel. Saying something I know he's wanted to say since we left Mineola.

"You can't really want to defend him on this Carson thing."

I smile because I can't keep myself from smiling. Because he's got me and we both know he's got me, the only thing left is to slap the cuffs on me.

"You're right, Cunniff. I can't tell you that."

"Shit," he says. "I was afraid of that."

We make the turn at Exit 70, getting on Route 111, the connector road that will put us on 27 all the way to my house in Amagansett.

"I knew I shouldn't have taken you there," Jimmy

says. "I should've known that being that close to the action would be like some kind of drug."

"Yeah," I say. "That's what I need these days. More drugs."

"Poor choice of words."

"But I can't lie to you, Cunniff. For a few minutes there in front of that courthouse, I actually felt like my old self again. Like I'm still the woman you refer to as Jane Effing Smith."

I don't tell Jimmy Cunniff the whole truth and nothing but, that there on those steps, I felt so alive I forgot I was dying.

That I didn't have effing cancer.

FOUR

DESPITE THE USUAL HAMPTONS traffic heading east, Jimmy gets me to my doctor's appointment in Southampton with plenty of time to spare.

When we pull up to Dr. Samantha Wylie's office, I ask if he wants to come in with me, and hear whatever I'm about to hear, so later he can't accuse me of holding back.

"Gonna take a hard pass on that."

I'd asked knowing the answer. The only people in the world who scare Jimmy, truly, are doctors. He'd rather have somebody pull a gun on him. The only doctor he tolerates is my boyfriend, Dr. Ben Kalinsky.

And Ben's a veterinarian.

Sam Wylie isn't my oncologist. Just my internist. But so much more than that. She's been my friend since junior high school. I sit down across from her desk, where she's been reviewing my latest test results.

I have stage 4 cancer. Neck and head. Mostly neck.

You know how people talk about the Big C? Trust me when I tell you something:

There's no Little C.

When I visit Sam's office, I sometimes imagine her as a professor about to tell me I'm flunking my major, and the final is just around the corner.

I've just gone through my second round of chemo. Against all odds, I've still got my hair. And don't plan to give it up without a fight.

I'm not giving up without a fight, period.

"Good news first, or bad?" Sam says.

"Surprise me."

"The good news is that your numbers haven't gotten any worse."

I go blood test to blood test. All cancer patients know the drill, labeled day-to-day like some injured athlete. It doesn't feel like living.

"Wait for it," I say.

"The bad news, unfortunately, is that they haven't improved to the extent that I'd hoped they would after two rounds of chemo. Or might."

Sometimes I feel as if the last really good news I received is when the jury foreman in Rob Jacobson's trial said, "Not guilty."

"So what do we do?"

"We keep doing what we're doing," she says. "At least we've slowed its progress, which ain't nothing, pal."

"You've talked about this with Dr. Gellis."

Who is my oncologist.

"I have started to feel, since the patient is my friend Jane Smith, that I talk to Mike Gellis more than I talk to my husband these days."

She then patiently explains to me, not for the first time, the confidence she has in Gellis. She hasn't changed very much since we went to school together and she was the smartest girl in our class. Even smarter than me. Not that I was going to admit that to her, then or now or ever.

"We both know what great physical condition you were in before this," she says, "when you were still training for those no-snow biathlons. And you're still young."

"Define young."

I thought that might get a smile out of her. It doesn't. Tough room.

"I'm not even classifying today's numbers as a setback," she says. "Just part of the process."

I smile at her now.

"You're one of the best friends I've ever had," I say. "So please don't bullshit me. Remember, we've got a deal about you not bullshitting me. So promise me again that you won't."

Her voice is suddenly small enough to fit in the palm of my hand.

"I promise," she says.

Then, just like that, she starts to cry.

Really cry. Chest heaving. Sobbing-type crying. Trying to get air into her and failing. Losing it.

Maybe I'm too stubborn, even now, to break down in front of her. There have been times, plenty of times, when I've lost it in the privacy of my own home. Or with Dr. Ben. Or on a beach walk with my dog, Rip.

Just never in front of her.

Before I know it, she's come around the desk and the two of us are standing in the middle of her office, arms around each other, her tears finally beginning to subside. She's the doctor. She's the one giving me what passes for good news these days. Only now I feel like I'm the one consoling her.

When we both step back and out of the hug, Sam Wylie's face is a mess for what I think is the first time in all of recorded history. She does manage to smile now, embarrassed.

"Sorry about that."

"Don't take this as a criticism," I tell her. "But you may think about doing some work on your bedside manner."

I get to the door, but then turn around.

"I don't want you to die," Dr. Sam Wylie says.

"Imagine how I feel."

FIVE

Jimmy

JIMMY IS SURPRISED WHEN he looks up to see
Jane walking toward his car so soon. But it doesn't
matter.

He knows that even if she's inside with Sam Wylie
until tomorrow morning, he'll still be out here waiting
for her. Jimmy has promised her he won't let her go
through this alone. He keeps his promises.

Especially to her.

"So how did it go?"

"Great," she says.

"You don't look great."

"Thanks for sharing."

"You know," Jimmy says, "people say that sarcasm is
the weapon of the weak."

"I am weak," she says in a quiet voice.

"No," he says, "you're not. You're tougher than me,
and nobody is tougher than me."

"Does that even make sense?"

"To me it does."

They're stopped at the light where Main Street merges into 27. He feels her eyes on him, turns so he can see her.

"What?"

"I love you," she says.

Then his girl smiles at him and it's as if all the seriously bad shit she's got going in her life suddenly has washed away.

Jimmy actually feels a catch in his throat as he remembers, all over again, how much he loves her right back.

Not *that* way, of course.

It was never that way for either one of them, even when they first started working together and he was coming off a divorce and Jane was coming off her second. He loves her like a sister. Or the best friend that she is.

Both, probably.

He'd always known he'd take a bullet for her if he had to, something that finally happened, twice, while he was working the Carson case. Knows in his heart that he'd take cancer of the neck and head for her if he could, without hesitation.

"How did it go for real?" he says when the car is in motion and going through Water Mill.

"Basically, no change, according to the good doctor."

"So, for today it's a push," Jimmy says. "A push isn't a loss, right?"

"Sure," Jane says, without much enthusiasm.

Then she tells him to take the back roads, she likes the back roads better.

By the time they get to Scuttle Hole Road, Southampton becoming Bridgehampton, she's asleep. Jimmy punches the button for the Miles Davis channel on satellite radio. He really only bought satellite radio because it makes it easier, this far from the city, for him to actually hear Yankee games in the summer.

Miles is playing "So What."

In a soft voice, covered by Miles's horn, Jimmy says, "You either beat this or else."

From the seat next to him he hears, "Or else what?"

He grins. "I've never been entirely sure. But it always sounds good."

In that moment he hears the little ping that means a text message. It's Jane's phone, not his.

She reaches into the pocket of her jeans and comes out with it.

"*What the hell?*" she says.

"What?"

"Text. Unknown number."

Then she reads it to him:

Wouldn't you just rather die in peace?

Jimmy turns down the radio, so it's quiet then in the front seat of his car.

Jane is still staring at her phone.

"Is that all of it?" Jimmy says.

"It's signed."

"By who?"

"Joe Champi."

"Excuse me?"

"You heard me. It's signed 'Joe Champi.'"

"Morelli is only *presumed* dead," Jimmy says. "Champi really is."

"I know," Jane says. "I killed him, remember?"

SIX

JIMMY TAKES THE THREAT seriously, even if it came from a dead guy.

Joe Champi: former NYPD the way Jimmy is, the guy Rob Jacobson called Uncle Joe. The guy who'd been a fixer for Jacobson from the time he was first cop on the scene when Jacobson's father killed a teenage mistress named Carey Watson and then himself.

Jimmy is convinced that it was Champi who made Nick Morelli's boat come back without him that day. And who made Gregg McCall, the Nassau County DA, disappear after McCall hired Jimmy and me to look into the murder of the Carson family.

Jimmy is also convinced that it was Champi who ambushed and murdered Jimmy's old police partner, Mickey Dunne, after Mickey started looking too hard into Rob Jacobson's past. Fixing for Jacobson until the end.

Jimmy makes calls to his former NYPD contacts

now, keeps making them after we arrive at my house. And keeps getting the same answer, that unless whoever sent the message is an idiot, it came from a burner phone.

"So absolutely no way to trace where the text came from?"

"Sure," Jimmy says. "Right after we put a trace on where the wind comes from."

Rip the dog goes crazy when we arrive. Being a trained investigator myself, I have come to suspect that Rip likes Jimmy better than he likes me.

But then most people do.

We're sitting on my back porch. Jimmy is throwing a tennis ball. Rip brings it back, every single time, as if he's willing to do this until the *end* of time. He doesn't bring it back quickly. The old boy has lost a step. Or two. But ask yourself: who hasn't?

"He doesn't do that for me," I say.

"Must be a guy thing."

Jimmy throws the ball as far as he can. Off goes Rip.

"I don't get a lot of text messages from dead guys," I mention to Jimmy.

"Especially not ones that you *made* dead."

Jimmy is heading over to his bar from here. Dr. Ben Kalinsky is coming over in an hour to cook dinner for the two of us. Ben's not a better cook than I am. He's nicer.

"Okay, Jimmy. Who sends me a text like that?"

"Jacobson?"

"Why? We both know he wants me to defend him again, even if he hasn't asked yet."

"It is still my opinion that he's batshit crazy."

"He's locked up now until his bail hearing. You can get a burner into jail?"

"Are you joking?" Jimmy says. "I'm surprised guys aren't starting their own YouTube channels from jail."

I check my watch.

"I'm sorry," Jimmy says. "Am I boring you?"

"Got a hot date. Need to take a shower, do my makeup. Then do hair, while I still have my hair."

Jimmy has his beer in his left hand. Keeps throwing the ball with his right. Rip keeps fetching it. Rip is supposed to be way past his sell-by date. But the old boy really is hanging in there.

Like he's beating the odds.

My hero.

"Whoever is messing with you," Jimmy says, "which means messing with *us,* knows who Champi is. Or at least knows about him. Could whoever it is know what Champi knew?"

I laugh now. "Are *you* shitting *me*? We don't even know what Champi knew."

I take the ball from Jimmy and show off my arm. Nobody ever accused this particular girl of throwing like a girl. Rip chases it down to the end of the yard. Then he turns around, gives me a look.

And drops it in front of Jimmy.

Screw him. Game over. I put the ball on the table and leave it there. That'll show him.

Jimmy finishes his beer, then asks me one more time if I'm sure I saw who I thought I did in Mineola.

I didn't get that good a look at the guy, I tell him, but it sure looked like Nick Morelli to me.

"Who knows, maybe it is a day for the walking dead," Jimmy says.

"Gee, there's a lovely thought on which to build a night of romance."

"Too much information," Jimmy says, and leaves.

I'm on my way up the stairs to start getting ready for my date when there's a knock on the door.

When I open it, Jimmy's standing there.

"You forget something?"

He wordlessly hands me his phone, so I can see the text on the screen.

I still owe you 2 one.

Uncle Joe

I hand Jimmy back his phone, asking, "Who knew you could get cell service like this in hell?"

SEVEN

BEN COMES THROUGH THE door with a bottle of wine along with the lamb chops he's going to grill, fingerling potatoes, a salad he gave in and bought premade at Citarella. When we're settled in on the couch, Rip on the floor in front of us, wineglasses on the coffee table, Dr. Ben wants to know why I haven't been answering his calls, and where the heck I've been all day. He really does say heck. And darn sometimes. And gosh. Me, I can swear like a champ. He hardly ever does. Part of his all-around niceness. He's too good for me and keeps finding new ways to prove it.

I don't tell him about my visit with Dr. Sam. I do tell him about the trip to the courthouse.

"Boy," he says, "you sure know how to show yourself a good time."

"What can I tell you? I'm a complicated girl."

He leans over and kisses me. "And one who looks

beautiful tonight, let's get that on the record right now, counselor."

"Liar."

"Nope, I'm a doctor. Our motto is do no harm, especially not with flattery."

"Down boy."

"You talking to me? Or Rip?"

He asks if I want him to heat up the grill. I tell him there's no rush.

"How did he seem? Jacobson, I mean."

"Worried, frightened. Maybe a little of both. He thought he was in the clear, and now this. I haven't seen the evidence, but there must be enough to charge him."

"Will he get bail?"

"With another charge like this right on top of his trial? I doubt it. And he's a flight risk even if he does make bail."

We both sip wine.

"But he's not your problem, right?"

"Totally not," I lie.

The Cabernet is Train Wreck. One of my favorites, appropriately enough.

"Do you think he did it?"

"You want to know the truth?"

"Why I asked."

"I have no idea."

"But then you're still not sure if he killed the Gates family, are you? Even though you got the acquittal."

"Even though."

He smiles at me. When he smiles at me like this, I feel as if my ability to breathe properly has been compromised. Something that seems to happen whenever I'm in the presence of this exceptionally good and exceptionally attractive man. With everything I've got going on, during the first trial and then its aftermath, I've got this vet in my life who makes me feel like a schoolgirl.

I do manage to get some air into me.

"I need to tell you something," I say.

He waits.

Another deep breath.

Out with it, girl.

Tell him you've got cancer.

It's a minor miracle you've managed to keep it from him this long.

So tell him, already.

"I think I might want to defend Rob Jacobson again."

EIGHT

AFTER DR. BEN IS up and out in the morning, Rob Jacobson calls from Nassau County Correctional. It's still only eight o'clock. I'm actually surprised the call didn't come earlier.

"I need to see you as soon as possible."

"Want, or need?"

"When it's you, Janie, it's usually both."

Ah. There's the old Rob.

"And just exactly what do you need to see me about?"

Don't make it easy for him.

Fair's fair.

Nothing's easy for me these days.

"You've probably figured it out. But I'll tell you when you get here."

He knows I'll be there and so do I. It's why he placed the call and why I answered it.

When I'm finally in another jailhouse visitors' room with Rob Jacobson two hours later, it occurs to me how little time has passed since Jimmy and I went to his house after I shot Joe Champi, and I played the recording I made before Champi died. The one where Uncle Joe told me that they'd just tried Jacobson for the wrong murders.

Jacobson is uncuffed when he sits down across the table from me. I've already told the guard not to worry, I might not be at full strength these days, but had no doubt I could take the prisoner in a fair fight if necessary.

"Look at us," Jacobson says. "A team again."

"We were never a team, Rob. Our relationship, if you can even call it that, was strictly transactional."

He leans forward, as if his wrists were still cuffed, and clasps his hands in front of him.

"I was set up."

"Not to put too fine a point on things, but for which murders?"

"All of them."

"Tell it to your new judge. And your new lawyer."

He smiles now. I know from experience how hard it can be to knock the smile off Rob Jacobson's face. I even tried, without success, to slap it off one time.

"We're still undefeated, you and me."

"Pretty small sample size."

"But one huge case."

I take a closer look at him than I had outside the courthouse. He definitely has lost weight. And a lot of what I once thought was a permanent tan. Or maybe they've taken away his bronzer. Hair a little grayer. Matching the color of his jumpsuit.

"You could get me out of here at my bail hearing," he says.

"Howie the Horse's problem. Not mine."

He leans forward a little more. I'm worried that if he gets any closer, he might try to kiss me.

"Let's cut to the chase," he says.

"Do people even still say that?"

"I'm saying it. And asking you this: How much will it take for me to get you back?" He shrugs. "You have to know that's why I asked you here."

"I do. Not exactly rocket science."

"But you still showed up."

"Maybe I'm just here for the begging."

"Won't be any. And want to know why? Because I know you as well as you know me."

He nods at me before he leans back.

"How are you feeling, by the way?"

I hadn't known that *he* knew about my cancer until after his acquittal. He and his dear friend Joe Champi both knew, as it turned out. Champi gave that up before he tried to kill me.

"None of your business."

Another shrug. "Fair enough. So what do you think about my offer?" He grins. "You know you miss the rush of being in the game. You miss the thrill *you* got when you got *me* off." Slight hesitation. "So to speak."

He's right. But I'm not going to tell him that.

"On that note," I say, "time for me to go."

"So what's your answer?"

I stand.

"I'll get back to you," I tell him when I'm at the door and the guard is opening it for me.

"Oh, you'll be back, all right," Rob Jacobson says.

"You're that sure of yourself?"

"All my girls come back sooner or later," he says. "At least the ones who are still alive."

NINE

I'M AT THE END of the bar with Jimmy, having already told him about my meeting with Jacobson. The Yankee game is on both television sets. No Mets tonight. It means Jimmy has pulled rank on me. But then he does own the place. There have to be some perks that go along with that.

"You're gonna do this, aren't you? It doesn't matter what I say to try to change your mind."

"Maybe I'll be the one to change my mind while I'm away."

"No, you won't. We both know you were gonna do it before they had the cuffs on him the other day, whether you gave him a firm answer today or not."

I point at the TV set closest to us. "Would you mind terribly putting on the Mets game?"

"Yes, I would mind."

"Try to be the bigger man for once."

"Bigger man than you? Impossible."

That gets a laugh out of me. I reach for his bottle and take a sip of his Montauk Summer Ale.

"Hey," he says.

I tell him not to worry, I'm not contagious.

"It really would make me feel better if I could watch the Mets."

"You're playing the sick card over a *ball game*?" But he reluctantly points the remote at the set and switches to the Mets.

"So we're doing this with Jacobson," Jimmy says. "I'll be a sonofabitch."

"We're both doing it."

"You know and I know that Jacobson sent Joe Champi to kill you, whether he'll ever admit that or not. Then we get to the fact how you're the one who keeps telling me that you want Jacobson to be innocent of killing the entire damn Gates family because you don't want to die thinking you got an acquittal for a guilty man."

He realizes instantly that he had just put "dying" into play.

"I didn't mean that the way it came out."

"I know."

"But you just said to me the other day that you still don't know about this guy. Jacobson."

"That I do know."

"So explain to me, in a way I can understand, why we're going back to work for him."

"I can't."

He grins. "Jesus, Janie," he says. "You really are sick. *In the head.*"

I look at him, my own face serious now. "And please don't tell me again that life's too short to waste on Rob Jacobson."

"Even if I want to?"

"Even if."

He asks me if I want something to drink. I tell him that I'm going to head home.

"You really ready for this?"

"You mean another trial?"

"You know that's not what I'm talking about."

He's talking about the trip I am taking to Switzerland in the morning, to the same cancer clinic outside of Geneva where my sister, Brigid, was treated. Targeted immunotherapy was on the table. Enhanced chemotherapy. Perhaps some experimental meds not yet FDA-approved. If I respond favorably to their treatment program, I'm only there two weeks. If I don't, then we see.

My sister and me. Both with cancer, if different kinds. I know. Some families have all the luck. My mother died of it, too. At least Brigid's is in remission for the time being.

"I'm as ready as I'll ever be," I tell Jimmy. "Mostly because I have nothing to lose."

In a soft voice, my tough-guy partner says, "I do."

He walks me out the back door to my car.

We hug for a long time.

"This has to work," I whisper to him.

"I'll mention that to God at Sunday Mass this week," he whispers back.

That gets me to pull back.

"Wait. You're going to church again?"

"Desperate times."

"Would you mind asking Her something for me?" I ask.

"You got it."

"Ask Her in a nice way if She could please stop screwing with me."

TEN

IT'S BEEN A LONG day for me, much more activity than I'm used to, at least lately. Tomorrow is going to be much, *much* longer.

But I'm not ready to go home yet.

It's the beautiful twilight time on the South Fork of eastern Long Island. What I think of as my own personal magic hour. It's the kind of night, and light, that reminds me why I wanted to live out here full time, a hundred miles from the big, bad city, twenty miles from land's end in Montauk.

It's September, my favorite month of the year, even though I'm about to give the best part of it away with both hands.

I go past the turn to my house, keep going to Indian Wells Beach, park my car. No other cars in the lot. Just the way I like it. My own private beach, free of charge.

I get out and take off my sneakers and walk down

toward the water, wanting to feel the sand underneath my feet.

There are a lot of beaches in this part of the world that I love. But I love this one the most, maybe because it's so close to my house.

Out here I rarely feel the urge to think out loud. Almost like I want the ocean to do my thinking for me.

I walk and I think, mostly about tomorrow, heading east toward Atlantic Beach, the next one up.

Just me and an ocean perfectly lit as if by a moon shining down on a movie set.

Built for the movie of my so-called life.

I keep walking, taking it all in, beach and water and moon and sky. There's a point, every single day, when I think the same thing:

This can't be happening to me when I'm going this good.

I've just won the biggest case of my career. I'm in love with Dr. Ben Kalinsky. Really in love, for the first time in my life. I told myself I felt the same before both of my marriages. I realize now I was only kidding myself, as if wishing could have made it so, both times.

I suddenly feel myself smiling, thinking about all the days and nights when I had Rip on this beach with me, walking and running and then walking a little more, watching him get stronger, if not a whole lot faster.

Like he refused to die.

Now it was going to be my turn, a long way from home.

Before I, the only person on this beach tonight, head for the parking lot, I suddenly stop and then I am shouting at the ocean, or maybe God Herself, about just how goddamned much I want to live.

Then I get back into my car and drive past the turn for my house one more time and keep going to the Springs.

I park my car in the driveway and ring the doorbell, remembering the first time I made a trip like this, to this same house.

When Dr. Ben Kalinsky opens the door, I say, "There are some things I need to tell you."

ELEVEN

WE SPEND THE NIGHT at Ben's. When we're in bed he tells me that he's known about my cancer all along.

"Why didn't you say something?" I ask.

"Because you were the one who needed to say something."

"Have I mentioned lately how much I love you?"

He leans over and kisses my hair.

"I'm sorry," he says softly. "I didn't quite catch that."

In the morning he follows me back to my house so he can pick up Rip the dog. Ben offers for about the tenth time to drive me to the airport. I tell him that Brigid has insisted. I'd finally told her about my cancer the night before, having waited as long as I could, aware that she had cancer problems of her own.

When we're saying good-bye on my porch, he says,

"Remember: You're not allowed to fall for some mysterious stranger with an accent."

"What if it's a hunky male nurse feeding me good meds?"

"Well, that's different," Dr. Ben says.

"Get out of here before I start crying."

"Because you're already missing me?"

"Missing Rip," I say.

I'm packed and ready to go when Brigid pulls up an hour or so later, after which we begin the two-hour ride to JFK.

Brigid could afford Switzerland because Rob Jacobson, her college friend from Duke and former lover, paid for it. And said he was willing to do it again if he had to. I can afford the Meier Clinic because of what Jacobson paid *me* for getting him acquitted. I'd called him by now at Nassau County Correctional in East Meadow to tell him that I was taking his case, but that he is sworn to secrecy until I get back.

Brigid and I are about ten minutes out from Kennedy when she says, "Rob is so pleased that you've agreed to represent him again."

"So much for swearing him to secrecy," I say.

"He says we're all family."

"The hell we are."

She's wearing her glasses. Hands at nine and three

on the steering wheel. Even her driving posture is perfect.

"He's still my friend, Jane."

I angle myself to face her, so she can glimpse my smile. "Everybody makes mistakes."

"You're the one going back to work for him."

Still smiling I say, "I worry sometimes that it's spread to my brain."

"He says he's innocent."

"Got it," I say. "And I'm just heading off to Switzerland because I had a sudden urge to look at a bunch of Alps."

Brigid finally pulls the car up in front of the United terminal. I get my carry-on from the back of her SUV. Since I don't expect to do much socializing, or having the need to dress up in Switzerland, I'm traveling light.

After we've finished our hugging and kissing, Brigid says, "I want you to remember one thing while you're away."

"Not to lose my passport?"

"Just remember that you're Jane Fucking Smith, and you do not lose."

Not even "effing."

And her the good girl.

TWELVE

Jimmy

AN HOUR AND A half later, Jimmy is in the back room at P. J. Clarke's, a New York joint where they shot a lot of the movie *The Lost Weekend.* Jimmy thinks the place should long have been awarded landmark status where it's still sitting—or maybe squatting—at the corner of 55th and Third.

Detective Craig Jackson, the best friend Jimmy has left at the NYPD now that his old partner Mickey Dunne is dead, is waiting for him.

They're here because Jimmy really was way ahead of Jane on Rob Jacobson and the weird connection there is between the two of them, whether she wants to admit it's there or not. Like some hold the guy had on her even before the hook was in her all over again, even though there had been a time during the first trial when she actually slapped the shit out of him.

Jimmy has decided to go all the way back to the

beginning with the mutt, which means the day when Jacobson's old man did shoot a teenage girl named Carey Watson before shooting himself.

Or so the police report said at the time.

Only now Jimmy is doing what all good cops do when they don't feel they've satisfactorily buttoned up a case. He is starting all over again. The back-to-square-one rule of detecting. He is doing it in Clarke's with Craig Jackson. Jackson, he knows, is here out of friendship, on his own time, because he believes in the brotherhood the way Jimmy does, even if Jimmy is no longer officially part of it.

Looks-wise he has always reminded Jimmy of another Jackson, Samuel L., even before Samuel L. really hit it big and seemed to be in every other movie and even more television commercials.

"I ordered for you," Jackson says to Jimmy.

There are two beers on the table.

"What if I want something stronger than beer?"

"Then go ahead and order it, cowboy. Just means more beer for me if you do."

They get right to it. Jackson doesn't like small talk any more than Jimmy does. He told Jimmy one time, when they were both still on the job, that if Jimmy wanted to know how his wife and kids were doing, wait for the Christmas card.

Jackson taps a finger on the folder between them on the table.

"This is the original file on the Lolita shit," he says, "which you might remember is what they called it at the time. I copied it for you, along with generously adding the notes I've made about what I've found out since you got me interested."

He drinks some beer.

"It turns out there was another kid there that day," Jackson says. "At Jacobson's town house."

"Wait," Jimmy says. "I never heard about that."

"You weren't supposed to." Jackson nods. "Was in the original file, but then it wasn't. Kid named Edmund McKenzie. Apparently left long before all the shooting started. I had to do some digging, but it looks to me as if McKenzie, who had a rich daddy of his own, managed to get himself whited out of the story at the time. Or white-boyed out. Now this may come as a shock to you, Cunniff, but I'm thinking that money might have changed hands to make it happen."

"I'm shocked," Jimmy says. "Shocked, I tell ya."

"The kid was a classmate and asshole buddy of young Rob. Along with being somebody who'd dated the Watson girl same as our Robbie did, before Jacobson's daddy, that old perv, decided he wanted a taste."

"But you say the McKenzie kid left the party early?"

Jackson smiles brilliantly now, teeth very white against very dark skin.

"The original version, which I eventually found,

being the kick-ass detective that I am, is that he did. But McKenzie's daddy is even richer than Jacobson's was." He shrugs. "Feel free to connect the dots."

"They ever question the kid?"

Jackson shakes his head. "Just his daddy."

"What the fuck."

"Beautifully said."

Jackson holds up a finger. "Gets better. There's something else in play, just not sure where. There was always a rumor that McKenzie's old man, big hedge fund guy now, Thomas McKenzie's his name, was connected when he was starting to build his fortune."

"Connected to who?"

"Sonny Blum."

"The Jewish Godfather? No shit."

"No one has ever been able to nail it down. But a story went around at the time that maybe Edmund McKenzie's old man had friends in low places to help him clean up any and all of his kid's messes."

"Like Joe Champi cleaned up for Rob Jacobson."

"Uh huh."

Jimmy waves the waiter over and orders a Jack Daniels. "You've been busy, Action Jackson."

"Fuckin' ay."

Jackson says it's all in his notes, but he'd rather tell the rest of it. A few years later, he tells Jimmy, there was a beach party at McKenzie's father's house in

Southampton. Everybody there young and rich and drunk and stoned and stupid.

"Sounds like a real slice," Jimmy says.

"Long story short?" Jackson says. "McKenzie gets accused of rape when the party's over. Then his daddy makes *that* go away. But after the girl gets paid off, which is what I'm sure happened, our friend Edmund started telling anybody who will listen that it was Rob Jacobson who raped the girl, and that he, McKenzie, had gotten set up. And was going to get even someday."

"Rape kit?"

Jackson smiles again. "Somehow it managed to magically disappear."

"Seems like there was a lot of that going around."

"Ya think?"

"You're telling me that McKenzie might have had a fixer in the department, too?" Jimmy asks.

"Or maybe Sonny Blum did, if he still had his hooks into McKenzie's old man."

"They didn't used to call it Fun City for nothing," Jimmy says to Craig Jackson.

THIRTEEN

Jimmy

CRAIG JACKSON WALKS OUTSIDE to 55th Street, saying he was going to make some calls to see if Edmund McKenzie might be in town and making his usual round of clubs.

While Jimmy waits for him to come back, he looks around and remembers the days when a little guy named Frankie Ribondo ran the back room like a small country; when some nights you had to wait for the men's room, with its old stand-up urinals, because two of Sinatra's guys were posted outside while he was inside.

It takes less than ten minutes for Jackson to announce he has managed to locate Edmund McKenzie, reminding Jimmy for the second time tonight what a world-class detective he is.

"Swear to God, a reporter from Page Six who I help out sometimes tracks him on her phone, so she's got a better sense of where the stupid might break out on a given night. It hasn't yet tonight, but McKenzie is currently pregaming at Bemelmans."

The Bemelmans Bar at the Carlyle.

Jane took Jimmy there a couple of times when they were celebrating big wins in court, back when Jane still thought she would keep winning forever, maybe at everything except staying married.

In the cab uptown Jimmy finds a couple of pictures of Mc-Kenzie on his phone, from Page Six, appropriately enough. And spots him right away at a small corner table facing the piano, checking his phone, highball glass in front of him, full.

McKenzie gives Jimmy a bored look when Jimmy sits down across from him. Calmly puts his phone down before taking a big pull on his drink.

"I'm saving that seat for my date."

"Good to know. But what you need to know is that I'm a cop and there are matters we need to discuss."

"Care to show me your badge?"

"Care to empty your pockets?"

McKenzie's eyes widen, in mock fear. "Oh no. Am I about to be arrested for possession, officer? What year do you think this is?"

McKenzie takes another sip of his drink. "So, what's got you all worked up? My old parking tickets?"

"I'm taking another look at the day your buddy Rob's old man died and took that kid Carey Watson with him," Jimmy says. "And what I'm wondering is if you were really gone from the town house before the shooting started."

"Who says I was there?"

"I say."

"And all this time later, you're here because of *that* shit?" McKenzie said. "You lose a bet?"

The piano player has just eased into "Stardust." Jimmy idly wonders how many times he's played it in bars like this, with hardly anybody really listening, or caring.

"You should be talking to your client, tough guy. Hear the guy's a real killer."

"My client?" Jimmy grins. "So you know who I am. Tough guy."

"I've got cable and everything."

"I'm told you and Rob were close once."

"*Were* being the operative word. You want to know how close we are now? Fuck him, that's how close."

"What happened to a beautiful friendship?"

McKenzie checks his phone again. "Long story."

Jimmy leans forward, grinning at him. "Actually, Eddie, I just now learned the story. Or at least the good parts about how he got you in a frame for a rape you say he committed. Do I have that right?"

"As rain." He drinks. "What other interesting things have you heard about me?"

"That you were going to get him back even if it took the rest of your life."

McKenzie brightens. "Like framing him for a triple homicide, or even two? Well, wouldn't that be a dream? Listen, I was actually kind of a hot-shit science whiz when I was still at Princeton. But that was before I went back to my two real majors: drinking and girls."

"What really did happen that day at Jacobson's place when that girl died, along with Jacobson's old man?"

"You mean what do I *think* might have happened after I was long gone? I think Rob went crazy and killed them both and then the scene got staged by a cop who went on his payroll that day and didn't get off till he was the one who got shot to death by that lawyer you work for." He grins. "Whew, a mouthful like that makes me thirsty."

He drinks.

He's no longer grinning when he puts his glass back down.

"You think you know so much about me, Cunniff. You don't know jack shit. Or who *I* know. Or what happens if I make a call about you thinking you can come here and jam me up like this."

Before Jimmy can respond, a young woman about half Mc-Kenzie's age, if that, appears at the table, wearing something Jimmy would call a dress if there were more of it.

"Amber," McKenzie says.

"Eddie," she whines. "I would have been here already if you sent the car like you promised."

McKenzie acts as if he hasn't heard and stands. So does Jimmy.

"Now beat it," McKenzie says to him. "Before I make that call."

Jimmy thinks about grabbing him by the lapels of the skinny, too-short blazer he's wearing and bouncing him into the wall. But there's no point, at least not tonight. Jimmy doesn't want to be the one on Page Six tomorrow morning for busting up Edmund McKenzie and the Bemelmans Bar.

He's on his way out the door when McKenzie calls out to him. "Hey, Cunniff."

Jimmy makes a half turn.

"How many times are the two of you going to let him get away with murder? Asking for a friend."

FOURTEEN

Jimmy

WHEN HE'S GOTTEN OUT of the city and is finally flying up the LIE, Jimmy has finally calmed down, knowing how close he'd come to bouncing McKenzie around, even in a bar full of cell phone cameras.

What he had done, though, before McKenzie knew it was happening, was get him up and out of his chair and into the small lobby between Bemelmans and the Café Carlyle, where Bobby Short used to play the piano in the old days.

Out there, nobody around except the girl in no clothes, Amber, making bird noises, Jimmy put McKenzie up against the wall.

"You got any other smart comments you want to make?" Jimmy had said to him, their faces close enough that he could smell the whiskey on McKenzie's breath.

"You have no idea what a mistake you're making," McKenzie said.

An older couple walked through the door from Madison Avenue, took one look at them, and left.

"It's the other way around," Jimmy said. "I'm the last guy in town you want up in your shit."

McKenzie had smiled at him.

"Well, maybe not the last guy."

"You think you're some kind of badass, Eddie?"

The smirk was back in place. "No," McKenzie said. "But I know some. Now get your hands off me before I start yelling for security."

Jimmy did. McKenzie walked out onto Madison, his girlfriend following him.

Jimmy gets to Southampton and cuts through Shinnecock Hills Golf Club; taking North Sea and then Noyac Road, the bay on his left, passing Ferry Road because he's not going down to the Shelter Island Ferry but into North Haven and the turn on his street.

He loves driving around at this time of night, hardly any other cars out, sometimes going a couple of miles without seeing any headlights or taillights.

As late as it is, he knows it's still too early in Switzerland to call Jane and tell her about his night. And before she left he promised her, and himself, that he wasn't going to give her daily updates while she was over there, even though she tells him it will take her mind off the reason she went there in the first place.

As if any update he was going to give her could do that.

He knows he needs to find out more about McKenzie, figure out how much badass he might have behind him, maybe even from Sonny Blum, who might still be in business with Edmund McKenzie's old man. Who might still be fixing things for the family.

One thing was certain: McKenzie had seemed pretty goddamned sure of himself, after he'd asked how many times Jane and Jimmy might let Rob Jacobson, his old high school pal, get away with murder.

Jimmy parks his car in the driveway, finally ready to sleep, as if driving back out has really driven the adrenaline he was feeling at Bemelmans right out of him.

They're waiting for him inside the front door, on him in the dark before he can throw the light switch.

A needle goes into the back of his neck then.

The last thing Jimmy hears is a voice behind him in the darkness saying, "Remember what this feels like?"

FIFTEEN

Jimmy

WHEN HE COMES TO, he feels as groggy as he did after Joe Champi—or at least Jimmy always assumed it was Champi—jabbed him at the home of Gregg McCall, the Nassau County DA who'd hired Jane and Jimmy before disappearing for good.

Except it's my goddamn house this time.

He can see enough, barely, to know they have him in his bedroom at the back of the house. It's dark enough that he can make out shapes, just not faces. There's a big guy to his right, the one who's just said, "Rise and shine." The woman, smaller, is to Jimmy's left. Jimmy knows it's a woman because he hears her say "You must be joking" when the guy asks if she's sure Jimmy's wrists are secure enough.

"You want to tell me what this is about," Jimmy says. "I was hoping to turn in early."

"And you did."

56

"You have a name?" Jimmy says, turning his head just enough to face the guy.

Nothing.

"You and Champi have similar games. The two of you ever work together?"

"Funny story," the guy says. "We started working together when we were involved in the same situation. Long time ago. Representing different interests."

"Whose?"

Nothing.

"Aren't you going to introduce me to your date?" Jimmy says.

Jimmy is bound to what he's sure is one of his kitchen chairs. Before he even knows she's on him, the woman hits him with what has to be a full wind-up slap across his face, nearly knocking the chair he's bound to over on its side.

"Do we have your attention now?" the guy asks.

"What," Jimmy says, "you got tired of sending texts and came here for a more hands-on approach?"

"Do you want a little more?" the woman asks.

"Not tonight, dear. I have a headache."

The guy chuckles. "I told you he's a funny bastard. Didn't I tell you this guy is a funny bastard?"

"Is there a purpose to this visit?"

"Now that you mention it," the guy says.

Jimmy thinks he even sounds a little like Champi.

Older voice. Raspy. Some New York in it. Almost like he could have come out of Jimmy's old neighborhood.

"I want you and your friend, when she gets back from Switzerland, to stop looking into things you don't need to be looking into. We like things we fix to stay fixed."

"You know about Switzerland?"

"Want to know which seat she sat in on the flight over?"

Jimmy feels his fingers losing circulation. Knocked out and tied up in his own home. First time for everything. If there were just one, Jimmy could try to bull-rush him, even with his hands tied behind him. But there's two of them. And there are guys Jimmy was in the ring with who couldn't hit as hard as this woman.

"You want to waste your time defending that asshole again, have at it. I kept telling Joe he wasn't worth it, but Joe just didn't want the gravy train to end. Either way, Jacobson's going down this time."

"You sound pretty sure of that."

"He did it. I thought Joe told you that."

"So what's in this for you?"

"My business, not yours. Let the trial play out. Then you and the cancer patient go on and live happy lives. Hers will be shorter, of course. Just stay away from Eddie McKenzie, starting now."

"Did McKenzie call you after I put him against the wall?"

Now the guy laughs hard enough that he starts coughing.

"You got no idea what you're into. No wonder you busted out of the cops. You still don't know what you don't know."

"I know you could have killed me tonight if you wanted," Jimmy says.

"I need you around, to get her to *come* around."

"And if she doesn't?"

"Then she unfortunately dies of something other than cancer," the guy says. "While you watch."

He shoves Jimmy hard enough that the chair goes over and he ends up on his back. The guy laughs again and they leave him there.

SIXTEEN

AS SOON AS I'M awake at the Meier Clinic, every morning, first thing, I check my hair.

My nose is nearly pressed against the bathroom mirror after I've made what I consider to be a full forensic examination of my pillows, making sure I haven't backslid, hairwise, overnight.

It doesn't mean I'm getting better, necessarily. But still having a full head of hair makes me feel better.

About me.

My father was born on the West Side of Manhattan, Hell's Kitchen, but grew up in Seaford, Long Island, and finally went to high school there, with the old basketball coach Jim Valvano. And the more Valvano won in college basketball, including a national championship, the better friends my father and the coach had been when they were kids. At least, that's the way my father told it. Valvano later died of cancer himself, young, at forty-seven. At the time it was treated like a death in *our* family.

But when Valvano did finally pass, he still had a full head of hair. I read up on his final days, an old cover piece from *Sports Illustrated*.

One line stayed with me:

"His hair, against all medical logic, had survived massive chemotherapy."

So has mine, at least so far.

I'm undergoing another round of what the Meier team describes as "gentle" chemo, along with a daily multidrug cocktail they call multitargeted immunotherapy. They are even trying intense, experimental nerve therapy in the area on the back of my neck where the tumor was first discovered.

"Perfect," I tell Dr. Ludwig. "A pain in the neck for a pain in the neck like me."

He's German, maybe as much as one person could possibly be. Dr. Stone Face. Head of hospital. I get no reaction out of him.

"Tough room," I say.

Still nothing.

"Come on, doc. You know I'm funny."

He responds in his thick accent. "Ya. But maybe I'm just not *sinking* you are funny."

Five days in, and I might be feeling a little less weak, but maybe that's just me wishing to make it so. I'm a little less tired. Less like a daytime drunk by the time I've finished my various treatments. Afterward, I make myself go for a long afternoon walk, even when I'm not feeling up to it, picturing Dr. Ben and Rip and wishing they were with me, pretending I'm at some kind of five-star Swiss hotel instead of one of the world's leading cancer clinics.

I talk to Ben Kalinsky almost every day. Jimmy, on the other hand, has told me that he'll call me at the end of my first week.

He's never been much of a phone person.

"Even if something develops?" I asked him.

"The only development I'm interested in is you telling me the Swiss cheese heads are getting my girl better," he said.

It's on Day Six that Dr. Ludwig informs me that my numbers have improved, with as much emotion as if he were announcing a change in the lunch menu. Not a big improvement. He shows me the charts, and the pretty pictures. But for the first time in months, a doctor gives me some legit good news. The tumor has shrunk, if ever so slightly. It ain't nothing, as my father used to say.

There's a gym here, and I force myself to work out with weights and on the machines at least every other day, whether I feel the energy or not. All this means I'm fighting the way my mother did, and the way Brigid is fighting, in a way I hope would make my ex-Marine

Pops proud, even if I always knew I was the jock daughter he really wanted to be a son. He never came right out and said it, but we both knew it was true.

As far as he ever went was to tell me, "Show some balls," when he thought somebody had pushed me around in a hockey game.

He was brave growing up with gangs all around him in Hell's Kitchen, brave enough to take a bullet to the shoulder for a friend when he was a teenager, in the middle of some gang beef that didn't involve him. He never talked much about it, never told us the kid's name, the way he never talked about being in the Corps. Just that his friend would have done the same for him. It was, he said, what friends did for each other.

If they had the balls.

But my mother was brave, too. Even at the end, when she had nothing left and weighed hardly anything and barely had the strength to get out of bed, it was as if she were still the strongest of all of us. And the bravest. As brave as the Marine she'd married. Never whined. No woe-is-me. Never complained even when her last house became a hospice in the end, because there wasn't enough money to send her across the world to some fancy clinic and buy her more time.

Through it all, I never saw her cry.

I don't cry here, even when I'm alone. At least not yet. And never in front of strangers.

Tonight is another night when I'm wide awake at a little after four. And even though I've been telling myself since the moment I arrived to stay present, stay even, follow coaches' orders about not getting too high or too low, out of nowhere I feel overwhelmed suddenly, about everything that's happened and everything that might still happen.

Now I feel the tears coming.

I squeeze my eyes shut, like slamming a door.

I try something else I'd learned in sports. I try visualization, try to take myself away from here. Picture myself at Atlantic Beach, or Indian Wells, with Dr. Ben and Rip. Or at the end of Jimmy's bar, watching a ball game with him. Any ball game.

I picture myself in the courtroom in Mineola, walking and talking and playing to the jury and the judge and even the gallery, back in my element, totally.

And the tears don't come.

And then I'm talking to God again, softly but out loud, hoping that this is the night when She's really listening.

"You've got my attention, okay? You've had Your fun. I've clearly cleaned up my act. Gotten my priorities in order. Now how about You go bother somebody else?"

No answer.

At least I'm finally starting to feel my eyes get heavy

with something other than tears, sleep finally on the way. It's a good thing. Some nights rest never comes and I feel even more like shit the next day, all day.

"Eff cancer," I say, cleaning up the language just in case God does happen to be listening tonight.

It would be, on Her part, about effing time.

SEVENTEEN

SINCE MY FIRST NIGHT at Meier, I've been dreaming about my mother.

I was fourteen when she died of ovarian cancer. Brigid was sixteen. But my sister, as brave as she was being in her own cancer fight, never could handle it with Mom, from the day we'd all gotten Mom's diagnosis, which was essentially a death sentence. So Brigid would look for any possible reason to be out of the house, look for any excuse to avoid being alone with Mom. She even went out for soccer her junior year of high school.

Dad took on part-time construction jobs in addition to bartending, because insurance was covering only a fraction of Mom's hospital costs before she finally made the decision that she was going to die at home. She never came out and said it, but I knew it was because of the expense.

Because she was Mom.

So while Dad was working two jobs and with Brigid rarely around, I became Mom's nurse and caregiver. And best friend. Mostly I was there to talk to her, and listen, and keep her company before she'd drift off again.

"I don't want you to be sad when I'm gone," Mary Smith would tell me, repeatedly. "I've been blessed with two wonderful daughters and a husband who loves me. My regrets are small ones."

I knew her regrets were bigger than that, that she'd always dreamed about being a writer, across all her years as a school librarian. But with being a mother and wife and holding down a job, there was never enough time for her to write.

To the end, she would hold my hand and smile and tell me that if there were one truth she wanted to pass on, it was how precious life is, even as her own was draining out of her.

Then she'd be talking again about her hummingbirds. I sometimes thought she loved the ones that used to come to the feeder Dad built for her when we were still living in Patchogue almost as much as she loved him, and Brigid. And me.

She even nicknamed me Hummingbird, my mother did, because she said I was in constant motion. I had a tiny hummingbird tattooed behind my left hip bone, but she didn't live long enough to see it. Dr. Ben didn't even notice it right away when we started sleeping together.

He finally ran a finger over it one night and asked what it was.

"It's me," I said, and told him the story.

"I'm the hummingbird," I said.

Mom's feeder moved with us when we moved back to the city, a couple of years before she died. An old friend of my father's had given him a better bartending job. On our tiny balcony overlooking 11th Street, there was even a place for Mom to hang the feeder. The hummingbirds never found it, and though she ended up taking it down, she could never bring herself to throw it away, just packed it in a box with the rest of her belongings, like she was packing for a long trip.

In my dreams, I never picture Mom as sick. She's in her bed. The drapes are open so she could feel the sun on her face. Most of the time—not all the time, but most—I dream of her as a young woman, the great beauty she'd been when my father first fell in love with her.

I mention all of this to Dr. Ludwig one day. He's already asked me if during my stay here I'd like to meet regularly with a therapist. I tell him that I'm strictly here for body and fender work which, of course, goes right past him.

"What do you think my dreams mean?"

"Maybe it's as simple as you wanting her to be strong for you now," he says. "And, even more, to be present."

I rarely wake up sad or anxious after the dreams. Sometimes I realize I'm smiling when I open my eyes, as if my mom were the one sitting next to *my* bed now.

I'm out for my afternoon walk on one of the trails that goes up into the hills and eventually winds its way back down, mountains and blue sky everywhere, when maybe fifty yards ahead of me I spot a woman I've seen around the clinic.

I'm walking much faster than she is and cover the ground between us quickly because I do walk fast, turning even my afternoon walk at a cancer clinic into a competition.

When I'm alongside her I ask, "Would you like some company?"

She's wearing a rainbow-colored bandana to cover what can only be a chemo-bald head and protect it from the high afternoon sun.

She smiles as if her day suddenly got a lot better and answers in a British accent. "Well, wouldn't that be brilliant?"

Her name is Fiona Mills. She lives in London, informs me that her husband is a news "presenter" for ITV. They have two teenage daughters, around the same age Brigid and I were when Mary Smith was losing her own battle with cancer.

She asks me about myself. I tell her I'm a lawyer from New York.

"Married?"

"Twice. Divorced twice."

"Did you love them?"

I smile back at her. "I thought I did."

She laughs. Laughter, like just about everything, sounds better with a British accent.

"Without prying," she asks, "is there a man in your life now?"

"Yes."

"Do you love *him*?"

"More than my husbands."

She laughs again. "Have you opened your heart to him completely?"

It is a serious question, one that demands a serious answer.

"Not as much as I should. There's still a lot he doesn't know about me."

"Don't wait too long to tell him."

We walk and talk. I tell her that I've been dreaming about my mother almost every night. All of it. She tells me that when she got sick, she used to have the same kinds of dreams about her father, who died of pancreatic cancer when she was ten.

"I used to sit with him and hold his hand and not want to let go," Fiona says.

"I used to sit with my mom and listen to her talk about her life," I say. "*Her* dreams. Until the day when she closed her eyes and never opened them again."

Fiona Mills talks about her children then, how the younger daughter is the strong one. I tell her I played the same role in my family. I tell her we can turn around whenever she feels herself start to tire. She says she's fine, that this is her favorite time of day and she'd rather lengthen it than shorten it.

I tell her I feel the exact same way.

"I get up here and pretend that I've left cancer down the hill," she says.

I tell her I feel the same way about that, too.

"Maybe," I tell her, "we should consider making a run for it."

"I'm afraid it's a smidge late for that."

Even with her head covered, and as thin as she is, she is quite lovely. Her eyes are this lovely combination of green and hazel, as if they can't decide.

"Sadly," she continues, "this is the end for me here. My last visit to Meier. They've done as much as they can do. At this point they can't make up their minds whether it's weeks I've left, or months. However much time it is, it will bloody well be spent with my family." She drinks in mountain air. "Life really is so damned precious. I realized that before I got sick, if not as well as I should have."

I tell her that my mother used to tell me the same thing, when there wasn't a place like Meier for her to buy more time.

Fiona tells me she has ovarian cancer. I tell her that's what my mother had. She asks about my prognosis. I share the news from Dr. Ludwig and the rest of the boys and girls in the band.

"So you've more time than I."

"Just how much more is to be determined."

I've downshifted to match her pace. Even with that, she is beginning to slow. When I ask her again if she's ready to turn around, she says, "A bit longer, if it's just the same with you."

I tell her I've got no place to be except back down the hill, where the cancer is waiting for both of us.

When we do finally begin to make our way down the trail, she asks, "Are you spending your own time wisely, Jane, if that's not too impertinent or personal of me to ask?"

"I'm working as hard as I ever have." No point in wearing her out with the details about the trials and extraordinary tribulations of Rob Jacobson. "When I get back home, I'll begin prep work for a new murder trial."

"When will it begin?"

"Going off the usual timetable, sometime next year."

She stops. So do I. In this light, her eyes seem more

hazel now. Almost opaque. She doesn't say anything. She doesn't have to.

"I'm going to ask the judge to move it up," I say. "Usually, lawyers want as much time as possible to prepare. I want less."

Fiona nods, as if I've answered her unspoken question. "Your work, does it make you happy?"

"It's the one thing that makes me feel as if I'm going to live forever."

"Even more than the man in your life?"

"Something else that's to be determined," I say, and she smiles again.

On our way back, the sun finally begins to set, dropping toward the mountains.

"I read somewhere that if there were only a handful of sunsets in our lives, how valuable would they be?" she says now. "Well, I try to approach every hour of every day like that." Fiona drinks in more air. "Make me one more promise that you will do the same."

"I promise."

When we've made our way back to the front door of the clinic, she says, "Thank you."

"For what?"

"For making this last hour even more valuable than I'd already planned for it to be."

I ask her if I'll see her again before she leaves.

"I think not. This shall be our one and only good-bye.

I've only got so many of those left in me. Good-byes, I mean." She smiles one last time. "I'm afraid I can only allow one to a customer."

Her room is on the fourth floor. I watch Fiona walk down the long hallway leading to the elevator, moving more slowly than ever.

It's as if she feels me watching her. She stops and turns and gives me a small wave.

"Don't forget your promises."

The elevator doors open and close and then she's gone.

"Good-bye," I say.

EIGHTEEN

Jimmy

WHEN HE FINALLY CALLS Jane, Saturday of her first week at Meier, he doesn't tell her about getting ambushed and jacked up in his own house. He knows how pissed at him she's going to be when he finally does tell her, noted control freak that she is, somebody who always wants to know everything, and acts insulted when she doesn't, as if somehow you were cheating on her. Or like she failed some test.

But what's he going to do while she's over there going through what she's going through? Tell her the last thing his attacker, the guy Jimmy thinks of as Joe Too, said and that she might actually be safer where she is?

So, he lets her talk, lets her set the scene at Meier, gets him laughing when she describes Dr. Stone Face, tells him about this great English woman she met. That's before she gets to the good parts, what he's waited to hear from her today, about how they're cautiously optimistic about her treatments, at least so far.

Then she wants to know what's happening with the case. Jimmy knows he has to give her something; she'll get suspicious if he gives her nothing. So, he tells her about his meeting with Edmund McKenzie, and what McKenzie said before he left Bemelmans that night.

"You think McKenzie's the one who sent the texts?" Jane asks.

"I'll ask him next time I see him," Jimmy says. "Problem is he seems to have disappeared."

Then he tells Jane that he hopes he has more intel on McKenzie the next time they talk, and that he loves her, but that he has to go, he's got another call.

The call is from Craig Jackson, who proceeds to tell him he can't locate McKenzie. The gossip police can't either, tracking his phone doesn't help, according to Jackson's reporter friend, because it hasn't left his apartment on Central Park West. The girl from Bemelmans, Amber, hasn't heard from him. The doorman on CPW hasn't seen him. Neither has the caretaker at McKenzie's house in Southampton. What seems like an army of bartender friends all over Manhattan haven't seen him in a week, because Jackson has interviewed most of them.

"Guy's in the wind," Craig Jackson says.

"Tell me something," Jimmy says. "When did you start talking like a TV detective?"

McKenzie's first wife lives in Paris now. She hasn't spoken with him since one of the alimony checks was late around the first of the year. Jimmy gets the second Mrs. McKenzie on the phone. "I haven't heard from him," she says, "but if you do before I do, please give him a message: *Die.*"

Jimmy is sitting at his kitchen table after his calls with Jane and Jackson, laptop open in front of him, nothing to do except modern detective work, which means going from search engine to search engine the way he used to go walking up stairs and knocking on doors. Wanting to know as much about McKenzie as possible when they do meet again, and why somebody wanted him to back up, and quickly.

Jimmy reads the coverage on the rape accusation, what there is of it until his hedge-funder daddy, Thomas McKenzie, clearly had the stories vaporized. The hits just keep on coming after that. There's the night he crashed daddy's Jag out in Water Mill. He just left the Jag wrapped around a tree, called a girl to take him home, never got Breathalyzed.

There are the gory details on Eddie's two divorces, which read to Jimmy like all the other cringeworthy celebrity divorces he's ever known or heard about.

There's the time the Jets backup quarterback beat him up after finding out McKenzie's current girl on the side was the quarterback's wife.

On and on.

A timeline of classic, modern, celebrity bullshit.

One of the stories quotes McKenzie as telling a friend, "Who knew that some of these bitches would be such bad sports?" He later denied saying that.

The truth is, Jimmy thinks, Edmund McKenzie is the bitch.

Same as Edmund's high school buddy Rob.

A brotherhood of bitches, Jimmy thinks.

Maybe both of them are crazy.

NINETEEN

Ten days later

I TELL ROB JACOBSON he can announce that I'm defending him again, the night before I leave for Genève Aéroport.

"I kept our secret until now," he said.

"Just like a big boy."

I don't leave the Meier Clinic with a clean bill of health, even if I do leave with my hair. But all of my markers keep improving, if imperceptibly, right up until my last day. Dr. Ludwig has been in constant contact with Sam Wylie and Dr. Mike Gellis, my stateside oncologist, and they're on the same page with the protocols going forward, including what Dr. Sam calls the kick-ass Meier meds I get sent home with, like they belong in the kind of goody bag you get when you leave a fancy party.

Dr. Ludwig walks me to the car. Before I shut the door, I ask him what he honestly thinks my prospects are, both short-term and — hopefully — long-term.

He takes more time to answer than, frankly, I would have preferred.

"Put it this way," he says. "They are being better than when you were showing up here."

And nods.

I tell him to stop being so emotional, which gets an honest-to-God smile out of him. "Basically, I am hoping, Ms. Smith, that maybe you are being too stubborn to die."

Jacobson waits until I'm in the air and then fires Howie Friedlander. By then Jimmy has posted a picture on our new Instagram account of Jacobson and me standing on the courthouse steps in Riverhead after his acquittal.

The caption is simple and to the point:

SHE'S BACK.

When I get through customs and pull my carry-on into the baggage-claim area, I see a TV reporter and her cameraman standing next to my ride, Dr. Ben Kalinsky.

"Is it true, Jane?" the reporter asks. "You're taking the case?"

I'm just glad she's not asking why I was in Europe.

"It's been a while since I've gotten to say this," I tell her. "But see you in court."

She must know that means in a couple of hours I'm going straight from JFK to Rob Jacobson's bail hearing, if the LIE doesn't screw us between here and Mineola.

Yeah, I am *so back.* I hug Ben and kiss him and he pulls my bag toward where he's managed to park his car right out front.

When we're inside his new Range Rover, I look over at the huge sign for Terminal 7.

Suddenly fixed on the word, not the number.

Terminal.

"What are you staring at?" Ben asks.

"Nothing," I say.

TWENTY

DR. BEN, EXHIBITING FORMULA 1 skills I didn't know he possessed, gets me to Mineola with time to spare.

Rob Jacobson is already inside the courthouse waiting for me, as is Jimmy Cunniff. So is the esteemed Judge Alicia Kane, whose reputation for being an all-time, all-world hard-ass is well documented in my world.

Any photographers walking through the parking lot after we pulled in might have gotten a good shot of the attorney for the defendant changing into court clothes in the back seat of Ben's Range Rover as he pulls up to the curb.

I lean forward and kiss Ben with enough force and feeling that when I finally pull back it's clear I'll have to redo my lipstick.

As I smooth my skirt and blouse and reach for my

makeup bag, Ben informs me that he plans to stick around, that he's ready to finally see me in action. I call Jimmy and tell him to save a seat for Ben.

"Good luck," he says.

"Feel like I'm owed at least a little."

"The papers have been saying there's no way he's getting out on bail."

"They were only still saying that when he was represented by someone other than your sweetie."

The proceedings about to begin have drawn a big crowd, even bigger than when Jacobson turned himself in. It's not just him they're packing the steps to see, all the way down to the sidewalk and nearly into the street. Today I'm as much the story as he is. Maybe more.

Ben waves as I get out of the car and dash up the courthouse steps, rocking the ridiculously expensive short leather jacket I bought yesterday in Geneva.

Definitely more media today, but who's keeping score?

Well, I am, actually.

Mommy's home.

Katie Phang, a legal analyst from NBC, calls out to me. "As I recall, Jane, the last time you were here you said you didn't miss this."

"Hold on," I say. "Doesn't a girl reserve the right to change her mind?"

"So you're here because you *did* miss the action?"

"I'm here because my client is innocent and shouldn't spend another night in jail, and I'll prove that for a second time."

Running on pure adrenaline at this point, I clear security, then make a quick stop in the ladies' room for a hair-and-makeup check. I drink some water out of the bottle in my bag, pat my cheeks, say what I always say before I walk into court:

"Showtime!"

Only this time, out of nowhere, I suddenly feel myself start to cry. I put my hands on the sink and try to deep-breathe the tears away.

A woman comes in and sees me standing there with red eyes.

"Are you all right?" she asks.

For some reason, I think of Fiona Mills, hear her voice inside my head.

"Brilliant," I say.

TWENTY-ONE

JUDGE KANE'S COURTROOM IS already packed when I step inside. As the door closes behind me, I look around, nod, and breathe deep. I've spent the last two weeks and change filling my lungs with the cleanest air on the planet.

Just not this air.

I shake hands with Kevin Ahearn, who is already seated at his table, before shaking hands with his second chair, a red-haired woman he introduces as Maggie Florescu. There's no second chair for me. I'm still doing a single.

I see Jimmy and Ben right behind our table as I take my seat next to Rob Jacobson.

"You look good, Janie," Jacobson says.

"Try not to sound so surprised."

"I mean, because of where you just came from."

Only he can wipe the smile off my face.

"You know what we're not going to talk about, Rob," I say, keeping my voice low as I lean closer to him, "today or ever? Where I just came from. Or why I was there."

Before he can even attempt to get a last word in, we're all rising because Judge Kane has entered the courtroom and is about to take her seat behind the bench. She is small, blond, pretty, full of commanding attitude, projecting without saying a word that she's not going to take any shit.

The only *empty* seats I see are in the jury box. But we're a long way from filling those. I'm a long way from having to explain away questionable evidence with an even more questionable timeline. Rob Jacobson's fingerprints on a murder weapon the cops found months after the fact. DNA matches on both Lily Carson and her daughter, made only after Jacobson became a suspect. And the magical appearance of a time-stamped photograph of Rob Jacobson outside the Carson house the night before the whole family got gunned down.

One of my old law professors once told me that jobs without problems generally don't pay very much.

For now, the only job that matters is getting Rob Jacobson out of jail before Kevin Ahearn tries to put him there for good, and forever.

Ahearn goes first.

"Your Honor," Ahearn says, "I'd like to begin with

an apology for wasting the court's time with this frivolous and rather outlandish request for bail from the defendant and his new attorney. Or should I say old?"

I shake my head, grinning.

"Who you calling old, Kevin?"

That gets a rap of the gavel. Today even that is music to my ears.

"Ms. Smith," Judge Kane says. "We're all aware what a noted wit you are. Save it for when you're back outside and addressing the media."

"Now it's my turn to apologize, Your Honor. It won't happen again."

Well, we all know *that's* a lie.

"I'm well aware that you're not much for boundaries," the judge continues. "Just *you* be aware that I'm a bear for them."

Less than five minutes in and I'm not just back on the ice, I feel like I'm on my way back to the penalty box.

As I listen to Ahearn, I'm reminded all over again what a good lawyer he is, even if I did take him to the place Jimmy calls Beatdown City the last time we faced each other. He still has that commanding courtroom voice, and presence, and good timing, even playing to a jury of one today.

He's also playing a much stronger hand than mine.

Maybe everything old *is* new again.

"I understand, Your Honor," he says, "that the

defendant's previous trial should, by law, have no bearing on this one. But as we all know, that's a mere legal distinction. Because how can the fact that the previous charges against him *were* for equally hideous crimes possibly be considered irrelevant to the matter we're here to discuss, however a previous jury found?"

He walks over and sits down on the railing in front of the empty jury box, dropping his voice down a couple of notches, turning his tone conversational, as if he and Judge Kane are the only ones in the room.

"This man *was* previously accused of murdering a father, a mother, a teenage daughter. A daughter, as a witness testified in open court, with whom the defendant was having a wildly inappropriate relationship before her death."

"Objection," I say.

"No objecting today, Ms. Smith." She shakes her head, slowly, almost sadly. "No sustaining, no overruling. But you know that, don't you? This is a *bail* hearing, not a trial. So please don't interrupt again."

"Sorry, Your Honor."

"If you've already had to apologize twice, we're not really off to a good start, are we?"

This is Killer Kane, in full. I did a lot of reading about her on the plane, after I finished writing out the remarks I'm about to make. I know she's someone you don't want to antagonize, but sometimes I can't help myself. My pop used to tell me that no maple tree he ever saw ever turned into an oak.

"In conclusion," Ahearn says, "let me remind the court that this man is about to stand trial for a second triple homicide—same MO as the first one. How many times has something like that ever happened in this country's justice system? *Never.* And never will again. So we aren't just talking about a potential flight risk here. We're talking about a potential serial killer. For those reasons alone, bail should be denied."

He is walking back to his table when he stops and points a finger at Rob Jacobson.

"You've heard the expression about locking up your daughters, Your Honor? This man makes us want to lock up whole families, until the state locks him up for good."

You done good, Kevin, I think.

You're just not as good as me.

TWENTY-TWO

I DON'T WANT THE last words Judge Kane heard from Ahearn to hang in the air for a moment longer. So I come in hot, making my voice louder than it needs to be.

"Opposing counsel makes it sound as if my client is being charged, in front of this court, with six homicides. Only he's not. My client stands accused—falsely, I might point out—of three murders, for which he will eventually be acquitted and for the best possible reason: Rob Jacobson didn't kill any of these people, because he's never killed anybody in his life."

I take it down a notch now, reminding myself to *slow* down, not get ahead of myself, not sound as if I'm trying my whole case in the next few minutes.

"I don't need to remind Mr. Ahearn, as painful as such a reminder might be to him, that Rob Jacobson *was* acquitted by a jury of his peers in that first trial. Lo and behold, he wasn't guilty until proven innocent, as Mr. Ahearn wanted him to be, when all the facts came to light."

I'm pretty sure I hear Ahearn say, "What facts were those?" to Maggie Florescu, but the judge doesn't hear him. Or doesn't care, maybe because she likes him better than she likes me. Wouldn't be the first time. Probably won't be the last.

As long as I last.

"Judge," I say, "it would not only be unfair to force my client to remain in custody, it would be cruel in light of the time he has already spent behind bars for previous crimes he absolutely did not commit."

I move back to our table and point to Rob Jacobson.

"Mr. Ahearn says this man, this innocent man, is a flight risk. *No, he is not.* On the contrary, he isn't going anywhere, because he is going to stay right here and fight to clear his name. *Again.* And I'm going to fight right along with him."

I'm walking back to the table, talking to Judge Kane over my shoulder, surprising myself with what next comes out of my mouth before I can stop it.

"Like we're both fighting for our lives here."

Judge Kane says we will have her decision shortly, and that no one should leave the courtroom. She's not lying. She's back in less than ten minutes. A jury of one coming back.

"I'll make this short and sweet," she says. "Bail is set at five million dollars."

I see Jacobson lean forward, feel the steam come off him, know him well enough by now to know that he's about to say something stupid, react like this is a restaurant and he's shocked at the amount of the bill.

I stop him with a grip on his arm strong enough to quickly cut off circulation.

"Shut up," I say into his ear. "And pay up."

Judge Kane then begins to explain the conditions of Jacobson's bail apart from the money, including his wearing an ankle monitor, and how he will be released from the jail in East Meadow as soon as he has paid the $5 million either by check or wire transfer. And that any violation, of any kind, will land him back in East Meadow, with absolutely no chance at supervised release until the trial begins.

"Do you understand these terms as I've explained them to you, Mr. Jacobson?"

"Yes."

"Do you have any questions?"

"No, Your Honor, I do not."

"Then we're done here, at least for now," Judge Alicia Kane says, before heading for her chambers as if being chased, the click of her heels sounding like gunfire.

When the door shuts behind her, I turn to Rob Jacobson.

"You're welcome," I say.

Then he's the one putting a hand on my arm and telling me we need to find a conference room because there's something important he needs to tell me.

"It's about Brigid."

TWENTY-THREE

ANOTHER CONFERENCE ROOM FOR Rob Jacobson and me. Flashing back to the first trial, at the courthouse in Riverhead, I can't remember a single time I felt better about things when walking out of a room like this than when I walked in.

"We need to make this quick," I say to him. "I'm jet-lagged, I need a hot bath, and then I need a hot meal with the man of my dreams."

"Dr. Dolittle," Jacobson says.

"Funny," I say, "since Ben thinks I'm the one who talks to the animals."

"Ouch," Jacobson says. "And here I thought I still had a chance to be the man of your dreams."

"Only *in* your dreams," I say. "Now please focus, Rob. What *about* Brigid?"

He hesitates, somehow looking at everything in the room except me.

"There's no easy way for me to tell you this," he says finally. Still not looking at me. "But we're seeing each other again. She wanted me to be the one to tell you. And to tell you at the same time the subject is not up for discussion."

I'm not sure what he thinks my reaction will be. I'm not disappointed in him. There's nothing more he can do to disappoint me. I *am* disappointed in my sister. She's shown shockingly bad taste. What's more, she knows this man's history with women, the younger the better.

That she won't even discuss this with me feels like catching a break.

"Aren't you going to say something?"

I put my hands on the table between us and push off it. It takes all the strength I have left in me to get to my feet.

"Just do me one favor."

"Anything," he says.

"Try not to hurt her."

"I won't."

"I mean with the ankle monitor, dumb-ass," I say with a twinkle, and head out.

A probation officer is standing just outside the door.

"He's all yours," I say.

I'm about to cross Main Street when I see Dr. Ben. I come to a dead stop. He's talking to someone whose back is to me.

Guy in a hoodie.

My breath comes out of me like air coming out of a punctured tire, remembering the last time I exited the courthouse and saw a hoodie just like this one.

Despite being as worn out as I am, I'm running across Main, toward the parking lot and Ben's Range Rover.

As I get to the car, the guy turns around, pulls the hood from his head, sticks out his hand.

"Hi, I'm Edmund McKenzie," he says. "I wanted to meet the asshole who's still defending Rob Jacobson."

"I heard you were missing," I said.

"Who told you that?" McKenzie says.

Ben steps away from the Range Rover. "Problem?" he asks.

"I've got this," I tell him, motioning with my hand that he's to stay where he is. To McKenzie I say, "Get out of my way."

He puts up his hands. "No problem," he says. "I just wanted to ask you something."

He still hasn't moved.

"Have *you* ever been raped?" he asks.

He winks at me. Then he walks away. I can hear him whistling.

TWENTY-FOUR

Jimmy

JIMMY IS AT THE end of his bar, nursing a beer. Jimmy has the Yankee game on both sets, but he's paying no attention.

Jane and Ben left about fifteen minutes ago and Jimmy is thinking about Jane — what McKenzie said to her at the courthouse, what Joe Too said that night at Jimmy's house, and what a shame it would be if Jane died of something other than the cancer.

If Joe Too and his girlfriend could get to Jimmy that easily, they could get to Jane if they wanted to. It really does seem as if that sonofabitch Joe Champi has come back from the grave to terrorize them all over again.

Jimmy finishes his beer and is getting ready to leave when his phone makes that marimba sound Jimmy is too lazy to change, the one that has half the people in the bar reaching for their phones every time they hear it.

UNKNOWN CALLER.

"Cunniff," Jimmy says into his phone.

"McKenzie," the voice at the other end replies, as if trying to imitate Jimmy.

"Oh," Jimmy says, "it's the asshole who called my partner one today."

"Just wanted to get her attention."

"Well, let me get yours," Jimmy says. "Stay away from her. Or the next time I see you I'll swing you around by your nuts."

McKenzie waits a beat before responding. "I'm just calling to tell you what a *thrill* it was for me to finally meet Jane. I saw her leave the bar. Next time you talk to her, tell her I'd do her in a heartbeat."

Jimmy calmly gets off his barstool and walks out the door. His eyes are searching Main Street, then farther, past Bay Street, to where the harbor begins.

No sign of Edmund McKenzie.

But he's out here somewhere.

"Since you're obviously in the neighborhood, why don't you drop in and I can start bouncing you around right now?"

"Wow. The attitude. And here I was just trying to pay her a compliment. I would think she'd be happy that all the miles she obviously has on her wouldn't be a deal breaker."

"Fuck you."

McKenzie just laughs.

"You and your partner need to know something, Cunniff, in case you don't already."

"And what might that be?"

"Things aren't always what they seem."

TWENTY-FIVE

JIMMY CUNNIFF LOVES LIBRARIES so much he's now a board member at the John Jermain Memorial Library in Sag Harbor. As a kid in the Bronx he spent time at the one in Morris Park to stay out of trouble when his friends weren't.

That seat on the board also has something to do with an old girlfriend who worked in real estate before realizing that Jesus would be back before Jimmy was ever going to propose to her. She moved away and married somebody else, but Jimmy remains on the board.

The annual Friends of Jermain fundraiser is one of the South Fork's social events of the year. Jimmy, Dr. Ben, and I are in the packed auditorium at Pierson High School with people who in season turn up at every event wanting to be seen, hoping to be photographed for

Hamptons magazine, and generally congratulating each other for having money to give away to good causes like this one.

That I normally wouldn't have been caught dead—even when I thought that was an appropriate choice of words—at a society event isn't particularly surprising or meaningful to me.

But this is:

The room looks like a who's who from Rob Jacobson's first murder trial.

Rob Jacobson himself is home with his ankle bracelet. It's been a few days since the bail hearing and I haven't spoken to him or my sister, even knowing I'll have to open the lines of communication with both of them eventually.

But Claire Jacobson, Rob's soon-to-be ex, is keeping her distance on the other side of the auditorium. Otis Miller, whom I unintentionally outed during Rob's first trial, is there with his partner. I'm blocked on his name but they're chatting away with Gus Hennessy, Rob's former friend and Claire's onetime lover, who nearly torpedoed us during that first trial.

"The gang's all here," Ben Kalinsky says.

Jimmy snorts. "The Westies were a nicer gang than this."

He points out the event's chairperson, Elise Parsons,

who finally outlived her elderly robber-baron husband but still lives for nights like this. Jimmy informs Ben and me that for years the relationship between Rob Jacobson and Elise Parsons has been an open secret in the Hamptons.

"Wouldn't it be easier to talk about who he *hasn't* slept with?" Ben asks. "Just to streamline things?"

I smile at him and proudly raise a hand.

"Was it still going on with Rob and Elise even after he ended up under house arrest?"

"I heard it ended badly," Jimmy says. "But at least nobody got shot."

Our plan is to stay about an hour. Ben and I are a few minutes away from the opening bid in the live auction and a clean getaway when Elise Parsons heads straight in our direction. The aging debutante is, bless her heart, the whole package: hair, makeup, not a bad body, lots of good Botox, enough jewelry to open a Tiffany pop-up store. She was probably a knockout back in the day. But for the catty life of me, I can't imagine which day that might have been.

"Well," Elise says when she reaches me. "I see the bitch is back."

I keep my smile in place.

"Nice to see you, too, Elise. Usually people get to know me a lot better before they call me that."

"I'm aware why your hideous client is unable to attend," she says. "What's your excuse for being here?"

She does a little toss of her head, hair unmoving, for effect.

"It actually did take nerve for me to show up," I say. "But not for the reason you think."

"You're really going to defend him all over again? Seriously? Just how much of a whore are you?"

Elise looks flushed, voice continuing to rise, as if she's already had too much to drink. Up to now, the event has been relatively sedate, even boring. The auditorium hushes to the unspoken thrill of listening in on a scene like this.

"Elise," Ben says calmly, trying to diffuse an impossible situation. "Please lower your voice."

She doesn't. We're way past that by now.

Suddenly a younger and much prettier version of Elise appears. Known as Ellie, she shares Elise's name.

"Mom," she says, "I heard what you called her. But there's no reason to insult any other whores here tonight."

"Is he screwing you, too, Jane?" her mother asks me, loud enough now for the parking attendants outside to hear. "Everybody on the South Fork thinks so."

I look at Elise Parsons, then her daughter, then back at Elise.

I motion her closer and lower my voice to a near whisper.

"It was you who married Gramps," I say, smiling sweetly at her. "So who's the real whore?"

And with that, the chairperson for Friends of Jermain hauls off and slaps me, the sound so loud it echoes off the polished floor.

TWENTY-SIX

A FEW NIGHTS AFTER all the fun at the library gala, I invite Dr. Ben over for dinner, telling him that I'm doing the cooking for a change.

"What are we celebrating?"

"How about me walking away from Elise Parsons after she got the first swing in? My dad used to tell me that if a hockey fight was about to break out, I had to be the one to throw the first punch."

"I'm still shocked you did. Walk away, I mean."

"Not as shocked as I was."

He's very good in the kitchen, with an imaginative flair for cooking. What he doesn't know is that he's not nearly as good as I am. One of the many secrets I haven't shared with him.

But not for long.

When Ben arrives, he immediately tells me how good the house smells.

"So, what's for dinner? You've failed to mention that."

"Beef Wellington."

I've already poured the wine, and hand him a glass of Caymus, a Napa Valley cabernet far more expensive than what I usually spend on wine, no matter what the occasion. It just seems worthy of the meal I'm preparing.

I see genuine surprise in his eyes.

"*You* are making beef *Wellington*?"

"Don't sound so shocked, Dr. Kalinsky."

"I just know how difficult it is to get beef Wellington right."

"You mean because of the chopping and dusting of the steak with the flour, frying it just right in oil, then slow-cooking the whole thing with the perfect blend of red wine and garlic and mushrooms and onions, before topping it with a puff pastry that only the bravest home cooks ever think about attempting? *That* kind of difficult, doc?"

He stares at me. "Who *are* you? Somebody must have taught you to cook."

"Martin."

"Who's Martin?"

"My second ex-husband."

I take a healthy sip of my wine.

"That sonofabitch," I say.

TWENTY-SEVEN

DR. BEN KALINSKY MAKES the fair point that until this moment I've never talked about either of my ex-husbands, other than to jokingly refer to them as Thing One and Thing Two before I change the subject.

I counter now by reminding him that he never talks about his ex-wife.

He grins. "Who?"

I check on dinner. We've still got some time. Rip has taken his usual spot at our feet.

"Tell me about Martin."

Back at the Meier Clinic, I promised Fiona that I'd do a better job of opening myself up. I do that now, for the man I told Fiona I loved even more than either of the men I'd married.

So I tell him.

About the time I decided that even with my career

beginning to take off after a couple of high-profile cases, I needed a new hobby. I considered learning to play the piano. I chose cooking classes instead. A Manhattan culinary studio called Home Cooking on Grand Street. The teacher, as gorgeous as his accent, was Martin Elian.

He was going to be famous someday, he said, when he finally had enough money to open his own restaurant.

"Maybe even as famous as you are going to be," he told me.

I sip my wine, say to Ben, "I could tell you a little more about browning the puff pastry just right."

"I want to hear about the chef."

"Brigid was taking the class, too. I was sure he'd go for her. Martin was a few years younger than both of us, but she's always been the pretty one. Trust me when I tell you this: he was prettiest."

"And swept you off your feet, the romantic French bastard."

"Did he ever."

Martin and I were married six months later. By then he'd opened a bistro in the West Village and both of our professional lives were taking off. I still thought we were happy.

That made one of us.

"No happily-ever-after, obviously," Ben says.

"Unhappily, no."

The marriage lasted three years. Really, it only went bad over the final six months. He eventually drifted into an affair with his sous chef at the new, bigger place he'd opened on the Upper West Side. But he had already moved out by then.

Moved out and moved on.

"I wanted to blame it on our careers, but even I knew that was a cliché. It wasn't careers, plural. It was just one. Mine. He said being a lawyer was all I needed. I told him he was wrong. He said that maybe he knew me better than I knew myself. Before he walked out, I told him I could change if he'd give me a chance; I hated how needy and desperate I sounded, almost like another person. He told me that I was incapable of changing. And left. And nearly broke my goddamn heart in the process."

I sip more wine. "You want to know why I don't cook? Because it reminds me too much of him."

Ben doesn't say anything. He somehow seems to know that isn't the end of the story.

It isn't.

"He told me he still loved me and probably always would love me. But that I was incapable of living with anybody."

"Anybody meaning him, the master chef."

"Anybody meaning anybody," I say.

I reach for my glass and realize it's empty. I reach for his glass and take a sip.

"And none of that is the worst part," I say. "The worst part is what he said to me on the day he moved out."

No going back now.

Tell him all of it.

Now or never.

"He told me that losing the baby was probably the best thing for both of us."

TWENTY-EIGHT

ONLY JIMMY AND BRIGID knew about the miscarriage, one month into my second trimester, in what also turned out to be the last trimester of my marriage to Martin.

Now Dr. Ben Kalinsky knew, too, and knew about how after the miscarriage I found out I could no longer have children.

It was going to be a boy.

Going to be the son my father never had, as badly as he'd wanted one.

I finally announce when we sit down for dinner that I'm through talking about Martin Elian for tonight and maybe until the end of time. The dinner, by the way, is a complete triumph in Ben's estimation, not just the beef but the sides of potato-fennel gratin and the honey-glazed carrots.

"Please tell me this isn't one of his recipes."

"Ina Garten!" I say.

Before we change the subject, Ben says he'd like to make one final observation about Martin.

"Because of what he said about you having lost the baby, I fully intend to punch his teeth through the back of his head if I ever meet him."

"And you a man of peace."

"Do you ever see him?"

"Never."

"Do you still hate him?"

"I have long since decided he's no longer important enough to hate."

After we've finally cleaned up the kitchen and loaded the dishwasher and treated ourselves to a shared glass of Hennessy, we're leaning against the kitchen counter and Ben pulls me into a kiss.

"So why *did* you finally show off your cooking skills?"

"Because doing that made me happy tonight. Mostly because you're not him."

We're in the bedroom a few minutes later making love. Ben has already announced he can't spend the night, because of a ridiculously early surgery. When he's gone, I lie there in the dark, listening to Rip snore, thinking about how much I told Ben tonight, and how much I left unspoken, embarrassed to tell him how even after the divorce I would go up to the Upper West

Side sometimes and stare through the window of Café Martin, hoping for a glimpse of him.

Hating him and loving him at the same time.

But then I go to a much happier place, thinking about Ben Kalinsky again, everything we've shared tonight, how easy things are between us, the opposite of the theme-park ride that my relationship with Martin Elian was, even in the good times. I think about all this even as I worry, constantly, that the only reason that I've found someone I *can* live happily with—making a liar out of Martin Elian— is that I know it's probably not going to last.

As if cancer has hedged my bets for me before I can do that for myself.

I did open up to Ben Kalinsky, in a way I haven't opened up to any man, not even Jimmy Cunniff, in a long time. Or maybe ever. Somehow it felt easier, safer, opening myself up, even a little bit, with Fiona Mills, a perfect stranger.

Tonight was different. This was me telling my secrets to the man I really am in love with and realizing in the process—maybe—that I needed more than my work to make me feel alive.

For an hour tonight, the kind of precious hour Fiona spoke of, I didn't feel the need to be tough-guy Jane. I wasn't Jane Effing Smith. I opened a door and let Ben Kalinsky in.

And honored my promise to Fiona in the process.

When I finally fall asleep, I dream about my mother again. She's still young, like we're sisters, and we're walking on the beach, smiling and holding hands.

Behind her, hanging outside the window, is her hummingbird feeder, swaying slightly in the breeze.

This time a bird is there.

She turns to see it and smiles, not looking as if she's sick or dying.

She looks happy, watching the bird suspended in midair next to the feeder, as if frozen in time, and memory, from before she got sick.

The last thing I remember before I fall asleep is her staring at the feeder, the glass looking as shiny and new as it was the day my father built it for her.

She's smiling and reaching for the bird, as if wanting to put it in the palm of her hand, when my phone wakes me up.

JIMMY.

"We got two more bodies," he says.

"Who?"

"Another mother-daughter deal."

I realize I'm already standing next to my bed.

"*Who,* Jimmy?"

"Elise Parsons and her kid," he says. "The other Elise."

"How?"

"Two each in the head."

TWENTY-NINE

JIMMY IS WAITING FOR me on the street in front of the mansion in North Haven. The late Carl Parsons, the guy I called Gramps to his widow, had built the home for his wife and their daughter with a spectacular view of Noyac Bay and Shelter Island.

The place is actually just a couple of miles from Jimmy's own house. Couple of miles. Like a different world.

Carl's view of the water, I'm sure, is much better.

There is a police cruiser with lights flashing just inside the gated entrance, then more cruisers leading up to the house. Somehow Jimmy, who seems to know all police in the area, has gotten word to the cop acting as gatekeeper at the end of the driveway that I should be allowed through. When I get near the front door, I notice a black Dodge Charger Pursuit with a State Police license plate.

Jimmy is leaning against the cruiser as if it and this crime scene are his.

"Considering our client's romantic history with at least one of the deceased, it's probably a good thing the state has turned him into a shut-in," I say.

"Both of the deceased," Jimmy says.

I nod at the house. "How did you find out what happened?"

Jimmy shrugs. "People like talking to me. Or maybe it's the free drinks I hand out to cops like I'm handing out flyers."

Cops keep walking out the front door with evidence bags. Somehow, even as they walk slowly over to the black East Hampton Police Department van parked in front of the garage, there is an urgency to it all. An intensity. A focus. The bags go into the van and the cops turn around and go back into the house. Jimmy says it all the time. Murder is still the main event.

"So if our horny client has an airtight alibi, why am I here, exactly?"

"Because half the town saw one of the victims bitch-slap you at the benefit. And because it got around pretty quickly that before you walked out, you told the late Elise Parsons that if she ever tried anything like that ever again, her face would need more than filler."

"I was joking!"

"Ha ha," Jimmy says. "You funny."

I now see a cop that I don't recognize. Tall guy, *Top Gun* aviator jacket, Ray-Ban sunglasses, coming straight for us after he removes his surgical gloves and booties. Long black hair. He appears to be vain enough to have taken some of the gray out, though there's more gray than black in his beard stubble, like it's a mismatched set.

He's talking on his phone, which he now puts away. Grinning underneath the shades as if the best part of his day is about to begin.

Even from a distance I can see that he's trying too hard to be cool.

Way too hard.

Like he felt he was going through life with the top down.

One of those.

"The reason they asked me to call you, Janie, as I believe you're about to find out, is that they've got some questions," Jimmy says.

I'm listening to Jimmy, but my eyes are on the guy in the Ray-Bans and Tom Cruise jacket, who has now made his way over to us and hears the last thing Jimmy said.

"Guess who the questions are for?" the guy asks.

THIRTY

LOOKS-WISE HE REMINDS ME a little of my ex-husband Martin. But once he opens his mouth his accent isn't French, it sounds more like 200 proof Queens, New York.

"Wow, I don't get to meet a lot of famous people," he says before he even introduces himself.

"You need to set the bar a lot higher than me when it comes to famous."

"Is that false modesty I hear?"

"Is there any other kind? And by the way, I don't believe I caught your name."

"I'm Danny Esposito. Homicide investigator, State Police. I work out of our office at the Republic Airport, over in East Farmingdale."

"I know where the airport is."

"'Course you do. You went to junior high school in Patchogue, right? Before you moved back to the city?"

"You've done your homework."

"Like I said, you're famous and I like to know as much as I can about famous people. I was the same way with my favorite ballplayers growing up."

"We seem to have locked that in at this point, your opinion about my celebrity status." My smile is so thin I barely feel my lips move. "I assume you want to talk about something other than that."

"Well, now that you mention it," he says, "it might have something to do with that scene you and the mother and the daughter had the other night, them now being deceased and all."

"You find that out in between getting the call on the murders and making it out here from East Farmingdale?"

He rubs his chin. His look must require some tending to get it just right, that sweet spot between a couple of days' growth and an actual beard.

"I've been following your exploits since the first Jacobson trial. I even sat in the gallery." He shrugs. "Anyway, now it turns out that as you were leaving the benefit, people heard you threaten Elise Parsons. The mom. Something about knocking the Botox out of her face. Did that happen?"

"You obviously know it did." I nod. "Are we skipping right past the part where she hit me?"

He grins and points a finger at me. "Right before

you threatened to harm her if she ever came near you again." Still grinning, he asks, "So did she?"

"Did she what?"

"Come near you again?"

I look over at Jimmy. There have been enough times in his life when he was the one asking questions at crime scenes. His eyes tell me to answer Esposito without going out of my way to antagonize him. It will only keep us here longer and neither one of us wants that.

"I never saw Elise again after the benefit. It was part of a much broader plan to never see her ever again, period."

Esposito takes off the sunglasses and puts them on top of his head. Maybe thinking he's showing off his blue eyes. I don't have the heart to tell him he's wasting his time with me.

"Are we really doing this, investigator? Is that a real title, by the way?"

"Call me Danny."

"I'm not a suspect here, *Danny*. We both know that. So why are we still even having this conversation?"

"How about we go with you being a person of interest. You like that better?"

"We know I'm not one of those, either."

He smiles what I'm sure he thinks is a flirty smile. "You are to me."

"I've got a question for you, if you don't mind?"

"Go ahead."

"This whole vibe you've got going, the pose, the come-on — does it actually work with other women?"

"More than you'd think, actually."

"Good boy," I say.

I look at Jimmy again and jerk my head in the direction of the street.

"Maybe I need to call a good lawyer," I say to Danny Esposito, and head down the driveway without looking back, knowing the hotshot from the state cops is watching me all the way down the hill, maybe starting to understand how far out of his league he is.

Or not.

THIRTY-ONE

Jimmy

JIMMY THINKS HE BRIEFLY saw Edmund McKenzie at the benefit after Jane left, but there were a few hundred people between them and by the time Jimmy made his way across the room, McKenzie—if it really *was* him—was nowhere in sight.

And is still nowhere to be found.

But if Jimmy is going to find out who jumped him and tied him up at his house, he knows he needs to find McKenzie. And if the guy Jimmy thinks of as Joe Too is working for McKenzie, or with him, *why* is he?

Loose ends.

They'd always driven him crazy and still do.

Jane is working on filing a motion to get Jacobson's trial date moved up. It's unspoken between them, but Jimmy knows why, of course he knows why. She doesn't want to start something she can't finish. If she had her way the trial would start the day after tomorrow.

But he can't help her with that. Can't find this chump McKenzie, at least for the time being, no matter how many calls he makes. So he tells Jane that until further notice he's going to work the Parsons case like it's theirs. He can't just sit around. It will drive him even crazier than a loose end. Even if Jacobson isn't a suspect, he's connected to more dead women.

What are the odds?

Once you start doing the degrees-of-separation thing, Jacobson is connected, some form or fashion, to all of it. The Gates murders. The Carson murders. Joe Champi. Who's obviously connected to the guy who broke into Jimmy's house with his slugger of a girlfriend.

He counts more than a dozen people dead. Six before they took Jacobson's case and seven since. He used to think the total was even higher, until Jane said she was sure she'd seen Nick Morelli outside the courthouse in Mineola that day, and where the fuck has he disappeared to since?

Truth be told, dead bodies seemed to follow Jacobson all the way back to high school, and his father and that girl.

You really did need a scorecard.

He tried to go back to the beginning with Jacobson and his old man. Now Jimmy tells Jane he's going another way, working back from the most recent murders. The latest mother and daughter. No search engines today. In the morning he drives over to North Haven and starts knocking on doors the way he used to. The fifth door, across Noyac Road from the end of the Parsonses' driveway, police tape still across the gate, is answered by a small, sassy white-haired woman not more than five feet tall who introduces herself as Geraldine Nason.

"Cop, right?"

"Ex."

She nods. "You still look like one."

"I keep trying to wash it off."

"The real cops, not that you weren't a real one, probably have been looking to talk to me. But I've been up the island visiting my daughter and the bum she married. Just got back a couple of hours ago. So, it turns out you beat them to it, you lucky boy."

"Why lucky?"

"Because of my security cameras, that's why."

"You have some?"

"Lots." She winks at him. "Can't be too careful on the mean streets of the Hamptons."

"Would you mind if I take a look at what you've got?"

"Be my guest."

And shows him in.

She says she's got a son who has an audiovisual store

over in Bridgehampton. He set up the system for her because she's eighty and lives alone. Geraldine Nason walks him through the first floor of her house, finally taking him into a small room off the kitchen featuring six different screens. She tells him her son has the same setup she has, looking at the same video feeds of her property. He sees something he doesn't like, the cops are there in less than ten minutes.

There's a high view of the street, looking directly across at the Parsonses' house, a low view, angles from both sides of the old woman's house, and from the back, facing south.

"My son says this stuff automatically gets erased every week."

It's all right, Jimmy tells her, the Parsonses were murdered four days ago.

Jimmy works off the laptop in the studio after she gives him the password, the system synced up with the cameras. He starts looking at the video from three days before the murders, focusing on the two cameras facing the Parsonses' house.

It's the night before the murders, and night of, when things get interesting.

The same car cruising the neighborhood both nights.

A blue Bentley.

Jimmy is pretty sure he knows the car. Just to make

completely sure, he calls his friend Detective Craig Jackson in the city and asks him to run the plates.

Jackson calls back within five minutes.

The Bentley belongs to Claire Jacobson.

Rob Jacobson's wife.

Hardly any degrees of separation there, Jimmy thinks.

Hardly any at all.

THIRTY-TWO

THE BLUE BENTLEY IS in the driveway when I arrive at the Jacobson home in Sagaponack.

When Claire Jacobson opens the door and sees it's me, she says, "If I had to make it clearer that I have nothing to say to you I'd have to hire one of those sky-writers you see over the beach on the weekends."

She then starts to close the door in my face.

I stop it with my foot. I'm wearing sneakers, but I'm not going to let her see the sting of applying that force. Claire Jacobson has been annoying me for a long time, getting up in my face with the skill of a prosecutor practically every chance she got during her husband's first trial. And I've done my level best to annoy her right back.

"This won't take long," I tell her. "But there are things we need to discuss."

I'm holding the door open with my hand now.

"Is this about Rob?"

"It's about you."

"What about me?" she says. "We have nothing in common except that we dislike each other."

She doesn't try to close the door again. Like I'm some old-time traveling salesman, I take that as progress.

"What I'm here to discuss is you cruising Elise Parsons's neighborhood a couple of the nights before she died, and me thinking you'd rather talk about it with me than the police."

Then Rob Jacobson's wife, who I had always seen as the ice-queen bitch of the world, surprises me.

She opens the door wide.

It's as if a switch has been thrown.

"I apologize for being rude," she says. "I'm glad you're here, because there's something I need to discuss with you. Please come in."

Please?

I feel the urge to ask her if she has lost a bet.

The living room is as spectacular as I remember it. I take a seat on one of the couches. She's across from me on another one, a truly magnificent antique mahogany coffee table between us.

"Why were you over in North Haven, Claire?"

I don't know how I expect her to respond, by acting defensive, or simply denying it without knowing what proof I have. But she surprises me a second time. She suddenly and quite unexpectedly appears to be on the verge of tears.

"I'd heard they'd started up again before he turned himself in," she says, "and I just couldn't take that. I don't know why they were the ones to push me over the edge. But they were. And I just wanted to see if I could find out for myself."

"You mean find out if he'd hooked up with Elise?"

"Or Ellie. Or, knowing them and their weird tastes and knowing my husband's, perhaps both of them at the same time."

She smiles weakly at me. At least no tears for now. I'm not sure how I'd deal with that. I'm having enough trouble processing the fact that she's acting like a human being in front of me, really for the first time.

"Kind of Rob's thing, mothers and daughters," she says, not sounding judgmental, just profoundly weary. Or just sad. "I wanted to see for myself, even if it made me feel like a stalker."

"But he's not allowed to leave the rented house without his ankle bracelet."

"Knowing my husband, I thought that where there was a will, there was a way."

And in this moment, I picture myself in the old days, night after night outside Café Martin around closing time, looking for the chance to see who my ex-husband might be leaving with on a particular evening. When I was the one who felt like a stalker. And a little bit crazy.

A sigh comes out of Claire now, loud and genuine. Like more sadness coming out of her. "I finally got back in the car, realizing how truly pathetic I must look."

Been there, I think.

Done that.

A single tear appears on one cheek now. Just the one. She brushes it away, as if it's one more embarrassment, even beyond the story she's telling.

Definitely a human being.

One I almost find myself wanting to like.

"I still love him," she says in a soft voice. Whether she's talking to herself or to me doesn't seem to matter in the moment. "I'm not sure I know him anymore." She shakes her head, her eyes fixed on some point behind me, maybe some of the amazing artwork on the wall. "But I still love him. Can you understand that? Or do you just want to laugh at me?"

"Actually, I can understand it. And have absolutely no desire to laugh at you."

"He's not a killer," she says, eyes fixed on me again. "Rob is a lot of things. A lot of quite unattractive things sometimes, as you know. But he's not a killer."

"You haven't always acted as if you believed that, Claire."

"But, in my heart, I think I always did, no matter how angry I was during the first trial. At him and at you."

I've assumed all along from her behavior that she couldn't wait to divorce him and walk away with pretty much everything she wanted.

Not feeling so sure about that now.

Because here Claire Jacobson is, in the house they once shared, defending him.

Telling me how much she still loves him.

"There's something else," she says. "Something that you need to know."

I try to soften my own voice, as if trying to make sure the two of us are at perfect pitch.

"What's that, Claire?"

She hesitates, but not for very long.

"Somebody just tried to kill him."

THIRTY-THREE

ON THE BEACH LAST night, somebody fired shots at Rob Jacobson. The house he's renting on Hedges Lane in Amagansett is less than a half mile from the beach. You can hear the water from his back patio even though you can't see it.

Claire told me what Rob had told her about the gunshots.

Now my client and I are doing a face-to-face and I'm about to get the full story directly from him. Rob Jacobson is trying to act cool, trying not to break character in the part he plays for me. But I can see that he's rattled.

Two brand-new human beings this morning, same marriage.

What *are* the odds?

"I didn't get much sleep." He forces a smile. "But not for the usual reasons."

He sips some coffee. He offers me some. I pass. I'm wired enough at this point.

"You sure you want to hear this?"

"As much as I might occasionally want to kill you myself, I'm not letting somebody else do it on my watch," I say. "And I haven't lost a client yet."

"I didn't tell you what happened because I didn't want you to worry about me," he says.

"Just tell me what happened last night and we'll worry together."

I had gotten him permission to do a route I knew they could track on GPS: drive into town for dinner with the ankle bracelet on and walk down to the beach afterward. But he didn't want to eat. He wanted to drink and didn't want to drink alone.

He says he had a few too many at the Main Street Tavern, but wasn't drunk enough to forget this was no time in his life to get picked up for a DUI. He walked the short distance to his house and was still so buzzed that he continued walking down to Indian Wells Beach to see if the ocean air could help sober him up before bed.

He did sober up then. But not because of the air. When he drunkenly kicked off his loafers, he did a full face-plant into the sand.

"Luck of the Irish whiskey, I guess. Because that exact same moment was when I heard the shot. Pretty sure I then heard the bullet maybe bang off one of the parking signs."

He's not the cool Rob now, the one who wants you to think he's the only one who gets the joke. By now I know what a good liar he can be. But I don't think he's lying now. He's reliving what happened to him. And how close he came.

"Could you tell where the shot came from?"

"Behind, I'm pretty sure. From the parking lot. Like I said: I sobered up pretty quick and rolled to my right and then I'm tearing ass into the dunes. It's a cloudy night, no moon or stars. You can barely see the ocean. I hear another shot. That one misses, too. I'm not the sprinter I was in high school, but I've done a lot of beach running in my life and I can still get it in gear when I have to. I must have been faster than whoever it was shooting at my ass. The shooting stops. But I don't stop until I get all the way to Maidstone."

"You walked all the way home from the country club?"

He shakes his head. And grins. For a moment this is the Rob I know, if not love.

"I called a friend and she came and got me and we came back here."

"Not worried that the shooter might come looking for you here?"

"You don't want to know this, Janie. But I've still got a gun."

He's right. I don't want to know that.

"You didn't consider phoning the police instead?"

"Don't feel as if I'm a white life that matters to them these days."

"Will you please be serious for once in your life, Rob? Because this actually happens to be life-and-death shit we're discussing."

"Sorry," he says. "I mean it."

"By the way? I don't suppose the friend you phoned was my sister."

He frowns. "Not exactly."

"Don't tell me you two crazy kids have broken up again."

"See, that's the thing, Janie. We might not have ever really gotten back together."

I stare at him, knowing I shouldn't be remotely surprised.

"So you lied to me about that."

He puts out his hands. "What can I tell you? It's like with women. Sometimes I can't stop myself."

"How do I know you're not lying about being shot at?"

I have slapped him in the past. He reacts as if I've just done it again.

"I'm not lying, goddamnit! Somebody tried to shoot me in my goddamn back!"

I'll never be sure when he's lying and when he's telling the truth. Still not sure, in my heart, whether he's capable of murder. But the same way I suddenly found myself caring about his wife, I also care about him.

And I'm scared right along with him.

"Any theories about who would want to take some shots at you? Or hire somebody to take them?"

"It would take too long to list all the people I've screwed in my life. Or screwed over. Or both."

"You need to be careful, Rob," I tell him. "Whoever came for you once might come again."

"See, Janie, you do care about me."

Slipping back into character, as if he can only stay serious—or act scared—for so long.

"Believe *me* on something," I tell him. "I'm as surprised about that as you are."

Before I head home, I drive up to Indian Wells and check the EMERGENCY VEHICLES sign in front of the fence between the parking lot and the start of the beach. There's no sign of a bullet hole anywhere on it, or on either of the other two parking signs.

As I pull into my own driveway, I see Brigid sitting on my front porch.

Before I can even apologize about believing Rob Jacobson when he told me they were back together, she says, "My cancer is back."

THIRTY-FOUR

Jimmy

DANNY ESPOSITO, THE STATE cop who annoyed Jane in almost record time at the murder scene, takes a seat next to Jimmy at his bar.

"I feel as if maybe we got off on the wrong foot," Esposito says.

"No wonder you made detective as fast as you did."

Esposito tells Kenny the bartender that he'll have what Jimmy is having. Kenny walks over with a Montauk Ale for Esposito and places it in front of him.

"Cheers," Esposito says, raising his glass.

Jimmy leaves his glass where it is.

"What do you want?" Jimmy asks. "You can buy a beer anywhere between your headquarters and here."

"I think there's a chance here that we can help each other out on the Parsons thing. You know the lay of the land out here a hell of a lot better than I do."

"True," Jimmy says. "So we've established I have

something you want. The problem is that you have nothing I want."

"You sure about that?"

He's out of his hip-cop look tonight. Black sweater. Jeans. The chin stubble looks exactly the same, but Esposito appears to have checked at least some of his attitude at the door. Maybe all. It occurs to Jimmy it might be one more pose because he does want something.

"My partner took an almost instant dislike to you," Jimmy tells him.

"Gotta admit," he says, grinning, "it'll only get worse once she gets to know me better."

Behind them is a big round table filled with cops, East Hampton cops tonight. But then there are almost always cops in here, from East or the Sag Harbor station just up the block. It was always one of Jimmy's goals, turning this into the East End version of one of his old NYPD bars in the city. Even when some of the local cops were royally pissed at Jimmy during the first Jacobson trial, they kept coming in, as much as they wanted Jacobson to get his ticket punched for murdering the Gates family.

Esposito turns and gives the cops a thumbs-up.

"Listen, we both know you wouldn't be here if you *didn't* have something you at least think I might want," Jimmy says. "If it's any good, I might buy you that beer in front of you."

"Are you trying to bribe an officer of the law?"

"Absolutely."

Esposito moves his chair closer and leans in. "It's about the dead woman's husband."

"Ah," Jimmy says. "Mr. Carl Parsons himself. Richer than shit, which means he fit right in out here. What about him?"

"Carl liked to gamble, as it turns out. Like maybe it was the only thing that got his motor running at the end."

"And I'm sure it was legal, him being a pillar of the community and all."

"No, sir, it was not."

Esposito is now wearing a truly world-class shit-eating grin.

"Seriously, it probably was the only fun the old bastard was getting at the end, because from what I gather he sure wasn't getting any from Elise. She was too busy screwing her way all the way to Montauk and back. But if it was on television, and just about every game is these days including cricket, old Carl had some action going. You should see his old-man cave at the house, which Elise looks to have left in place as some kind of shrine, maybe to remember the only room in the house where Gramps was happy. Six flat screens. I wanted to freaking move in myself."

"You gonna get to where you're going while your beer is still cold?"

"I drove all the way out here. Let me tell it my way."

According to Esposito, Parsons's gambling only turned up because his name turned up in another Suffolk County investigation. "You can't turn on the television these days," he points out, "and not be bombarded with commercials about that DraftKings shit."

"I actually found myself wondering, all this time after Parsons kicked," Esposito continues, "if Elise might have put a pillow over his head before he blew any more of what she stood to inherit."

"So he was betting big."

"To the end, and with both hands," Esposito says. "But that's only partly what I drove out to tell you."

"You may have noticed, and maybe against all odds, that you now have my undivided attention."

"The name Artie Shore ring a bell?"

Hank Carson's bookie. Lieutenant in Bobby Salvatore's operation. As in mob operation. The same Artie Shore who shot himself in Garden City after Jimmy and Jane first started looking into the murders of Hank Carson and his wife and daughter. Shot himself with Jimmy on the other side of his door, trying to get inside. Artie died knowing things Jimmy wanted to know.

"You know I know who Artie Shore is."

"What you don't know is that Artie was Carl Parsons's bookie, too."

"Which means that old man Parsons was doing business with the mob, too," Jimmy says.

"Small world, isn't it?" Esposito says.

Jimmy tells Esposito that his beer is most definitely on the house now, as he finally does get around to clinking his glass against Danny Esposito's.

Finally, and with a flourish, Esposito takes a folded-up piece of paper out of his wallet and smooths it out on the bar in front of Jimmy.

"What's this?"

"This, my friend, is Artie's old client list," Esposito says. "Or at least as much of it as we could put together after the fact."

There's one other name on it besides Carl Parsons that Jimmy recognizes.

Jumps right off the page, like they say.

Edmund McKenzie.

THIRTY-FIVE

BRIGID INFORMS ME THAT she is flying back to Switzerland, to the Meier Clinic, tonight.

If I wasn't so scared and angry at her truly awful news, I'd ask her if she's looked into the two of us signing up on their family plan.

But I *am* scared and angry.

For both of us.

So, I don't make any jokes because there is nothing funny about this.

It's an aggressive form of non-Hodgkins lymphoma for Brigid, by the way.

"The official name, in my current circumstances, is refractory lymphoma," she says.

"I know what they call it, Brigid. I've done as much research on your cancer as I have my own. If this is a course in cancer, I'm passing with flying colors."

I smile at her. It's taken a while, but we've both finally stopped crying.

If only for now.

"It's also known as relapsed lymphoma, when it comes back," I continue.

"Look at you," Brigid says. "And Dad always called me the smart one."

Brigid is separated from Chris, who used to be the principal at Pierson High and is now a headmaster at some fancy prep school in Connecticut. They separated during Rob Jacobson's first trial once he found out about the affair between Brigid and Rob. Brigid says she called Chris last night to tell him about her return visit to Meier. He offered to go with her. As hurt as he is—he's told me how she hurt him—he still loves her.

People love Brigid even when they don't.

"Mom's cancer killed both her and Pop in the end, like they both got hit with the same bullet," I say now. "That's not going to happen to us, sis."

She smiles back at me, but it's a forced smile made out of hardly anything at all. It's still enough to make me remember why she wasn't just the smart one, but also the pretty one, when we were growing up.

The pretty one even now, as thin as she is.

"I'll drink to that," she says.

Inside the house, I open a bottle of white wine, because I can't think of one good reason not to.

We both drink. Rip is next to Brigid on the couch. She's stroking his neck. He looks blissful. Rip loves her, too.

"We're both beating this," I say. I grin. "Even if it kills us."

"You know that makes no sense."

"Totally."

"But unfortunately, sister Jane, you can't beat up my illness—or yours—the way you used to beat up the mean girls bothering me in grade school."

"I still hate those bitches."

Brigid laughs now, until just like that, she's crying again. We both are, all over again.

Her plane, the same United flight I took, leaves at eight. I've offered to drive her, but she says she's already booked a car from East Wind and it's picking her up around four.

I ask if the doctors at Meier have given her any sense of how long she'll be over there.

"Until the fuckers get it right this time."

That gets a laugh out of me. Brigid always does when she drops an f-bomb.

Once she's gone, I cook dinner for myself. Nothing exotic tonight, no degree of difficulty, no showing off for Ben, just pasta with an array of vegetables from Balsam Farms.

When I've cleaned up, I put Rip the dog into the car and we drive to Indian Wells Beach. I hope that nobody will be shooting at me tonight, it's been enough of a monumentally shit day already.

It's cold and windy for this time of year, so even with a lot of light left in the sky, the beach is empty in both directions.

I throw a tennis ball for Rip. He even brings it back to me a few times, as if he's an emotional support dog tonight, and senses I needed all the support I can get.

I keep picturing Brigid waving to me from the front seat of the town car—she still gets carsick if she sits in the back—the way she waved good-bye to me from Dad's car the day they drove to Duke before the start of her freshman year.

Despite the wind, the water is surprisingly calm. I'm not. My sister was supposed to be getting better. Only now she's not.

It is no longer in dispute that God is officially starting to pile on.

I walk down to the water's edge. Standing out here in the magic light between night and day, the shore and the water, always seems better here than anyplace else.

It's time for another talk with God.

"Okay, Missy," I say, knowing She can hear me perfectly over the soft sound of the wind and waves. "You're the one starting to act like a mean girl now."

Rip and I head back toward the car. Before we get to the parking lot, I stop and look up at the sky one last time.

"Don't make me come up there," I say.

THIRTY-SIX

AFTER BRIGID LEAVES, I spend two days in the house, most of that time in bed.

Not just a reaction to her cancer.

A reaction to mine, too.

More mine than hers in this case.

It happens occasionally, and there's nothing I can do to stop it, nothing I can take. I just have to wear it. Either the drugs aren't working the way they're supposed to. Or they're working too well. Whatever the reason, I get knocked down and feel the fight go right out of me, at least temporarily.

It's a reminder, even after any stretch when I do start to feel better, about what's going on inside me.

The elephant in the room.

The whole herd of elephants in the room.

The medical definition, you can look it up if you want to, of my current condition: absolute crap.

Rip is always right next to my bed, or the couch, occasionally staring up at me to see if I'm still breathing. Probably thinking back to when we met, and he was supposed to play the part of sick dog.

Ben Kalinsky has been in Boston for a veterinary convention, due back tonight. I haven't told him how lousy I've been feeling, because even with his expertise at treating sick dogs, he's far away.

I've told Jimmy, because I tell Jimmy pretty much everything, even more than I tell Ben. Even when I don't tell Jimmy things, he usually seems to know anyway. He says it was the same way with his cop partners, all the way back to Mickey Dunne.

Brigid says she'll call from Meier when she knows more. I'm honest enough with myself to know that I *am* at least partly feeling the way I'm feeling because of her, because of how much I hate what she's about to go through all over again.

Jimmy calls from the city, after spending the last two nights at my apartment on Christopher Street in the West Village. He says he has a new dirtbag update.

"On McKenzie?"

"Joe Champi."

"Tell me he's still dead."

"Very much so," Jimmy says. "But it turns out he had a partner from back in the day."

"Another dirty cop?"

"Yup. Name of Anthony Licata. King of the dirt-bags, from what I'm told. I'll tell *you* all about him when I get there."

I tell him if it's going to be too late, we can do it in the morning. He says he won't be that late, he's about to break his own speed record once he gets off the LIE at Exit 70.

As soon as I hang up, Rob Jacobson calls.

"Since the night of my beach walk, the court wouldn't give me another furlough even when I told them I wanted to drop in on my lawyer," he says.

"I didn't like you dropping in even before you were wearing the ankle bracelet," I say.

Rip starts barking as if he knows who I'm talking to.

"I think I can help you."

"Have you cured cancer since I was over at your house?"

"You told me to get serious, and that's what I'm doing. I think I can help you solve this."

"*This*? I'm afraid you're going to have to be a lot more specific than that, Rob. Which case?"

"All of them."

I wait for him to drop a funny line on me. Or one he thinks is funny. But he doesn't.

"What if it's all one thing?" he asks.

THIRTY-SEVEN

Jimmy

JIMMY IS NEARLY TO Amagansett when Jane calls to tell him she's making the short drive over to Jacobson's rental house.

Jimmy tells her he'll meet her there. Jimmy knows Jacobson prefers meeting with Jane alone, but Jimmy's convinced Jacobson has the hots for her, whether or not he's ever verbalized that. Even the idea of them together gives Jimmy the creeps.

"Somebody take another shot at him?" Jimmy asks.

"I'm sure he would have mentioned it."

"Can't blame me for being a dreamer," Jimmy says.

She looks more tired than usual when Jacobson lets him in, as if she needs getting out of the house about as much as she needs a hole in the head. But she's here, and Jimmy knows why.

Because she's Jane.

"Rob seems to think that everything that's happened and keeps happening might all be connected."

"Yeah, it is," Jimmy says. "Connected to his sorry ass."

Jimmy sees Jacobson start to say something, then swallow it. It has been a while since Jacobson went out of his way to piss Jimmy off.

"Listen," Jacobson says. "I know you don't like me, or like working for me. But we're still on the same team here."

"Even though I keep asking myself who chose up these sides," Jimmy says. "And for the record, how were we all on the same team when you knew Joe Champi was ready to take her out one day when he left the big house you used to live in?"

"*I couldn't control him. Nobody could!*"

"So you were just going to let Jane put him out of *your* misery."

"This isn't getting us anywhere," Jane says, sounding like a referee. "So, before I fall asleep in this chair, Rob, why don't you explain why you got me over here?"

"I think the whole thing actually runs through Eddie Mc-Kenzie," he says.

He talks for a long time then about McKenzie, how he was like a little brother Jacobson bullied. About how obsessed Mc-Kenzie was with him, wanting everything Jacobson wanted, starting with girls in high school.

And how obsessed McKenzie became later after the kid he treated like his hero set him up on the rape.

"So he waits all this time and starts killing people just to frame you?" Jimmy asks him.

"In a word? Yes," Jacobson says calmly.

"So he's the mastermind of a conspiracy as complex as the plan to get bin Laden?" Jane asks. "Seriously?"

"I'm not saying he did it by himself," Jacobson says. "But I've done some checking."

"Leave the investigating to us, hotshot," Jimmy says.

Jacobson ignores Jimmy and turns to Jane. "May I finish?"

She nods. "Proceed."

"So, I asked around and found one more thing that scared the shit out of me, as if that was even possible after I nearly got my ass shot off."

"What did you find out?" Jane asks.

"Not what as much as who," Jacobson says. "Turns out there was a guy who was a body man for Eddie and his old man, the way Joe Champi was for my dad and me. I just never knew until now."

"A fixer, you mean," Jane says.

She throws a nod at Jimmy.

"The guy who jumped me talked about fixing things, and for us to not go around trying to unfix them," Jimmy says.

"Licata is his name." Jacobson is looking at Jimmy now. "Ex-cop. You ever hear of him?"

"As a matter of fact, I think I ran into him not long ago," Jimmy says.

"Where?" Jacobson asks.

"My house."

THIRTY-EIGHT

THIRD STRAIGHT DAY OF my latest round of chemo. The new Phillips Family Cancer Center in South-ampton is right there on Route 27, before you make the hard left toward Water Mill. Locals, not just New York people, needed a first-rate place like it out here.

I consider myself both.

The good news is that once I'm done for the day, I don't get hooked up again for three more weeks.

Ben Kalinsky came with me the first two days, spent both nights with chemo-weak me back at my house. But I'm driving myself for treatment, and when I get home I'm cooking dinner for two.

"How do you know you're going to be up to that?" Ben asks.

"We've gone over this."

"Of course," he says. "You're Jane Effing Smith. How could I ever forget a thing like that?"

I power through my three hours in the chair. When I get home, I go over the presentation I'm making to Judge Killer Kane in two days, asking that the trial date be moved up. Way up. Without asking her if she can help out a girl with cancer. There's already enough drama surrounding this case. I don't need to provide any more for social media and the tabloids that are still standing.

I can see the headlines now:

CANCER-STRICKEN LAWYER FIGHTS OWN DEATH SENTENCE.

I don't put it out there because I don't want anybody's pity. I just want to win, the sooner the better.

I text Jimmy when I'm leaving Phillips, a little after five, to tell him I'm stopping by the bar on my way back to Amagansett. I know he'll be there, as the bar is the closest thing he has to an office, especially when there's hardly anybody around to bother him in the afternoon.

I've decided that I'm going to celebrate being off the needle for the next three weeks by stopping by and letting him treat me to a shot of his very best whiskey, Midleton Very Rare, before I go home and cook up dinner for Dr. Ben and me, nothing particularly elaborate tonight, just teriyaki salmon with a tomato-and-zucchini casserole on the side. A choice of red or white wine.

You only live once.

I'm nearly to Sag Harbor, having gone past Elise Parsons's old house, when Jimmy calls and asks how close I am, there's somebody he wants me to meet when I get to the bar.

When I walk in, I see that he apparently wants me to meet Jesus, much sooner than I'd anticipated.

THIRTY-NINE

THE BAR IS CROWDED because it's one of Jimmy's happy hours, drinks half price for the after-work crowd until six o'clock, even though it always seems to be a soft deadline once he gets to the top of the hour. Jimmy and his guest are at Jimmy's normal post, far end of the bar. There is some kind of late-afternoon ball game going on. Not the Yankees. But in Jimmy's view, any baseball is better than none.

"This is Dave Wolk," Jimmy says when I get to them.

I grin.

"Are you by any chance related to the son of God?"

He grins. "Not even by virgin birth."

"Actually, Dave's a thief," Jimmy says.

"Reformed," Wolk corrects him.

"There's an old football coach who used to say you are what your record says you are," Jimmy tells him.

Wolk grins again. "Well, then I'm not an *adult* thief, put it that way."

There's a distinct laid-back, surfer-dude vibe to him. Long hair, beard, deep tan. Dark eyes. Tall even sitting down. In his twenties, I'm guessing. MAIN BEACH T-shirt, cargo shorts, sandals.

"I'm Jane," I say, and put out my hand.

"Nice to meet you, Jane." Before I can do anything about it, he slides off his stool, ignores my outstretched hand, and hugs me.

"Dave a friend of yours?" I ask Jimmy.

"Call it a relationship that's suddenly evolving," Jimmy says. "It has come to my attention that Dave here broke into Elise Parsons's house a few months ago, even if he didn't get pinched for it."

"Allegedly broke in," Wolk says. He shrugs. "And none of the missing jewelry was ever found, if that makes you feel any better."

"You just said you were reformed," I tell him.

"I might've had a slip." Another grin. "Allegedly," he adds.

"Fascinating," I say.

Jimmy asks if I want that shot. I tell him I'll wait. I'm interested to hear why Jimmy wanted me to meet this guy.

"As it turns out," Jimmy says, "Dave seems to have

had a history of B&Es when he was still trying to find himself as a teenager."

Wolk smiles at me now. Full wattage. Young and good-looking and cool and clearly proud of it. He reaches for his shot glass and empties it. Smacks his lips. "First of the day."

"I hate to interrupt," I say. "But would either of you care to explain what we're all doing here?"

"We are all of us here," Jimmy says, "because one of my many drinking buddies from the East Hampton cops told me about the alleged break-in, even though they couldn't pin it on him. And then my friend further tells me that the reason they wanted to talk to Dave was because him and a couple of his thrill-seeker pals used to do a lot of B&Es when they weren't surfing in the summer and chasing hardbodies in bikinis up and down the beach."

Wolk holds up his glass and gestures with it toward Emmett, who usually works days behind Jimmy's bar. Emmett pours more Patrón.

"I'm sure there's a point to all this, because I have to get home and start dinner."

"Almost there," Jimmy says, "I promise."

He loves it when he knows something that I don't. And he clearly does now.

"It was just fun," Wolk says. "Screwing with rich

people for the pure, 200 proof fun of screwing with them. Taking a few of their toys. We had a way to fence a lot of shit, and so we were making decent money, which beat cutting fucking lawns. But getting in and getting out? I swear, it was a better rush than getting high. Until I was the one who got caught and ended up at juvie in Westbury for what was supposed to be my senior year."

"Your accomplices got away?"

"Let's just say that when the shit finally hit the fan, my boys didn't exactly embrace the concept of no smash-grabber left behind," Wolk says.

I turn to Jimmy. "Again, this all sounds fascinating. Truly. But what does it have to do with me? Or us?"

"Glad you asked. You need to ask him who his accomplices were on his teenage crime spree."

"Who'd you work with, Dave?"

"Well, Nick Morelli was the boss of us," Wolk says. "So I guess that technically I worked for him."

Boom.

"You know who he is, right?"

"I know who he is," I say. "Used to be dead, but apparently got over it."

"Wish he'd stayed dead," Wolk says, suddenly serious, verging on angry, no laid-back vibe now.

"No longer a fan?" I ask him.

"I used to think Nick was good crazy. He's not. He's just crazy. And dangerous."

"A danger to you?"

"To everybody."

We all let that settle. I have more questions about Morelli, but it's clear there's more to the story. You cross-examine enough witnesses in your life, you know better than to interrupt once they pick up a head of steam.

"Now tell her who the third musketeer was," Jimmy says to Wolk.

"Eric Jacobson," he says. I stare at him again. Speechless for the second time in a few minutes.

First Morelli. Now this.

"Rob Jacobson's son," I say.

"One and the same," Dave Wolk says.

"Jesus Christ," I say.

FORTY

Jimmy

DAVE WOLK IS LIKE somebody talking about all the big games he played in high school, like all the houses they robbed were the highlight of his life.

"Doing it, I mean when we started, was Nick's idea," Wolk says. "He was always bad-ass, from the time we were in junior high."

"I thought he was a fisherman," Jane says.

"Well, a mobbed-up fisherman," Wolk says.

"Excuse me?" Jimmy says. "You must have left that part out before Jane got here."

"His father's brother was this guy named Bobby Salvatore."

I think: *And the hits just keep on coming.*

Bobby Salvatore, we knew by now, had been Artie Shore's boss. The mob guy with whom Hank Carson was underwater in debt. The guy we now discover is related to the not-so-late Nick Morelli, a star witness in Rob Jacobson's trial until he wasn't.

"You want to know why I didn't rat him out when I was the one who got caught?" Wolk says. "Because who would be stupid enough to rat out anybody related to Bobby Salvatore?"

Jimmy sees Jane texting. He asks her what she's doing. She grins and says that she's telling Dr. Ben to get over to her house and start dinner, she might be a few minutes late.

No stopping our new friend Dave Wolk now.

"So I went to Westbury and did my time in a way I hoped Nick's family would respect."

"I'm sure they were very proud," Jimmy says. "A made man, practically, just like a big boy."

"What I don't get," Jane says, "is what was in this for Eric Jacobson?"

"He fucking hated his father," Wolk says. "Told me he loved that his old man had to buy him out of trouble the way his daddy's old man had done the same when his dad was a kid. Like closing some kind of weirded-out circle."

"Why did he hate him so much?" Jimmy says. "Other than the obvious reason of his old man being an asshole."

Wolk looks down at his glass and seems pleased to find it not quite empty.

"His father had been calling Eric a loser his whole life," Wolk says. "You're not this, you're not that. Be a man. All that dad shit. I mean, I'm a loser, too. But what guy wants to hear that from his father? We'd get drunk on the beach and Eric would get going and talk about how someday he was going to fuck his father up bad. One time I asked, 'You mean beat his ass?' And he gave me this funny look and said, 'I mean *kill* his ass someday.'"

"Where's Eric now?" Jane asks Wolk. "He never showed up for his father's trial. We heard that he was off looking for the perfect wave in Micronesia or someplace."

"Well, yeah," Wolk says. "That's what he wanted everybody to think."

FORTY-ONE

IT'S SEVEN THIRTY BY the time I'm leaving Jimmy's bar.

By then Wolk has sworn to us that he doesn't know where Eric Jacobson might be, just that a girl he knows in the city is sure she saw Eric drinking at The Otheroom on Perry Street the week before.

Jimmy tells me not to worry, he'll find the kid, and McKenzie, and maybe even Anthony Licata before he's through.

"What about Amelia Earhart and Judge Crater?"

"I found out what happened to both of them a long time ago," Jimmy says. "I just didn't want to make the whole thing about me."

I kiss him on the cheek and tell him I still love him madly.

"I know," he says.

With light traffic on Route 114, it takes a half hour

to get from Jimmy's bar to my house. I take it even slower tonight. I'm feeling a little lightheaded, even though I never had my shot of whiskey. Tonight, it's not because of my physical state, though I often start to fade at the end of the day.

No, tonight my head is spinning because so much information has just come into my brain I feel as if I should be on notice that I need to purchase more storage space.

Did Rob Jacobson know Eric was back? Could he *not* know? Rob suggested the crimes might all be connected, and now here comes Dave Wolk, who may have broken into the Parsonses' house, saying he and Eric and Morelli once robbed houses together.

Could it be possible that Jacobson is just now learning that Joe Champi and this Licata guy were in business together?

I plan to ask my client about all of that.

Just not tonight.

Tonight is dinner with Ben and then sleep. A lot of sleep. He spent the last two nights at my house so I know he won't mind me kicking him out—in a sweet way—after we eat. After that, the only male companionship I want is Rip the dog, even though his snoring is a lot worse than Ben's. My own version of white noise.

With my brain spinning to process new information, I nearly miss my turn on Floyd Street. I realize

I'm on my way toward Northwest Harbor, the long way home.

An hour later, I'm in such a rush to get into the house that I don't pay any attention to the Mercedes up the street from Dr. Ben's car.

When I'm inside, I see immediately that Dr. Ben and Rip are not alone.

But I'm not looking at them, frozen in place, a couple of feet inside the front door.

Not believing my own eyes.

Ben tries to break the ice, even though he would need a pickax at the moment, offering a feeble—and doomed—attempt at humor.

"I believe you two know each other," he says.

"Hello, Jane," the other man in the room says.

"Hello, Martin," I say to my ex-husband. "Long time no see."

FORTY-TWO

Jimmy

JIMMY FOLLOWS DAVE WOLK when he leaves the bar.

He offered to call the guy an Uber, not sure how many tequilas Wolk had downed. If Wolk has some kind of accident between Jimmy's bar and his next stop, Jimmy will face the consequences, but Wolk says screw Uber, it takes a lot more Patrón than he's thrown down tonight to get him shit-faced.

Jimmy wants to know more about Dave Wolk, how his activities relate to Nick Morelli and Jacobson's kid. In the morning, he plans to put in a call to Organized Crime, see what they know about Bobby Salvatore's crime-family tree. In Jimmy's distant memory, he heard that Salvatore had come up in Sonny Blum's outfit on Long Island before branching out. But he can't remember the details.

He doesn't like not remembering. But then who the hell does?

Wolk parked in back. Before he left the bar, Jimmy got Wolk's number and put it into his own phone, telling him he'd be in touch. The last thing he asks Wolk is where he's spending most of his time these days.

"Wherever the best waves are out here, brother," Wolk says.

"Hang ten," Jimmy says sarcastically, and then watches the beat-up Corolla pull out onto Bay Street.

Wolk said something about a crash pad in Napeague. Maybe he's heading there right now. Jimmy doesn't care. He's got nothing but time, so he puts a car in between him and Wolk as the Corolla bears left off Division and onto 114. Wolk is taking it slow, probably worried about getting pulled over no matter how well he thinks he handles his booze. They all think they have it under control once they walk out of the bar, until they don't.

When he gets to East Hampton, he doesn't go through town, makes his way around it instead, to Town Lane and then Abraham's Path, not far from Jane's house, and then a left to put him on Route 27 eastbound.

No cars between Jimmy and the Corolla now.

Wolk has picked up a little speed.

They go past the Lobster Roll on the ocean side of 27, where they once filmed some TV show about Hamptons couples screwing around on each other. Jimmy has never watched the show, the only reason he even knows the thing exists is because he once dated a woman who worked on it before she dumped him for the lighting director.

Maybe it was the assistant director.

Jimmy can't remember that either.

Eventually they're moving up on the place where 27 forks, and Old Montauk Highway takes you to Gurney's Inn.

Wolk bears right. Maybe Wolk's headed there, Jimmy's aware that there's always a good bar scene at Gurney's, older than the drunk-stupid teenage crowd in Montauk village.

Before they get to Gurney's, Wolk makes a left, heading up into one of the neighborhoods on the north side of Old Montauk, not on the ocean, but close enough.

Jimmy stops at the corner of Fir Lane and Elm, watches Wolk pull up in front of a house on Elm.

Jimmy can't see the number. He can come back in the morning and find out later, and find out who owns it, if it matters. Maybe this is the crash pad if Jimmy needs to find Wolk again.

Wolk doesn't even get out of the car, just waits on

the street for a small woman to get into the passenger side of the Corolla.

The woman with the guy Jimmy is sure was Licata was small.

Wolk turns around in the driveway. Jimmy has already pulled into the driveway closest to him, shutting off the engine and lights of his sporty new Jetta convertible.

Wolk goes right past him. By the time he makes the turn onto Old Montauk, heading west, Jimmy is behind him, at a decent distance, keeping his headlights off for the time being.

Wolk floors it.

I've been made, Jimmy thinks. *By a tequila-swigging, Jesus-looking beach bum.*

Then Wolk is back on the highway, but not for long, making a hard right onto a dirt road into the dunes, just before what Jimmy knows is the turn for Napeague Harbor.

Fuck it.

The beach bum has officially annoyed him.

Jimmy follows him into the dunes, opening his glove compartment as he does, pulling out the Glock 9 he keeps in there.

Now he sees the Corolla's headlights go off as Wolk slows to a crawl and heads deeper into the dunes.

Jimmy thinks: *I've come this far.*

He is about to get out of the car and follow them on foot when he sees headlights back on, lighting up the sky, Wolk having turned back around toward the highway. Maybe they got lost. Maybe Wolk thought this was the road leading to the harbor. Or got stood up.

Wolk isn't heading for the highway.

He stops his car about fifty yards from Jimmy's. Then Jimmy—too late to get out of the Jetta or turn it back on and throw it into reverse—sees the small woman get out and leave the front passenger door open.

She disappears behind it.

Not for long.

When she straightens up, Jimmy sees the gun in her hand.

He is throwing himself across the front seat as the bullet hits the windshield.

FORTY-THREE

A REPORTER COVERING ONE of my old trials once wrote in the *Times* that I could talk the way Gaga can sing.

But right now I have no urge to do either, because for once in my life I'm speechless.

I stare at my ex-husband. He stares at me. I assume Ben is staring at both of us.

No one moves, as if we've all suddenly calcified.

My ex-husband smiles finally, as if the scene is the most natural thing in the world, and why doesn't someone mix up a pitcher of martinis?

"Hello, Jane."

"Are you lost, Martin?"

How long has it been since we were in the same room together? How long since I've actually *seen* him, if I don't count the nights when I tried to get a glimpse of him through his restaurant window?

Then I remember.

Of course.

It was the day we signed the divorce papers at the lawyer's office.

Before Martin can respond, Ben says, "I should probably leave."

"Please don't," I say, the words sounding to me as if I'm pleading with him.

"I guess you could say I was in the neighborhood," Martin says.

He still looks like a movie star. Still has the French accent, which I know he can make much thicker when he wants to. There was a time, and a good long time ago it was, when the combination of looks and accent and his goddamn Gallic charm made me feel as if the world had started to spin.

Not anymore.

I motion for him to take the sofa closest to him. Ben and I sit on the one facing the television set. Rip takes his usual seat at our feet. He isn't growling at my ex-husband. Maybe when he gets to know Martin better.

"You were in the *neighborhood*?"

"Allen Reese and his wife, Paige, had a dinner party tonight," Martin says. "Allen has the biggest real estate business out here, I'm told. Even bigger than your client's."

I've heard Rob Jacobson mention Allen Reese more than once. Never without the words "lying" and "thieving" or "scumbag" finding their way into the conversation at least once, and that's when he was trying to be kind. Rob's company *had* been prosperous before his trial. Not nearly as prosperous as Allen Reese's. Nobody's out here was.

"Well aware," I say.

"Allen and Paige have an amazing home over on Further Lane," Martin says.

"Happy for them."

"Anyway," Martin continues, "they occasionally come into my restaurant, and asked if they could auction off a dinner cooked by me for God's Love We Deliver. It's such a good cause, and so I agreed. Tonight was the night for me to come out. And, as I said, since I was in the neighborhood..."

He made this fluttery gesture with his hands, as if that somehow explained everything.

"And here I am," he says finally.

"Here you are," I say.

More gray to the hair and beard. More lines in the face. But still Martin, acting as if sitting in my living room were as comfortable for him as being in his own kitchen.

Maybe I ask him to go in there now and help out with dinner.

"So how are you, Jane?" he asks.

Fine, Martin, discounting my cancer. What about you?

I take a nice, deep breath. An old yoga teacher used to talk about her nighttime routine of "moon breathing."

I wanted to be on the moon right now.

"Martin," I say, "what's the French word for awkward?"

He smiles, with his eyes, mostly. *"Genant."*

"Well, this is about as *genant* as it gets, wouldn't you say?"

"I should go," Ben says again. "So you two can talk."

Now I smile at him. "I'll pay you to stay."

Has Martin somehow found out that I'm sick? Is that why he's here?

"I would have called," Martin says. He shrugs. "But I was afraid if I did, you'd tell me not to come by."

I wonder if he had worn his white chef's coat at the hedge funder's house.

"Is there wine?" he asks.

"There is," I say, but make no move to get off the couch, instead gently placing my hand over Ben's to keep him right where he is.

"This was obviously a mistake," he says. "But even though I did want to say hello, my visit actually does have a purpose."

"You always did take your time getting to the good

parts," I say, and immediately wish I hadn't, hoping that I'm the only one hearing a double meaning.

"It was an interesting and eclectic group around the table," Martin says.

"Now I'm happy for all of you."

I've heard about the colorful parties Allen Reese and his wife throw, featuring everybody from rappers to hard-core Republicans like them to jocks to the hot TikTokers.

"Have you ever been to one of their parties?" Martin asks. "It sounds like anybody out here who's anybody does eventually."

"I don't hang with people like the Reeses," I say. "I defend them."

He chuckles. Too cool to laugh.

"Is there a point to this story, Martin? Ben and I need to have dinner and then get to bed."

Take that.

"Two of the guests said they knew you, and to send along their best," Martin says. "I thought they might have come together."

"Names please?"

"One was named Edmund McKenzie," he says.

I sit up a little straighter.

"The other?"

"Bobby Salvatore."

Jimmy's right.

The world just keeps getting smaller.

And perhaps more dangerous.

"Martin," I say. "You suddenly have my undivided attention."

Another smile. "I didn't have it before?"

"Finish the story, Martin." It's a tone I'm sure he remembers along with everything else from our marriage.

"Allen Reese said something odd: that Mr. Salvatore was his bookie. I couldn't tell whether he was joking or not."

"He likely wasn't joking."

"So it was even more of an eclectic group than I first thought," Martin says.

Quietly Ben Kalinsky says, "You have no idea."

"Before Mr. Salvatore left, I asked if he was really Allen's bookie."

"What did he say?"

"He said problems were his specialty," Martin says. "I asked if that meant solving them or creating them. He smiled and said, 'Both.'"

FORTY-FOUR

Jimmy

HIS FACE IS BURNING, bleeding he's sure from the shattered windshield. But there's no time to check.

He's just happy nothing has hit him in the eyes, and that he can still see.

He's below the dashboard when a second bullet comes thudding into the leather behind the steering wheel.

No point in calling 911. Pinned down and taking fire, Jimmy knows he's outnumbered and maybe outgunned and tries to figure out how not to remain a sitting goddamn duck.

The third shot doesn't come, at least not right away.

Maybe she's waiting to see if he's been hit.

Or for him to show himself again.

For all Jimmy knows, she's in the dunes, circling around and closing in on the Jetta right now.

Jimmy doesn't know if Wolk has a gun of his own

or is just hunched down below his own dashboard, waiting for the woman to finish the job.

Not knowing where the shooter is, Jimmy unlatches the passenger door, using *it* for cover now. Then he's the one rising up from behind it, firing one shot, then another, and then two more after that, not aiming at anything in particular. He can't see the woman. He's just providing cover for himself, even as he's blinded by the Corolla's high beams.

Now the woman fires again and hits the door.

Jimmy leans out to the side, trying to refocus her gaze if only for an instant, then puts a bullet of his own into the Corolla's windshield, and hears it shatter.

And hears Wolk scream.

"Son of a *bitch*!"

"Get down, you fool," the woman shouts.

Two more bullets hit Jimmy's passenger door.

Jimmy doesn't know what kind of gun she has. Or how many rounds it has in it. But Jimmy is shit sure he's got seventeen rounds in the Glock if he needs them.

He waits.

If you're a cop for even a day of your life, you're good at waiting, even in a firefight like this.

Jimmy is about to put his gun back over the top of his door again when he hears the other guy make the next move.

The Corolla's engine ignites. High beams still on.

Jimmy fires again, then again, as he sees the car in motion, the crazy bastard gunning it, the roar of the engine filling the distance between them as Wolk drives straight for the Jetta.

Jimmy's surprised at the pickup.

From zero to me.

FORTY-FIVE

MARTIN LEAVES FIRST. ONCE he's gone, Ben doesn't even raise the possibility of spending the night.

The man I love now and the man I used to love were both in one room with me and somehow I felt as alone as I ever had in my life.

Dr. Sam has given me pills to help me sleep when and if I need them. But I don't take them. Or reach into the kitchen cabinet for the bottle of Jameson.

To process the events of the evening, I walk Rip, lock up the house, set the alarm. My Glock 27, the new one Jimmy got me for Christmas for being both naughty and nice, is in the top drawer of my night-stand. Ben saw it there one night and asked if I thought I needed the gun to protect me from him.

"Other way around," I told him.

I think about Martin now. Not only out here, but in

the same room with Edmund McKenzie and Bobby Salvatore before he was in the same room with me.

I think about Bobby Salvatore, hiding in plain sight at an Allen Reese party. The same Allen Reese whom my client called his sworn scumbag worst enemy.

As tired as I am, it's almost too much to process.

The only sound in the bedroom is Rip snoring softly on the throw rug at the end of the bed.

Sure, at least he can go right to sleep after a night like this.

Finally, perhaps by the grace of God—about time She gave a girl a break—I'm asleep and dreaming. In this one, my mother is with me again. Only I'm the one in the bed and she's sitting next to me, holding my hand.

Then she's leaning forward, close to my ear. She has something important to say, something she's been waiting my whole life to tell me.

Before she can, the moment is shattered by a ringtone and I'm wide awake all over again.

Rip is sitting up now. I can see his head over the foot of the bed, and he's wide awake, too, and panting.

It's my phone. I've finally ditched the Boston College fight song and gone with a normal ringtone.

At first, I can't hear the voice at the other end of the line.

Then I realize it's Jimmy.

"You . . . need . . . need to come get me."

"Jimmy, what happened?"

"A lot."

He tells me where he is before the line goes dead.

FORTY-SIX

THE PASSENGER-SIDE DOOR FROM Jimmy's Jetta is on the ground next to the car when I get to the dirt road just past the entrance to Napeague Harbor.

When I walk around to the front of the car, Glock in my hand, I see that the windshield is mostly gone and when I look inside, I see the broken glass on the front seat.

The tan-colored leather is bloodstained.

I yell Jimmy's name and wait.

Nothing.

I walk up the road, dunes on either side of me.

"Jimmy Cunniff, you told me to come, now where the hell are you?"

I often get mad when I'm as scared as I am right now. *"Jimmy?"*

I turn around and look at the car. Windshield gone. Door on the side of the road. Bullet holes in the door.

If Jimmy has been shot, it would be the third time since we took on Rob Jacobson as a client, which has to be some kind of record.

Where is he?

I jog back to my car and get the flashlight that I keep in the glove compartment along with my gun, and go back to his car, pointing the flashlight at the ground near the detached door.

The trail of blood begins there.

FORTY-SEVEN

Jimmy

WOLK'S CAR DOESN'T HIT Jimmy's head-on, he's going for the door Jimmy was using for cover, obviously hoping Jimmy is still behind it.

When Jimmy realizes that Wolk isn't bluffing, that he's not going to stop or even slow down, he dives underneath the Jetta, feeling the impact, hearing the screech of metal-on-metal, and tries to crawl all the way to the other side as the Jetta gets spun around, the front wheels hitting the right side of his chest, and he worries that the car is about to roll over on top of him.

He manages to get out from underneath, the Glock somehow still in his hand. *Screw it.* He's going down firing. He comes up and puts the gun on top of the convertible roof and starts firing at Wolk's car again, not sure whether they're going to stop or keep going.

This time he hits the back windshield and shatters

that, and then Jimmy is running for the dunes in case the crazy bastard turns around and comes back.

He trips and lands on ribs that he's sure are busted or at least cracked, manages not to scream.

It's finally quiet then.

He manages to raise himself up, sees the taillights of the Corolla now as Wolk puts the car back on the highway and heads east.

Maybe she didn't try to finish the job and was counting shots and wasn't sure how many rounds Jimmy had left.

Jimmy touches his face and feels the blood, not just from the windshield now, but from when his face hit the rocks and dirt as he dove under the car.

His chest feels like it's been hit with all the worst body blows he ever took in the ring. But he gets his phone out and manages to call Jane before he passes out.

The light shining on his face is what wakes him up.

Jane standing over him.

"Does that white light mean this is heaven?" Jimmy asks.

"You wish," she says.

She sits down next to him in the dirt then, leaning over to kiss him on the forehead before telling him she needs to call 911.

"No," he says.

FORTY-EIGHT

JIMMY'S CAR HAS BEEN towed by a friend of theirs, Lenny Morrell, who owns a gas station on Springs Fireplace Road. By now I've driven Jimmy—at his request—to the office of Dr. Ben Kalinsky, who has X-rayed Jimmy and taped up his three cracked ribs, cleaned and bandaged the worst cuts to his forehead, and told him it's a miracle he doesn't need stitches.

When Ben tells Jimmy he's really going to need to take it easy for a few days, they both hear me snort.

"I'm sure you both have your reasons for not calling the police," Ben says.

"I don't want them to be the ones who find the guy driving the car," Jimmy says, "or Annie Oakley."

I grin at Ben. "He's always been very inner-directed."

"And extremely inner banged up," Ben says.

"I've already filed a report with a cop," Jimmy says. *"Me."*

I drive us back to my house, after Ben points out once again what a full and interesting life I'm leading. The sun is up by now. I tell Jimmy I have some pain pills he can borrow. I've been hoarding my own for a while. He says it only hurts when he laughs, and since none of this seems particularly funny, he'll be fine.

What I do give him is coffee enhanced by a healthy shot of the Kentucky Owl Straight Bourbon I keep in the house for him. It's not as pricey as Pappy Van Winkle. But not cheap, either.

Jimmy drinks some of his bourbon-laced coffee. He picks the mug up with his left hand and then gently places it back on the table, making sure to take care with even the smallest moves. I've been there. I broke two ribs playing college hockey and for the next month was worried about taking deep breaths and became more afraid of coughs and sneezes than I was of snakes.

Jimmy has awakened Detective Craig Jackson, asking him to find out anything and everything he can about Anthony Licata, and if he might have a female partner now that Joe Champi is among the departed.

Jimmy has the call on speaker.

"Anything else you need?" Jackson asks.

"You've always been a giver," Jimmy says, and ends the call.

Jimmy carefully raises his mug to his lips and drinks.

"I like your triple shot better than the kind you get at Starbucks," he says.

"Breakfast of former Golden Glove champions."

We sit in silence. I've told him I'll drive him home when he's ready. He says not yet.

He coughs now, nothing he can do to stop it, and bends over in pain, which I can see only makes things worse.

"You're supposed to be the sick one," he says when he straightens up. "You know that, right?"

"You're the one who keeps getting shot at."

"Trying to quit," he says. "But at least now I know I owe this woman, whoever the hell she is, a good slap."

Before I can respond, he grins. "Sorry, I know that sounds politically incorrect," Jimmy says. "Actually, I meant two slaps."

"A lot of bad people out there, JC. Circling us like buzzards."

"And multiplying like rabbits," he says.

I tell him that it must be the bourbon making him mix his metaphors. Then ask how he's going to get around after I drop him in North Haven, since I know the last thing he's going to do is take it easy. He says he's going to try to sleep for a couple of hours, then call a buddy who runs the Hertz place at the little East

Hampton Airport and rent a car, and put it on Rob Jacobson's tab.

"Then what?" I ask after helping him up and into the Prius, giving him a pillow to put between him and the door.

"Then you don't want to know."

"Try me," I say.

"I'm about to get woke, or die trying," he says. "W-O-L-K."

"Even with broken ribs."

"It will make it more of a fair fight when I catch up with him."

"What if that woman is with him?"

"All the better," Jimmy says.

FORTY-NINE

SAM WYLIE AND I are at a restaurant we both like, Highway, on 27 in Wainscott. The place sits in front of the VFW post, and standing guard from across the parking lot is a venerable World War II tank. Highway features an interesting menu and a good bar crowd on most nights.

"I do believe there's a couple of studs at the bar checking us out," Sam says.

She's dressed up more than I have, in a silk summer dress she informs me she bought at J. McLaughlin in Bridgehampton for the occasion. She's clearly had her hair done, no point in me asking, it's there for the whole room to observe. She's not Dr. Sam tonight. More glam Sam.

"They're too young and we're too old," I tell her.

"Speak for yourself," she says. She turns and smiles at them. They raise their glasses in response.

"Don't encourage them, unless you're considering adopting them."

"Just because I'm married doesn't mean I can't check out men the way I used to when we'd go bar hopping," Sam says. "Remember the time—"

"No."

"That sounds like plausible deniability."

"Doesn't sound like," I say. *"Is."*

We both order white wine. We have an understanding that tonight we're not going to talk about my condition, the resumption of chemo in a couple of weeks, none of it or any of it. I don't tell her about what happened to Jimmy, because he wants to keep the circle tight for now as he tries to track down Wolk and figure out who the woman shooter is.

When the wine is delivered, Sam raises her glass. "To better days."

"When?"

We both drink. When we put our glasses down, neither one of us making a move to look at the menu, she says, "Tell me about Martin. Leave nothing out. Take as much time as you want. My darling husband says I have no curfew tonight."

I describe the scene at the house when I walked in and found Martin with Ben, tell her why Martin was out here, how he'd ended up at the same dinner party with Rob Jacobson's old classmate Edmund McKenzie and a bookie whose name keeps popping up for Jimmy and me.

"I'm sure the bookie person and the other person are fascinating to you," Sam says. "But Martin is the one who fascinates me."

"You act like this is still high school."

"As it should be."

Sam leans across the table, trying to act conspiratorial. "Was it still there?"

"Was what still there?"

She grins. "What my grandmother used to call the old zookety-zook."

"You want the truth?"

"You're practically required to be truthful with your personal physician."

"No."

"Really?"

"Really. And even if I did still have feelings for him, which I don't, they wouldn't matter because I'm with Ben now. Who loves me for who I am, instead of what I'm not."

"Who was it that said the heart wants what it wants?"

"Woody Allen," I say. "You still want to play that particular card?"

We both laugh. It feels good, if fleetingly.

Then, almost in the next moment, I start to cry.

I wouldn't do it in her office. But I'm doing it here. The tears come freely and in full force, nothing I can do to stop them, no point in even trying. Our waitress is on the way back to us, probably to tell us about the special. She turns right around and heads back toward the kitchen. My hands are pressed firmly on the table, as if I'm afraid to lose my balance or further lose control. Sam reaches across and covers them with her own.

I'm no longer making any noise, but my shoulders continue to rise and fall as I try to get enough air into me, and not make more of a scene than I already have.

"It's okay, Jane," Sam says softly. "It's okay."

My voice is practically a whisper.

"I want to live so much."

We sit there like that, at the window table, her hands still over mine. I don't know what the other people at Highway think, how many of them might recognize me from all the television airtime I'd gotten during Rob Jacobson's first trial. For as long as I've known Sam, she's always told me there's nothing I can't tell her, nothing I should hold back, no matter how private or personal.

I don't hold back now.

"I want to be happy," I say. "Is that too much to ask?"

Then I'm crying again.

FIFTY

"WELL," I SAY AFTER a lengthy trip to the ladies' room, "that was embarrassing."

"Don't feel embarrassed on my account, pal." Sam smiles. "As I remember it, I cried for a week after Tommy O'Neill broke up with me in high school. I thought I was going to have bags under my eyes for the rest of my life."

We both order appetizer salads as entrées, even though I've pretty much lost my appetite.

"I frankly don't know how you've managed to hold it together this long."

"Fake it till you make it."

"Jane Smith," Sam says, "you're the toughest person I know."

"Everybody going through what I'm going through is tough. I'm not better or braver than anybody else."

"How about we go with *as* tough as anybody I know?"

"What if it doesn't do me any good in the end?"

Our glasses are empty. But Sam holds hers up anyway. I feel as if I have no choice but to do the same.

"Let's not drink to that," she says.

We both pick away at our salads. The waitress comes by and sees how little each of us has eaten. I tell her to blame us, not the chef.

I wink at Sam when the waitress has walked away. "At least don't blame *her* chef."

My breathing is back to normal, even if I feel as if I've thrown a brick through our night out together.

We sit there quietly until she says, "Can you see yourself marrying him? Ben, I mean."

"You mean marry him and live happily ever after?"

"Yes."

"Before I answer, maybe you could tell me how long 'ever after' is."

"I'm your friend and your doctor, Jane. But not a prophet."

"How about an informed opinion?"

"My opinion, as your doctor, is that you just keep doing what you're doing, with the same strong attitude you've always shown, and we'll both see where that leads us."

"The witness didn't answer the question."

We smile at each other. This is more like it. More us being us.

"You're just afraid I'm going to have another crying jag," I tell her. "You weenie."

"*Totally!*" Sam Wylie says. "You know the deal. Doctors are supposed to do no harm."

She picks up the check, over my objections. She got to the restaurant before me, so her BMW is parked so close to the front door she's almost at the hostess stand.

We hug before she gets into her car and then she tells me to go home and take two shots of Irish whiskey and call her in the morning.

"I love you," she says.

"I love you, too."

"Is it as easy telling Ben that?"

I grin. "Easier," I say. "Much, much easier."

I think about calling Jimmy on the way back to Amagansett, just to see how he's feeling and if he's managed to stay out of trouble tonight. But then I decide I've done enough talking for one night. And definitely enough crying.

I lock up and set the alarm and take a hot shower, which helps me sleep sometimes, and get into bed and for once fall asleep right away.

I'm awakened by the sound of Rip barking from somewhere else in the house, definitely not the end of the bed.

When I sit up, that's where I see the outline of a man.

"You need a better alarm system," the voice in the dark says. "And a better guard dog."

His voice is very soft.

"And if you're thinking about reaching for your gun," he says, "I already have it."

From outside the bedroom door, I can hear Rip's low growl. I want to do the same.

"Who are you?" I manage.

"We haven't met," he says. "I'm the prodigal son."

FIFTY-ONE

MY FIRST THOUGHT?

I may be dying.

Just don't let it be tonight.

"There's no reason to be alarmed," he says.

I remember Rob Jacobson once quoting me the late Joe Champi, about how anybody can get to anybody. Now Rob Jacobson's son has gotten to me.

The room is dark enough that he's just a shape standing next to the bed. I like it dark in here. Jimmy dog-sat for Rip, slept here when Dr. Ben and I decided last month to spend a night in the city, and called it the "cave of doom."

"I just want to talk," he says.

For the second time tonight I'm trying to get my breathing under control.

"Call and make an appointment," I manage. "I'll make sure to fit you in."

I'll be damned if I'm going to let him know how scared I really am.

I can't see Eric Jacobson very well but can still hear Rip's low growl from outside the bedroom door.

"Could you please let my dog in here? He's worried about me, and too old to attack you, even if he wants to."

"The dog's fine," Eric Jacobson says, "even if he did promise to keep quiet after I gave him the treats I brought with me."

"You mean after you got in through one of my locked doors and managed to disable my alarm."

"Alarms were always easy." He chuckles. "Gazillion dollar–homes out here and alarms installed by amateurs."

No need to tell him that Jimmy installed mine and that he is anything except an amateur.

"I'll be sure to ask the alarm company to have my next bill adjusted."

I've seen pictures of Eric, so even in the darkness I feel as if I have a visual. A younger version of his father. But you could always see a lot of Claire Jacobson in him, too.

"It must be pretty important if you choose this way to take a meeting with me."

I slowly sit up, so my back is against the headboard now.

"Careful," he says. "I've heard what a tough guy you think you are."

"Somebody told me once that tough is the one with the gun."

"You never know. Smart people do dumb things. My father thinks he's smarter than everybody and look at the dumpster fire he's made of his life."

You're the one not as smart as you think you are.

"Now that you're here," I say, "I might as well mention that your old partner, Dave Wolk, and his girlfriend tried to kill my partner tonight."

"Doesn't surprise me. He always was a dumb-ass. Why do you think Dave the Dude was the only one of us who ever got caught?"

He's so sure of himself. A smug bastard like his father.

"Let me ask you something, junior," I say, unable to help myself. "Do you think I'm going to let you get away with this?"

His voice is suddenly so loud it's like my window just shattered.

"Don't call me that!"

"Sorry."

His voice grows softer. "Trust me on something, Jane. You don't want to make me mad."

There's a glass of water I always keep by my bed. But no way to get to it. And he's still the one with the gun.

"Why are you here?"

"You need to quit this case."

"Be*cause?*" I say, dragging the word out.

"Because you can't let him get away with murder twice, that's why. He hurt more people after he killed the Carsons. And if you get him off again, he's never going to stop." I hear him take a deep breath and slowly let it out. "He needs to pay."

I try to see the outline of *my* Glock in *his* hand but can't.

"You really believe he's a killer?"

The voice is soft again.

"Maybe it runs in the family," he says. "Maybe something for you to consider."

Before I can answer, he continues. "But maybe you're just one more person looking the other way on this freak because the money just keeps flowing in?"

He reaches over and puts his hand on my cheek and I recoil.

"Unless he's not the only freak in the family," he says. "Something else to consider."

I think about all the things that have happened to me and to Jimmy and all around us since I first agreed to take on his father as a client.

How did I get here?

"Don't touch me," I say.

"Or what?"

He silently moves to the foot of the bed, a tall shadow now facing me directly, towering over me.

I can hear Rip's low growl again from the other side of my bedroom door. Some watchdog he turned out to be.

"There's no way you could have known he killed the Carsons when you took his case," Eric Jacobson continues. "But now you have no excuse."

"How can you be so sure about all this?"

"Because if he can kill his own father, he can do anything."

His voice barely above a whisper now in the dark room.

This kid in his own dark place talking about his own father.

"I'll make you a deal," Eric Jacobson says. "You walk away and I'll do the same thing. And you won't hear from me ever again. Or my boys."

"How come Morelli's not with you tonight?"

"I told him I could handle this. And, counselor? Trust me on something. You'd much rather deal with me than him."

There's so much more I want to ask him. But I sense that I'm running out of time.

"It's that important for you to see your father go down?"

"He's a predator," Eric Jacobson says. "A violent sexual predator, no matter how much he wants to be the coolest guy at the cocktail party. He wanted my girlfriends. He wanted mothers and their daughters. He wanted somebody's wife, if only because she *was* somebody else's wife." A pause. "Why do you think I'm the way I am?"

"He may be the prick you say he is. But that doesn't mean he did it."

"He told me he did, you stupid cow!"

Somehow I've touched a nerve.

Another nerve.

"Told you what?"

He's whispering again. "Everything. Like he wanted somebody to know. Like he was bragging."

We hear the sirens then, and junior now knows what I've known all along, that he isn't nearly as good with alarms as he thought he was, or as smart. Because Jimmy Cunniff is no amateur.

Somehow the sirens don't seem to rattle him very much.

"I forgot what a rush all of this was," he says.

Then he gets next to my ear. I can feel his breath as he adds, "I'll be in touch."

He walks over to the window closest to him and opens it. Before he climbs through and out, he says,

"One thing I inherited from my father? We both think we can get away with anything."

Then he's gone.

I get out of bed and open the top drawer to my nightstand.

The Glock is still there.

FIFTY-TWO

Jimmy

JANE IS ON HER way to Mineola for the hearing in which she'll ask Judge Kane to move up the trial date. She hasn't told the East Hampton cops the identity of her intruder, only that he ran off when he heard the alarms and thanked the cops for their service.

Jimmy knocks on the door of Rob Jacobson's rental house in Amagansett.

A tall girl wearing a St. John's sweatshirt that barely covers anything south of the equator answers.

"Who are you?" she asks.

"The truant officer," Jimmy says. "Where is he?"

"Still in bed. Where I should be, by the way. But he made me come answer the stupid door."

"Tough shit. Go get him. Unless you want me to call your parents."

She gives him the finger over her shoulder as she heads up the stairs.

Jacobson comes walking down a couple of minutes later, wearing a white T-shirt with a penguin on the front and tennis shorts. Jimmy hasn't seen an ankle bracelet in a while. It's bigger than he remembers, or maybe it's just Jacobson's skinny chicken legs. If he still had the tennis court at his old house, the thing would probably hamper the shit out of him rushing the net.

"All I have to say to you," Rob Jacobson says, "is that I got nothing to say to you."

But being Jacobson, he has to add, "I did hear you had some car trouble?"

"And where would you hear something like that?"

"A friend."

"Wait," Jimmy says. "You still have friends?"

"You just met one of them."

"You mean illegally blond?"

"I've got an idea," Jacobson says. "You got anything else you want to ask me, talk to my lawyer."

He turns around, like he's on his way back upstairs, when Jimmy grabs him by the shoulder and spins him around, feeling the immediate spasm of pain through his rib cage, but not caring because spinning this guy makes the pain well worth it.

He raises his hand just slightly, so he now has Jacobson by the neck. As he does, he hears the girl in the sweatshirt make a chew-toy squeak from the top of the stairs.

"This is not the day for you to annoy me more than you already have, for too many reasons to list," Jimmy says, his mouth close to Jacobson's ear.

"I have pointed this out before, but I can fire you," Jacobson says, through clenched teeth. "You know that, right?"

"And I've pointed out to you that you fire one of us, you fire both of us," Jimmy says as he lets go. "Now let's go sit in the living room without me having to pull you in there by your ear."

Jimmy can hear the girl walking around upstairs. Jacobson takes the couch. Jimmy lowers himself down, carefully, into a wicker chair.

"Okay, what's got your hair on fire this time?" Jacobson asks.

"Your son broke into Jane's house last night and threatened her."

Jimmy sees genuine surprise on Jacobson's face, even knowing how little is genuine with this bastard, other than maybe the fear he showed Jane after he'd gotten shot at.

"Wait . . . Eric was at Jane's?"

"In her bedroom. In the middle of the night."

"What the hell for?"

"He told her to quit your case. Told her that he couldn't let dear old dad get away with murder twice in the same lifetime."

Jacobson sadly shakes his head. "I can't believe I'm saying this, but he may be even more of a loser than I thought. And still dumber than cement."

"Jane found him pretty persuasive when he was talking shit about you, and what he says you're capable of."

"Rotten apple doesn't fall far from the tree. Eric could always fake sincerity even better than I do."

Before Jimmy can respond, he sees a familiar sneer. "Broke in, huh? At least the kid is still good at something besides riding the waves."

Jacobson yells up to the girl. "Bethany, come down here and get me some coffee."

"Get it yourself," they both hear from upstairs. "I'm walking to the beach."

Jacobson shrugs. "Kids today."

"Why didn't you tell me *your* kid was back in the country?" Jimmy asks. "Or that he used to be a thief?"

"I didn't know he was back this time," Jacobson says. "But if he is back, I'll hear from him eventually, because he'll want money. But spoiler alert? He's through getting it from me. The last time he came back he said he owed some bad people. I asked him if they were the same bad people from the last time and then told him to get lost."

"One of his house-looting buddies was the one who tried to kill me the other night."

"Wolk or Morelli?"

"Wolk."

Jacobson snorts. "I wouldn't have thought he had the balls."

Jacobson starts to get up off the couch. "We done now?"

"We're done when I tell you we're done."

"Least I know you've got some balls on you."

"How come you didn't tell Jane or me after Morelli testified against you that he and Eric were partners in crime?"

Jacobson doesn't answer right away. The leg with the ankle bracelet is stretched out on the coffee table, and Jacobson is staring at it suddenly, curious almost, like maybe he can't believe that after the pampered, rich-boy life he's led, he can't buy his way out of this.

"I knew Morelli was going to disappear," Jacobson says finally.

"And why was that?"

"Because his uncle wanted him to disappear after his face got plastered all over the media," Jacobson says. "I assume by now you know who his uncle is."

Jimmy nods. "Something else that never came up before."

"You want to know why? Because I got a call from his uncle, that's why. At which point he told me to keep my mouth shut for once in my life and if I did, I wouldn't hear from the kid again until the trial was over." Jacobson grins. "I'd rather piss you off than Bobby Salvatore, any day of the week. Starting with today."

Jimmy stands up too quickly and immediately wants to double over in pain. But thinks he manages to hide it.

He turns around when he gets to the door.

"As it happens, the other night Salvatore was at a dinner party thrown by a guy you know."

"And which guy might that be?"

"Allen Reese."

"Speaking of gangsters," Rob Jacobson says.

"Meaning what, exactly?"

Jacobson smirks at Jimmy in a way that reminds him of a chimp.

"You know what they say in the movies, Cunniff. Follow the dirty money."

FIFTY-THREE

KEVIN AHEARN AND I are in Judge Kane's chambers at the Nassau County Courthouse by ten. No robe for the judge today, just an exquisitely tailored pantsuit.

I'm already halfway through my presentation about why it would make sense for all concerned to move up the trial date. I began by telling her, and Ahearn, about having a conflict that may at some point down the line affect my ability to responsibly conclude the trial if it doesn't begin for six or more months.

The judge asks what kind of conflict.

"Personal," I say.

"Can I assume that you're talking about your sister's health concerns?" Judge Kane asks.

You don't know the half of it, sister.

"Yes, Your Honor," I say with a straight face, "this is very much about cancer, unfortunately."

"But I have to point out, and with all due respect, Ms. Smith, that you were aware of your sister's cancer when you chose to resume your defense of Mr. Jacobson, knowing that the trial was scheduled to begin next spring."

"I did know," I say. "But my sister's situation is only one element of my request to the court, if you'll allow me to continue. Because we're talking here about the professional as well as the personal."

From there I throw everything I have at her. It's another founding principle of lawyering, one they really should teach even at the best law schools:

Throw enough shit at the wall and the law of averages says some of it will eventually stick.

All of it, if you're lucky.

And even as a kid, my dad told me I had a great arm, and not just for a girl.

I tell Judge Kane that the more intense the media coverage of Rob Jacobson, now that he's been charged with two consecutive triple homicides, the less chance I have of getting him a fair trial.

"Not because of you, Your Honor. Absolutely *not* because of you. But all of us in this room know that no matter how much you tell the jury to ignore the coverage, it's pretty much impossible in the modern world. It's not like in the old days, when you could tell them to stay away from newspapers. It doesn't work that way any longer, not when they're on their phones before they make it to the bathroom."

I can stand now, as if we're back in court and I'm in front of her bench, and not her desk. As I do, she actually smiles.

"In one of my favorite old movies," she says, "I believe it was the Sundance Kid who said he was better when he moved."

I move to the right of the desk, so both she and Ahearn can see me.

"The bottom line," I say, "is that the only fair trial my client can get has to begin as soon as possible. I know this is an old legal chestnut, but it applies in this case: Slow justice is no justice at all."

And sit back down. I look over to see Ahearn smiling at me.

"Note to self," he says. "If I'm ever accused of killing three people, my first call needs to be to Jane Smith."

"Very funny."

"Wasn't trying to be funny," he says.

"Is there anything *relevant* you'd like to add, Mr. Ahearn?" Judge Kane asks.

"No, Your Honor. It's the state's belief that everybody's interests are best served by not waiting until next year." He smiles at her now. "If necessary, I'd be ready to make my opening statement this afternoon.

So, for once, and maybe for the last time, Ms. Smith and I are in agreement and our interests are aligned."

Judge Kane leans forward and hard-looks at me.

"Just to be clear, Ms. Smith. Is there some other reason, one you haven't shared here today, why you want to fast-track these proceedings?"

"No, Your Honor."

Not the first time I've lied to a judge.

She says she'll check the court calendar and maybe get back to me as early as this afternoon. I thank Judge Killer Kane for her time and walk out of her chambers smiling. Not because of the lie I just told her. No. It's because I know I've done my job today. I've been a good lawyer.

All I've ever wanted to be.

In sickness and in health.

I walk down the hall to an empty ladies' room and lean against the wall. I don't cry. I just close my eyes and think about what I've done, because I have just hidden behind my sister's cancer and not told either the judge or the district attorney about my own.

It is another choice I've made. Cancer isn't. The way I live my life is. In the last six months, I've been shot at and had my house broken into and been threatened. Jimmy Cunniff could have been killed on multiple occasions. My sister told me I should concentrate on this case and let God sort out the rest of it.

But a normal person would be doing what Brigid is doing, concentrating on my recovery, letting someone else defend Rob Jacobson, and taking myself and Jimmy out of the line of fire.

Fight for my life and not his.

I push off the wall and walk over to the mirror and smile into it.

"That's what a normal person absolutely would do," I say in the empty room. "But you're not."

FIFTY-FOUR

IN EAST HAMPTON, ALLEN Reese, who is big and fit and brown and bald, greets me at the door as if he's been expecting me, even though I didn't call first.

I'm feeling more than a little salty today.

"I've actually been wanting to meet you," Reese says as he walks me through a living room that opens into a sunroom and finally a back patio, the two of us having passed what feels like a Met's worth of art. And not the New York Mets.

Some Hamptons homes have private beaches. Allen Reese somehow seems to have arranged a private ocean.

"I'm actually not all that interesting," I tell him.

"To me you are," he says. "Put me down as one more person out here wondering why in the world you'd defend a prick like Rob Jacobson."

"But my client speaks so highly of you."

"Well, yeah, but from behind bars," Reese says.

Reese makes a gesture now that takes in the back lawn, the dunes, the water, everything from heaven on down. "It's not much, but we call it home," he says, and then laughs, as if he's just amused the hell out of himself. I suspect it happens a lot.

We both sit in expensive deck chairs. There is a setup for iced tea, with two glasses. Maybe he doesn't want to get caught short when it's time to play host.

"My ex-husband cooked for you here the other night."

"Marty? Yeah, he told me the two of you had been married."

Never until this moment had I heard him called Marty. The nickname is, I'm sure, a way for Reese to make him sound like the help.

"After the first or second course of all that cutesy-poo food," Reese continues, "I wanted to point at the grill and ask him for a couple of well-done burgers with bacon and cheese."

"I'm curious," I say. "Whose idea was it to have him come out?"

"My wife's, who do you think?"

He pours us both iced tea without asking what I want in mine, puts my tall glass in front of me, drinks down half of his and smacks his lips.

"So, I finally get to meet the great Jane Smith," he says.

He finishes his iced tea in another swallow. "So, what can I do for you?"

"You can tell me about your relationship with Bobby Salvatore, for starters."

He doesn't change expression, just pours himself more iced tea, drinks some. Smiles. Salesman at heart.

"Not much to tell. He's just one of my many and rather colorful acquaintances. I collect interesting people at this house."

"Lucky you," I say.

"An old baseball guy once said that luck is the residue of design."

"Branch Rickey," I say.

"I'm impressed."

I let that go.

"I'll try to bumper-sticker this for you, Allen. Bobby Salvatore keeps wandering in and out of my case. Which really means in and out of my life, and uninvited. You call him colorful. I call him a criminal. Which may or not make you a criminal as well, at least by association."

He nods. "I've heard about what a mouth you have on you."

I angle my chair so I'm facing him now, tearing myself away from the spectacular view.

"Bobby Salvatore was the bookie for Hank Carson, whom your friend Rob Jacobson is accused of murdering, along with Hank's wife and daughter. He was the bookie for Carl Parsons, also deceased, husband and father to the two Elises. Also dead. In addition, he is uncle to another criminal and world-class punk named Nick Morelli."

I reach for my iced tea and drink. It's very good. I always forget to add mint. "How am I doing?"

"Are we getting to the place where this has anything to do with me?"

"We are, as a matter of fact."

"Thank God you're not billing me," he says. "Christ, you lawyers talk the way fish swim."

I move my chair a little closer to his. "Here's what I know about you and Mr. Salvatore, without talking *too* much. I know that you were on your way to being the king of real estate out here way back in 2008, a time when you were attached at the hip to Bear Stearns." I shake my head sadly. "Also deceased. But then everything came crashing down on you and a whole country full of big guys like you. I know that when the mortgage crisis hit, your problems suddenly became their problems. And when the shylocks at Bear Stearns realized you couldn't cover your sudden and impressive debt, they told you that your business was about to become their business."

Danny Esposito did some digging and discovered that Allen Reese and Bobby Salvatore have been business partners for quite some time. He shared his intel with Jimmy, who immediately called to share it with me.

As I tell Reese, I see something change in his eyes, the way Rob Jacobson's eyes always change when he doesn't like something he's hearing from me. The look is fairly reptilian. Guys like this can only shed so much of their skin, no matter how rich they are.

"Is that all of it?"

"Not quite," I say. "When you couldn't find a bank to bail you out, Bobby Salvatore, ever impervious to market fluctuations, did."

Reese stands now, so he's suddenly towering above me. His face has reddened. He is breathing hard.

"Before I show you out," he says, "explain to me what any of this has to do with your prick client?"

It hurts my neck staring up at him. So I stand, too, moving back out of his air space, toward the railing behind me.

"I keep asking myself who benefits the most when Rob Jacobson's business craters the way it has. Everybody knows that his former friend Gus Hennessy has benefited mightily with his own real estate firm. But not nearly as mightily as you have."

"Okay, now we really are done here."

"Rob keeps saying he was set up," I say. "You know who could handle something like that no problem? Your friend, Bobby Salvatore."

"I told you he was an acquaintance, nothing more."

"Sure. Go with that."

223

He briskly leads me back toward the front door, to the point where I'm nearly jogging my way back through the living room to keep up with him.

But when I reach to open the door, he holds it shut.

"You are messing with the wrong people," Reese says. "All in the name of somebody who's getting exactly what he deserves."

He's still holding the door shut.

"I am going to give you a piece of free advice, even though I hate to give anything away," Reese says. "If I were you, I'd be careful about saying any of this bullshit about me to anybody else. Or have it get back to me. Or to Bobby Salvatore."

The look is even more feral now.

"Is that a threat?" I ask when he finally does open the door.

"Call it an appraisal contingency," Allen Reese says before he slams the big door behind me.

FIFTY-FIVE

THE NEXT AFTERNOON, I spend over an hour driving on Route 27 to my regularly scheduled appointment with Dr. Sam Wylie. She has nothing new to report, nor does my oncologist, Dr. Gellis. She just wants to make sure I'm still good with resuming chemo, even with the trial date being moved up.

"Can't wait!" I say.

"I'm immune to your sarcasm by now," Sam says. "You know that, right?"

"It had to happen eventually," I tell her, before hugging her good-bye and reminding her that I love her madly.

The trip home takes an hour. I do a couple of hours of prep work on the case, then consider driving over to Three Mile Harbor to do some running and shooting. I haven't done much of either lately, mostly because I've abandoned the idea of competing in my no-snow biathlon in the fall.

I still like to run and shoot.

Instead I take Rip the dog, who continues to defy his own bleak prognosis and keeps getting stronger — one of us has to — for a long walk on the beach, Indian Wells to Atlantic and back.

It is a beautiful afternoon, one of *those* afternoons out here, and I am happier than ever to be making this walk with my dog, happy to be walking these beaches, wind in my hair, ocean at full voice, hardly any clouds in the sky.

I put Rip into the car and then walk back down to the water, not wanting to leave until I offer one of my quiet prayers — the praying always seems to go better here — for this not to all be taken away from me.

Not just these beaches.

"I like my life now," I say quietly, talking to God or to the ocean or to both of them. "I finally like *me*."

I've just gotten out of the shower an hour later when I get the call about what happened to Dr. Ben.

FIFTY-SIX

SOMEBODY BROKE INTO DR. Ben Kalinsky's office, swung away at him with a baseball bat, then fled. He awakened long enough to call 911 before passing out again.

When the cops and EMTs got there, a little after eight, Ben was still unconscious near the back door, bleeding from the head. I knew he was always the first to show up in the morning and the last to leave the office at night.

A friend from the East Hampton cops called Jimmy and told him that the locked cabinet where Dr. Ben kept his drugs had been broken into and apparently cleaned out.

"He only keeps heavy-duty pain pills in case of an emergency," I tell Jimmy.

"Addicts don't care how many, or how they get them," Jimmy says. The last thing Ben remembered, according to the first cops on the scene, was walking to the back room to lock up, hearing a noise, and seeing the bat coming for his head.

The EMTs got him into the ambulance and on his way to the trauma center in Bridgehampton.

"How bad is it?" I ask Jimmy from the car.

"They're trying to find out how much swelling there might be near the brain, and whether they might need to go in as a way of alleviating it," Jimmy says.

It's just Jimmy and me in the waiting area when I arrive at the trauma center. No other patients tonight except for the kindest man I've ever known, somewhere inside with his head cracked open like a walnut.

Maybe because of me.

By now I've told Jimmy about Allen Reese warning me that I was messing with the wrong people.

"You think he called Salvatore after you left him?"

"It's what I would have done," I say. "Maybe he was afraid that I might go around and tell people that he and Salvatore were besties."

I stare down at my hands, inspecting what's left of my last manicure, not even sure what the color was when I'd had the nails done. Wanting to think about anything except what's happening with the doctors on the other side of the double doors.

"What's taking them so long?" I ask.

"He was pretty banged up."

I'm too angry to cry. And too scared.

"Maybe it was just supposed to look like a robbery," I say to Jimmy. "Maybe whoever did this was just there to deliver a message to me."

Jimmy takes one of my hands and puts it in his own. "Or it really was a break-in and they were looking for drugs. *Newsday* reported that local vets' offices are frequent targets. Maybe he was just in the wrong place at the wrong time."

"Maybe the wrong place for Dr. Ben is *me*," I say. "And the wrong time is right now."

After what seems like about three lifetimes, the doctor finally comes through the door. It's not Raymond Williams, who treated Jimmy after he was shot. Tonight it's a small woman with big red hair and what looks to be a sleek runner's body.

Dr. Byrne, her name tag reads.

"He's awake," she says.

"Are you going to have to operate?"

She shakes her head. "No. Even though his skull is fractured."

"Good Lord."

She smiles. "Let me finish," she says. "Fortunately, it's a linear fracture and not what we call a depressed fracture. So, no surgery."

"So that means he's going to be okay?"

She pauses. After everything I've been through over

the past several months, I'm not crazy about doctors hitting the pause button, even for a beat or two. Every time they do, I feel like I might be slip-sliding toward the end of the world.

"He's very lucky, let's put it that way."

"Is that an answer?"

"As a matter of fact," she says, "it is. Because this could have been so much worse if he hadn't somehow regained consciousness long enough to make that call, and they didn't get him here as quickly as they did."

I decide not to press her further. She's on Ben's side, after all. And I don't want her to feel as if she's on the stand.

"Can I see him?"

"He wants to see you," Dr. Byrne says. "But be aware that the drugs have him feeling no pain."

"Good," I say. "I just need to tell him something."

Before I follow Dr. Byrne inside, Jimmy gently takes my arm.

"*What* do you need to tell him that can't wait?" he asks quietly.

"How sorry I am."

"I'm sure he knows that."

Now I'm the one pausing.

"And that as soon as he's out of here I'm breaking up with him."

FIFTY-SEVEN

Jimmy

AFTER THE SHOOTOUT AT Napeague Harbor, Jimmy's Jetta should have been tagged do-not-resuscitate. Miraculously, he'll be picking it up from the shop in a couple of days. For now he drives out from the trauma center in his rented Hyundai, toward Montauk.

He retraces the route he took the night he was following that prick Dave Wolk, takes the same right on Old Montauk, pulls up in front of the house on Elm where Wolk had picked up the woman. No lights on inside. No car in the driveway. No sign of life. When he gets out of the Hyundai, he discovers there's no mail in the box. The front door is locked. Same with the sliding doors in back. And all the windows.

It just means that the beating he owes Wolk, the Big Kahuna, will have to wait.

He drives home and gets undressed and carefully

lowers himself into bed, where he can only sleep if he keeps pillows on both sides to keep him from rolling over on his ribs.

In the morning, he is at the East Hampton Town Hall, first customer in the Town Clerk's office. An old girlfriend who works there will know how to sift through public records and find out who owns the house on Elm Lane. Jimmy was very good at most cop things. Paperwork was never one of his strong suits.

"Long time no see," he says to Carole Gavin.

"Only if you count three and a half years as a long time."

"You look good, Carole."

She presses hand to heart. "Oh, thank you, Lord," she says sarcastically. "He still thinks I look good."

They eyeball each other silently, and awkwardly, until she relents and asks why he's there.

"I need a favor."

"Then you've unfortunately been directed to the wrong desk."

"I need to know who owns a particular house in Montauk, because the other night somebody came out of it and then tried to kill me."

"And sadly didn't succeed."

He knows he is just going to wear this. The bad ending between them was his fault. But then endings to his relationships usually were.

"Please, Carole," Jimmy says. "It's not just me who's in danger. It's Jane."

Jane always got along with Carole, much better than with Jimmy's ex-wives.

"I'm more worried about her than me," he continues.

"Same," Carole Gavin says. "And I don't even know what the issue is."

He gives her the address. She disappears into another office. Jimmy remains standing. It would hurt too much to lower himself into a chair and then have to lift himself out of it. It's fast reaching the point where he's convinced that his ribs are never going to heal.

When she comes back, she wordlessly hands him an official East Hampton Town Clerk envelope.

"You're welcome," she says, and walks away without another word.

He waits until he's outside to open the envelope and look at the property and tax records inside.

He gently leans against the side of the rented car and whistles at the name he sees at the bottom of the printout.

"Well, I'll be a sonofabitch," he says.

The property owner is Anthony Licata.

Joe Champi's old partner.

Speaking of sons of bitches.

FIFTY-EIGHT

THE DAY I TAKE him home from the hospital Ben Kalinsky continues to tell me he won't let me end our relationship.

"What if I told you I'm just not into you anymore?"

Dr. Ben grins. "Then I'd be convinced you'd suffered a traumatic brain injury."

He's recovering nicely, Dr. Byrne has told him, but he still needs rest, and a lot of it.

Of course he ignores her prescription of no work for at least a week and makes his first trip into the office this afternoon.

"If you'll be serious for a minute," I say, "I can't live my life worrying about protecting you."

"Not asking you to," he says. "And by the way? You couldn't protect Jimmy from getting shot and nearly run over. You couldn't protect yourself when your house got broken into. You couldn't protect your client from getting shot when he was going for a beach walk. Should I go on?"

We're in his living room. Maybe he thinks he's eventually going to talk me out of this, and that we'll be back together when he's fully recovered. But he can't because I'm not going to let him. It may not be the best thing for him. But it's the safest.

"You got shot in the head because of me," I tell him now. "Now somebody takes a baseball bat to the same head. I'm just trying to save you..."

"What, from myself?"

"From *my*self!"

"I knew what I was signing up for."

"The hell you did, doc. Even I didn't know what you were signing up for, and that means on top of my cancer."

He shakes his head, once, twice, very slowly and very carefully. "Not accepting your proffer, to put it in legal terms."

"Not a proffer. It's an offer I'm not letting you refuse."

He gets out of his chair and comes over and leans down and kisses me lightly on the lips. There's still a small bandage near his hairline.

"If I was going to run, I would have run when you finally told me about your diagnosis."

He kisses me again.

"Counsel is leading the witness, Your Honor."

He smiles. It is still some smile. "Now please go into the kitchen and start banging around some pots and pans for that dinner you promised me. Doing that woman's work thing."

"Sexist pig."

"What are you going to do, dump me?"

"I give up."

"Finally."

After my world-famous chicken pot pie, and after I've insisted on cleaning the kitchen, he kisses me one more time. What I've always thought of as his heater. When I finally pull back, I say, "Not tonight, dear. You have a headache."

I'm driving home past the East Hampton Golf Club when I get an incoming call.

UNKNOWN.

I answer it anyway.

"It's Claire."

Her voice is barely above a whisper, as if she's afraid of being overheard.

"What's wrong?"

"You told me to call if I was ever in trouble," she says. "I think there might be someone in the house."

"Then call 911 and get out of there," I say, letting

her hear the urgency in my own voice. "I'm on my way."

When she speaks again, it's clear she's no longer talking to me.

"What are you *doing here?"*

Then the line goes dead.

FIFTY-NINE

NO POLICE CARS OUT front when I get there. Plenty of lights on in the house. Blue Bentley in the driveway. My Glock in my hand as I get out of my car.

The front door is unlocked.

Maybe she called the police. Maybe it was a false alarm, though it was clear to me before the call ended that she was speaking to someone she knew.

What are you *doing here?*

Only one way to find out.

I step inside.

"Claire! It's Jane."

Nothing.

"Claire!"

Louder this time.

Still nothing from the big, quiet house.

Upstairs or downstairs?

I stay down here, walking slowly into the showroom

they call a living room. I've been here plenty of times before. Rarely under pleasant circumstances, no matter which Jacobson I was with. But then last time I sat with her in this room, I almost liked her. She almost acted like a human being, a wounded one, for the first time, at least in my presence.

Before I left that day, I told her to call if she ever needed help.

Now she has.

But what kind of trouble?

And where is she?

"Claire! Talk to me."

I step out onto the patio and under the floodlights flashing onto the back lawn. I once saw a young woman running away from Rob Jacobson out here.

Now, at the very edge of the property, I see a man running away, the light briefly hitting one side of his face before he lowers his head as if he's the one being chased.

For a moment, I think it might be Claire Jacobson's son, Eric.

But then he's gone, in the direction of the beach. There's no one else in sight.

Too late to stop him by firing a warning shot, *I* stop.

In the middle of the swimming pool is a body, slowly sinking.

Clearly a woman.

SIXTY

THE FIREHOUSE IN EAST Hampton offers a CPR course. Three summers ago, I earned my certification. If ever I was walking the beach or swimming in the ocean with no lifeguard on duty and saw somebody drowning, I'd be ready.

I was a good student but never had the opportunity to use what I'd learned.

Until right now.

"You need to be prepared if there ever comes a day when the shit gets real," one of my instructors, Shawn Roney, had told me.

Without hesitation, I kick off my sneakers and toss my cell phone next to my gun and dive into the pool.

I swim to her and lift her head, no idea if she's dead or alive, and somehow manage to get us both down to the shallow end. It then takes all my strength to lift her out of the water and onto the deck. I roll her onto her back. She doesn't appear to be breathing.

She can't have been in the water very long. But it doesn't take very long to drown. Maybe it took me fifteen minutes to get to her. Maybe a little more.

I feel for a pulse.

There is one.

Just not much of one.

But she's alive.

For now.

"He—or she—who hesitates loses the victim," Shawn told us in the CPR clinic.

I start doing chest compressions with both hands. Thirty, rapid fire. CAB, they call it. Compressions airway breathing. I go through the process now, keeping count in my head.

Then I start mouth-to-mouth.

Rescue breathing.

Tilt the head. Pinch the nose. Breathe in.

"You're not kissing them, you're sealing their mouth with yours," Shawn had taught me.

I breathe into Claire Jacobson's mouth once, then twice.

Nothing.

"Breathe!"

Like I'm shouting at the night.

Or the ocean.

Thirty more compressions, as quickly and firmly as I can. A little harder than before. Or maybe more desperate than before, not worrying that she might be the one who ends up with cracked ribs.

Just worrying that I'm running out of time to bring her back.

"Breathe, goddamn you!"

One more round of compression.

One last shot at mouth-to-mouth.

I pull back, gulping in air myself, even though I'm not the one who needs it.

No movement to her chest.

Eyes still closed.

I'm convinced I've lost her.

Then she coughs, just barely.

And opens her eyes.

SIXTY-ONE

A GEYSER OF POOL water splashes upward. Claire rises up on her elbows, streaming a spray that narrowly misses my face.

Now she's the one greedily drinking in air, slowly at first, then faster, as if chasing the feeling that she's still alive.

Her eyelids flutter closed and then open again.

"Jane," she says weakly.

"I was in the neighborhood."

There are things I need to know about how we both ended up here.

With great difficulty, she lifts her right arm. She looks disoriented, her eyes unfocused.

I take her hand and help her into a sitting position. "What happened?" I ask.

She frowns as if she's not thinking clearly. Or hearing.

"I don't know..."

"Who put you in the water?"

She takes in more air, almost panting now. "We've always...there's a lot...a lot of money in the house."

"Somebody tried to rob you?"

She closes her eyes again. I still haven't let go of her hand.

"Did you hear me?"

"What?"

"Claire," I say. "The last thing I heard you say on the phone was 'What are you doing here?' Were you talking to a stranger? Or someone you know?"

She starts to answer, then stops, and frowns. "I don't recall saying that."

I stare at her incredulously.

"Claire," I say. "Are you actually lying to the person who just saved your life?"

Suddenly she seems completely, intensely, present. And aware.

"Thank you," she says. "Now please get out of my house."

SIXTY-TWO

ROB JACOBSON ASKED HIS court-appointed officer for permission to meet me for lunch at il Buco al Mare, on Main Street about a mile from his rented house.

The restaurant's open design gives the feeling of eating outside on a beautiful day. Jacobson convinced the host to bend the no-reservations policy and booked one of the front tables. In the Hamptons, any kind of celebrity is better than none.

He arrives wearing fashionable, string-tied white slacks. The cut, I notice, strategically hides his ankle bracelet. I've recovered from last night's near-death experience for his wife, which feels as if it happened to me.

"The money and gold in the house, that's my wife's version of mad money," he informs me.

"How much money are we talking about, exactly?"

"A couple of million or thereabouts. She keeps it in a safe I used to call Fort Knox."

We've both ordered salads. He's having a glass of white wine. I'm having an iced tea.

"Didn't you used to take mad money with you on dates, back in the pre-Uber days?"

"Didn't need it. I usually had a gun in my purse."

A few minutes ago, I spotted a photographer on the south side of the street, discreetly taking pictures. The restaurant's manager had probably given him a call. Mobsters eating at your restaurant, or getting shot in front of it, is as good for business here as it is in the city.

"Who else knows where the safe is?"

"Just Claire and me," he says. "And the kids."

"Do the kids have the combination?"

He looks shocked. "Are you on drugs?"

"As a matter of fact."

"You know what I mean," he says.

"Before I noticed Claire in the pool, I saw somebody running away. I thought it might have been your son."

"Maybe he got tired of her turning down his requests for money and decided to take things into his own hands. Literally."

"Why wouldn't she tell me it was him?"

"A rare burst of maternal instinct?"

"After he left her for dead?"

"My loser son, having blown through his trust fund, seems to be getting increasingly desperate," he says. "About a week ago, he tried to strike a bargain. If Claire would just give him some money, one last time, she'd never hear from him again. She laughed him off, told him that's what he always says. That's when he threatened her, said he'd kill her if she didn't give up the combination to the safe."

He shrugs. "As soon as you told me what happened, I called her, asked if her attacker was him. Eric. She insisted that the person concealed his identity by wearing a mask."

"But this person knew about the safe."

He nods. "She told me she tried to get away, remembers only being hit in the back of the head until you brought her back from the great beyond."

The best of families.

"Is it worth me going back at Claire on this?" I ask.

He laughs. "All she seems to care about is that she refused to open the safe and nobody got her money. She's taking the win on that, even if it nearly got her killed."

My lunch date grows quiet, oddly so for someone who regards an unspoken thought as being against the law.

"Something else on your mind today?" I ask him.

"As a matter of fact, there is."

Now he's the one leaning forward, lowering his voice. I idly turn my head and see the photographer snapping away, not even trying to hide in plain sight.

"I need to tell you something, just in case none of us makes it out of this alive."

"Now there's a cheery thought."

"I think I'm falling in love with you," Rob Jacobson says.

SIXTY-THREE

A FEW DAYS LATER I'm still reeling from Jacobson's profession of undying love, or whatever that was.

"I've told you before, we're more alike than you think," he said.

"And I've told you on multiple occasions, no, we're not. Never have been and never will be."

"I knew I probably wouldn't get the response I wanted."

"Here's my response: *Get over it*!" I snapped. "And in case you've forgotten, I already have a boyfriend."

It turns out my breakup with Dr. Ben continues to be the least successful in recorded history, which is how the following Sunday I end up accompanying him to the annual Hampton Classic Horse Show in Bridgehampton.

Ben used to ride as a kid, even rode in the Classic a few times. Still loves horses. Still attends the Classic every year. I've never been, but he assures me I'll like this show-jumping circus more than I think I will.

"And it will be a nice change of pace for you," he says, "dealing with horses instead of horse's asses."

The Classic's showcase event, Grand Prix Sunday, is held the day before Labor Day in the big ring closest to Snake Hollow Road. As a way of fitting in with the rest of the swells, I've even purchased a new straw hat for the occasion.

"Are we arriving early so I don't miss batting practice?" I ask after we've parked.

"You promised to be a good sport."

"I might have lied."

"How are you feeling today, by the way?"

Lately I've been complaining to him about the fatigue he can see for himself when we're together. It's as if my body already knows I've got another round of chemo staring me smack in the face.

"I feel like a million damn dollars," I answer, lying about that, too.

Ben has VIP passes for us. Once we're inside, wearing our festive cloth bracelets, I see Claire Jacobson across the crowded tent, holding a champagne flute, laughing at something Congresswoman What's-Her-Name has just said.

I know Claire sees me, but when I wave, she immediately turns away with a phantom wave at somebody else, or nobody at all. That old proverb, if you save a person's life, you're forever responsible for it, is made to be broken.

I point that out to Ben.

"I'm convinced she knows who put her in that pool," I tell him. "She just won't say."

"Whatever her reasons are, they belong to her," Ben says. "And maybe, just maybe, we can stroll around the tent, mingle with some people I know, and enjoy the horsies."

"I know enough people," I tell him, kissing him on the cheek. "I'd rather stick one of the toothpicks from the appetizers in my ear than do this scene."

He heads in one direction and I head in the other, toward the bar, to order a Bloody Mary, knowing midday champagne will make me feel even sleepier than I already do.

After I've collected my drink, I think I see Edmund McKenzie standing where Claire Jacobson had been, but Larry Calabrese, the East Hampton police chief, intercepts me. Maybe McKenzie saw me coming, but he is long gone by the time Larry and I have finished making small talk.

While I wait for Dr. Ben to make his rounds, I make my way outside and toward the closest ring. I don't know what the time on the clock means, but I know the tall young rider has his horse moving fast by the way his hair flows from underneath his helmet. He gets around the course without knocking down any rails and the crowd cheers.

When I turn back toward the tent, Bobby Salvatore is standing in front of me. I know what he looks like because I have googled him, on multiple recent occasions.

"Let's take a walk," he says.

SIXTY-FOUR

HE DOESN'T PARTICULARLY LOOK like a gangster. But I'm not quite sure what that meant any longer, not since internet nerds looking like past presidents of the Science Club came along and started acting as if they ran crime families.

Salvatore is tall, broad, tanned, a lot of wavy gray hair, striking against the royal-blue shirt and pocket square he's paired with a cream-colored summer suit and the white-rimmed black leather sneakers now accepted as formal wear.

"What if I don't want to walk anywhere with you?"

"Come on, counselor," he says. "You had to know we were going to meet sooner or later. It's just me who picked the time and place."

"You had no way of knowing I'd be here."

"You'd be surprised at what I know." He chuckles. "And what you don't."

If there's a New York accent going on here, he's either hiding it pretty well or has lost most of it along the way. Maybe just a splash of Brooklyn.

"Come on," he says. "You'll be back with your date before you know it."

We start walking in the general direction of the barn area.

"Sorry to hear what happened to him," Salvatore adds.

"I'll bet."

"You got me all wrong."

"Somehow I doubt that."

We pass another ring, the riders inside looking like children.

"I got a granddaughter who rides," he says. "Sport's not cheap."

I stop briefly and look up at him. He has the darkest eyes I've ever seen, the color of night.

"This is how we're gonna do it, Bobby? Really? Making small talk about horses?"

"Just trying to break the ice."

"How about we have a conversation instead about all the dead people I've encountered who seem to have had some connection to you, all the way back to Hank Carson and your old friend Artie Shore?"

He grins. "What can I tell you? It's a dangerous world out there."

We arrive at an empty ring, the jumps already stacked against each other off to the side.

"Let me ask you something?" he says, his voice mild. "What's it like, knowing you're going to die?"

You'd be surprised at what I know.

I'm not sure what kind of reaction he expects. But I don't give him one.

"My father loved boxing, that's something I'm sure you don't know," I say. "And loved old fight films just as much. His favorite was *Body and Soul,* starring the guy he called the great New York actor John Garfield. Dad let me watch it with him when I was old enough. At the end, maybe you saw it yourself, Garfield doesn't take a dive and guys like you threaten to kill him."

He nods. "Guys like me."

"And you know what the great New York actor John Garfield says? 'Everybody dies.'"

Salvatore nods again. "But we all want the same thing, whether we got the cancer or not. We're looking for it to be later rather than sooner. Am I right?"

I hear a voice in the distance, an announcer calling the names of riders and horses to assemble at the Grand Prix ring. I know it's thoroughbred racing they call the sport of kings. But that's what it feels like here. Kings and queens.

And me.

And Bobby Salvatore.

"You think you know me, but you really don't," he says. "You think you know where I figure in all this, but you don't."

"So educate me."

He smiles. "My education, at I guess what you could call the school of hard knocks, came from a man named Sonny Blum."

"You still work for Blum? I heard you'd moved on long ago."

"I did. But before I did, he taught me well."

"I'll bet."

"And one of the things he taught me was to understand where you fit in the grand scheme of things. That no matter how big you think you are, there's always somebody bigger. Like Sonny, for example."

I was about to thank him for his crash course in the mob but thought better of it. Our date was going so well.

"What do you really want to tell me?" I ask, even though there's so much more I want to ask him.

In the next moment, he reaches over with a big hand and gently strokes my cheek. His touch makes my skin crawl. I want to recoil. Or give him a good slap. But I don't want to give him the satisfaction. And the last thing I want to do at the Hampton Classic, with media everywhere and a cell phone in every hand, is make a scene.

He takes his hand away as quickly as he put it there, then leans down to whisper in my ear.

"It's not me you're after," he says. "No matter how much you want it to be."

SIXTY-FIVE

Jimmy

JIMMY AND BEN KALINSKY alternate days of driving Jane to Southampton and sitting with her in the hospital, three hours at a time, the chemo drugs this round seeming to knock her down more than they ever have before. It only serves to piss her off more than ever before, since she's trying to keep working. Still in contact with the two young kids she's hired for Jacobson's trial, Estie and Zoe, who are doing their level law-student best to come up with alternative theories about who could have murdered the Carson families. The same game as always on their side of things. My guy didn't do it but here's somebody who could have.

These days Jane is feeling so punk she's even starting to second-guess herself for moving the trial date up, complaining that she's not going to be ready.

Something else to piss her off.

Jimmy Cunniff would rather wrestle a grizzly than spend a whole lot of time going back and forth on shit like this with cranky Jane.

But he sits there and holds her hand while the drugs are pumped into her. He doesn't bring a book. He doesn't make calls or listen to music. He is totally present for her.

"You need to be getting better," he says.

"When does that happen, doctor?"

Then apologizes almost as quickly as she's snapped at him.

"You know you don't ever have to apologize to me."

Another mistake.

"You don't get to tell me what to do."

Jimmy smiles at her and squeezes her hand and says, "Did we get married and I wasn't informed?"

That gets him a small smile in return. After that she closes her eyes and lets the drugs do their job without further comment. Neither one of them can believe she still has her hair. Minor miracle. But neither one of them talks much about that, for fear of jinxing things with the hair gods.

Jimmy wants to be working today, too. But she needs him here, and so here he is. He can't find an address for the mysterious Anthony Licata other than the one on Elm Lane. He can't find Nick Morelli and

Dave Wolk. Or Eric Jacobson, who may or may not have tried to off his own mother, even though she won't admit that or call the cops on him.

He's got Danny Esposito, his new best friend, looking for any sign of an email presence, or social media presence, or phone records, for Eric Jacobson and Morelli and Wolk. But if they're in contact with each other by phone, they're using burners. And have otherwise gone dark online. At the same time, Esposito hasn't gotten a single credible lead on the murders of Elise Parsons and her daughter, the ones who brought Esposito into Jimmy's life in the first place.

Jimmy feels like a mouse on one of those spinning wheels. Or a rat in a maze. Either way. Through it all he keeps coming back to some basic questions:

Could Rob Jacobson have killed them all?

And if he didn't, who did?

Or were Jimmy and Jane looking for one killer and not two?

Jane told him the last thing Bobby Salvatore had said to her at the horse show, playing off her line to him from that old movie.

"Everybody *lies*," Salvatore had told her.

Nobody Jimmy had ever encountered could lie the way Rob Jacobson could. Guy lied like Jeter used to play shortstop.

The nurse finally comes in and unhooks Jane. She's

a lovely Jamaican woman named Christine, and Jimmy
has already commissioned her as an angel.

"See you tomorrow, Miss Jane," Christine says.

"If I'm late," Jane says, sounding like herself, "start
without me."

But the spunk, that brief spark, is there and gone.
Jimmy feels as if she's a little more wobbly than usual
as he walks her to the car. At one point she starts to sag
and Jimmy steadies her by putting an arm around her.
She lets him keep it there until she's inside the
good-as-new Jetta, Jimmy wishing it were as easy for
the doctors to do bodywork on Jane.

When they're heading east, Jimmy asks if she'll be
okay by herself when they get to the house; he's got
some work he needs to do.

"You're worried I can't take care of myself?"

"Maybe not today, Janie."

At times Jimmy has thought they were doing a piss-
poor job of taking care of each other. Or anybody.
Including Ben Kalinsky, whom Jimmy knows Jane
would never let go of.

"Okay," she says quietly, and puts her head back and
seems to fall asleep.

Jimmy shuts off his Bluetooth, not wanting to wake
her if there's an incoming call. Goddamn, she looks
pale. And as tired as he's ever seen her.

They're stopped at the light in the middle of

Bridgehampton when Jimmy hears his phone buzzing. He's tossed it in the console. But can clearly see the screen.

Esposito

He'll call him back after he drops Jane off. They're almost at the house when she finally opens her eyes.

"You're awake," Jimmy says.

"Wasn't sleeping," she says. "Just thinking."

"About what?"

"About how I can't do this anymore."

"The chemo? This round is almost over, kid."

She shakes her head so slowly Jimmy imagines it being as heavy as a bowling ball.

"I mean the case," she says.

"What are you saying?"

"That I'm done."

SIXTY-SIX

BEFORE I GET OUT of the car Jimmy says, "If you quit, the terrorists win."

"Watch me," I say.

"You're always telling me that it's lawyering that makes you feel most alive."

"Only now I feel as if it might kill me and everybody I care about. Starting with you."

He starts to open his door. I tell him I don't need help getting into the house.

"You're just having a bad day," Jimmy says.

"They're *all* starting to feel like bad days. Ben could have died because of me. *Again.* You could have died on me. *I* could have died because of me."

I come around to his side of the car. He's got his window down. He tells me he'd never try to talk me out of something I really want to do.

"I'll have your back until somebody does take me

out," he says. "But I'll just leave you with this: I've always said that you should never make a big decision when you're drunk or tired. I think we can add being on chemo to that list."

I walk toward the front door, trying to will myself into looking stronger than I feel. Unlock the door. Disable the alarm. I never used to set it during the day. Now I do. Another reaction to all the bad days I've had recently. Jimmy has redone the system yet again, telling me that even the Army Corps of Engineers couldn't get past it, much less a punk-ass bitch like Eric Jacobson.

When I see Rip the dog standing there waiting for me in the front hall, tail wagging, I can't help but smile. But when I crouch down to scratch his ears, a wave of dizziness comes over me.

So I lie down on the floor, telling myself I'll stay there until the feeling passes.

My dog lies down next to me.

"I'll tell him I'm quitting in the morning," I say to Rip the dog.

We both go to sleep right where we are. It's dark out when I finally awaken and find out I slept through Jimmy's call from Esposito, about the body.

SIXTY-SEVEN

Jimmy

THE SURFBOARD ABOUT THIRTY yards away from the body, the lifeguards long gone, it would have looked like some kind of early-evening surfing accident at Ditch Plains Beach in Montauk if not for the bullet somebody had put in the middle of Dave Wolk's forehead, center cut.

"This the guy who tried to run you over?" Esposito says.

"One and the same."

Esposito and Chief Larry Calabrese are sharing the scene, even though it's technically Calabrese's jurisdiction. So they're playing nice, which is why Calabrese waited for Jimmy to arrive before allowing the body to be bagged.

"Big-ass storm blew through here about seven o'clock," Esposito says. "Everybody on the beach cleared out. A couple of kids in search of big-ass waves found him, freaked, called 911."

"This was an execution," Jimmy says.

He thinks about the way his old partner, Mickey Dunne, took one to the forehead in the Bronx, the murder still unsolved, Jimmy still certain Mickey had died at the hands of Joe Champi, Jacobson's former fixer, the one Jane took out.

How many people connected to this thing are going to die?

Esposito walks Jimmy away as the ME's people bag the body.

"I gotta ask, just on account of you having history with this guy."

"I've been with Jane all day." Jimmy doesn't tell him where or why. "You can ask her. I'd just dropped her off at her house when I got your call."

"Didn't think this was your style."

Jimmy looks out at the water. The waves are still huge.

"Bullet?" Jimmy asks.

Esposito shakes his head. "In the front door, out the back, nowhere to be found. Maybe the ocean swallowed it. No shell casing, either. Small caliber from the looks of the entry wound."

"You think he was surfing before he got shot?"

Esposito gives a who-knows shake to his head.

"Why not? Maybe the surfer dude felt as if he had the best waves out here all to himself. But somebody must have followed him and waited for him to come out of the water, and then got it done."

Jimmy walks back to where the body was.

"Just the two kids out here after the fact?"

"Still here," Esposito says, and points to the two of them, sitting on a piece of driftwood, the boy's arm around the girl.

High school kids. Maybe college. Jimmy has a harder and harder time telling the difference. Esposito tells him that the boy's name is Jared Willson. The girl is Missy Gomes. Both from Montauk.

Jimmy goes over and introduces himself. They look up at him, seeing him but not seeing him, as if still in a state of mild shock.

"I'm with the cops."

Technically true.

"All we wanted to do was come look at the waves," Missy says.

She looks as if she's been crying and might start up again if Jimmy says the wrong thing.

"Is there anything you can remember, other than what you've told the cops already, that might help us figure out who did this?"

They look at each other. "We called 911 right away!" Jared says.

Like he'd earned them a merit badge.

"Nobody else around when you parked your car?"

They look at each other, shake their heads, no.

"Wait," Missy says. "There was one other thing we maybe forgot to mention, we were both so creeped out when they were asking us questions. There *was* one other car, but it wasn't in the lot up top. Leaving as we were coming in."

"You happen to notice what kind of car?"

They both shake their heads again.

"Just that it looked like it had been in some kind of accident," Jared Willson says.

Jimmy Cunniff's voice is low enough that he wonders how they can hear it over the sound of the water.

"Did you by any chance get a look at the driver?"

"It was a woman," the boy says.

SIXTY-EIGHT

I NO LONGER WANT to represent Rob Jacobson. I have to tell him to his face. It's the right thing to do. So a little before eight o'clock I walk the couple of miles from my house to his rental. I spent hours last night sleeping on the floor next to Rip the dog, so the walk does my stiff back and neck good.

"Are you alone?" I ask Jacobson when he opens his door.

"Not exactly," he says.

Anticipating his reaction to my news, I feel myself smiling.

"But I thought you wanted to pledge your heart to me."

He shrugs, turns his hands palms-up. His eyes are puffy, either with sleep or from drinking, because I know for a fact he's been hitting the bottle hard.

"If you can't be with the one you love..."

"Love everybody you can get to stay still long enough?" I'm already moving past him as I add, "May I come in?"

I don't want to know who he's sleeping with in the upstairs bedroom and don't much care.

He shows me out to the back patio. There's a coffee mug on the table. He asks if I'd like a cup.

"I won't be staying that long," I say, "but we need to have this conversation in person."

"That doesn't sound good."

"It's not."

We take seats across from each other at the table. Over the past several months, I have spent more hours in this man's presence, in court and in jail and in this house and in the much bigger house he still owns in Sagaponack, than I care to count.

"You need to find a new lawyer," I say.

His eyes don't look nearly as sleepy now. But he collects himself quickly, the way he did the day I gave him a good slap.

"I'm a little too tired and a little too hungover for jokes," he says, and sips some coffee, trying to act casual.

"It's no joke. I'm quitting. For good this time."

He stares at me, eyes even bigger and more alert than before.

"You're serious."

Jacobson is shaking his head now, and not just to get rid of the cobwebs.

"I understand this is probably a shock," I say. "You can go back to Howie the Horse."

"Howie's not a horse. He's a jockey."

"Or I can make some recommendations."

"You'll be wasting your time. I don't want another lawyer. I want you."

"I hear you," I say. "I thought that I was still Bring It On Jane. But I'm not. And I can't." I sigh. "So I'm out."

He's still shaking his head. "No," he says. "No... no... *no*."

"It's not just one thing," I continue, knowing I'm giving him more information than he needs, or really deserves. "It's my treatments and the trial and putting people I care about in danger."

He reaches underneath the print edition of the *Wall Street Journal* next to his coffee mug and comes up with a thin silver flask. He pours some of whatever's in it into the mug. Takes a big gulp now.

"This is because of what I told you at lunch about falling in love with you, isn't it? You're just throwing it back in my face."

"What? No, Rob. It might shock you, but this isn't about you. It's about me. I've always told my clients that I'd be willing to fight to the death for them. Well, not anymore."

He snaps then, just like that, pounding his hand down on the table, veins popping in his neck, spilling some of his coffee. Shouting. *"It will make me look guilty if you quit!"*

"That's not true," I say quietly, trying to dial things down. "And if you want to tell people that you fired me, I'll back your story."

"Nobody will believe me," he says.

"You're the one always telling me that you could sell an oil slick if you had to."

He leans across the table now, trying to get himself under control. Hands clasped in front of him. He even manages a thin smile.

Suddenly he's negotiating with me. It seems to help him get his bearings.

"You want more money?" he says. "Done."

"Rob," I say. "It's not about money." Now I'm the one shaking my head, eyes closed. "You're not listening to me. This is about my life, not yours."

"And you just now arrived at that conclusion?"

He pounds the table again, less forcefully than before.

Voice rising again.

"This isn't fair!"

Like he's a little boy not getting his way.

"I'm sorry," I say. "I really am."

"No," he says, "you're not."

We stare at each other, clearly having reached an impasse. But something has changed in his eyes. A look appears in them that I've seen before, one that's made me think, and more than once, that he could have done it. A weird light in them, the clearing before the storm.

I need to end this.

"I've made up my mind."

"Unmake it."

"You're making this harder than it needs to be."

He barks out an unpleasant-sounding laugh. "Wait. I'm the one making things harder than they need to be?"

I stand up. "I'll call you later and explain the process to you, with the judge and the court and all that."

But as I come around the table, he's standing, too, and grabbing me by the arm.

I look at him, then down at his hand before calmly removing it.

"Don't," I say quietly.

He's still between me and the patio doors. The odd light still in his eyes somehow darkening the color of his pupils.

"Nobody walks away from me," he says before finally getting out of my way.

SIXTY-NINE

Jimmy

JIMMY NEEDS INFORMATION, AND in a hurry, about Anthony Licata, ex-partner to Joe Champi. Letting the game come to him has never been his strength so he goes to the city to work his friends in the department and their friends.

He can now connect Licata, wherever the hell he is, to the late Dave Wolk. Whose lady friend might have turned her gun on him. Or she was really Licata's lady friend, the one who slapped Jimmy that night when they had him tied up at his house.

Everything connected.

But how?

Jimmy meets Detective Craig Jackson and Dick Kelley, a retired detective older than both of them, at Dorrian's Red Hand. The Second Avenue bar became famous back in the 1980s when a kid named Robert Chambers left with a girl named Jennifer Levin, who ended up dead a couple of hours later in Central Park. Dick Kelley was one of the cops who caught the case of the Preppy Killer, as Chambers quickly became known. Craig Jackson said it was Kelley who picked the East Side bar, still popular with kids, as tonight's meeting point. Maybe Dorrian's reminded him of his glory days.

A cop's cop, everybody always said about Detective Dick Kelley. He was tall, thin, completely bald, one of those guys who'd probably looked old when he was young.

Kelley orders a tequila. So does Craig Jackson. Jimmy knows from his own bar that more people than ever are drinking tequila. And knows why. Calories for a jigger of tequila are about the same as a light beer, low sugar, no carbohydrates. Drinkers can make a lifestyle choice and still look cool. Win, win. And still get just as shit-faced in the end.

Jimmy orders a nonalcoholic beer. He doesn't want to make the hundred-mile drive home any harder.

They make small talk about Chambers, who pled guilty to manslaughter, served fifteen years, then went back in for an even longer bit on drug trafficking, the moron.

"Tell me about Anthony Licata," Jimmy says finally.

"You know that he and Champi finally partnered up over there on your dark side, right?" Kelley says. "Turned themselves into freaking legends, just not in a good way. A problem got in *your* way, they removed it, for a price."

Kelley drinks some tequila. He says he walked here from his apartment on 81st and Second.

"Licata and Champi figured out something even before they left the cops and became what you would call entrepreneurial," he continues. "Rich guys in the big city *like* having bad guys as body men, or fixers, or muscle, or whatever. Gives them that dark-side thrill. No one's sure who started it, but before long they were together. Somehow Champi got with your client's old man before the old man shot up his house that day. With him gone, it was like the kid inherited him."

"When Champi and Licata were both still with the department?" Jimmy asks.

"Just Champi," Kelley says. "Paul Harrington, commander of the detectives at the 24th, had already booted Licata's ass out of the precinct and out of the department by then."

"Did the kid really kill his father and the girl?"

"It looked like a murder-suicide, the story had a boldface name, the whole thing was instant tabloid gold. Lieutenant Harrington ran point because the case was so high-profile, and he was as good as it gets. He could never find anything to make them doubt the kid's version of how it went down."

Champi put in his papers not long after that,

according to Dick Kelley. Then Champi and Licata just kept expanding their client list, and their grift, managing to stay a step ahead of their old friends in the NYPD. Team owners, ballplayers trying to stay off Weinstein Island, when that first became a thing. A former network president who got a teenager pregnant. Construction guys. Restaurant guys and real estate guys. Publishing big shots like Rob Jacobson's father.

"All under the radar, I'm assuming," Jimmy says.

Kelley nods. "They just kept finding more high rollers who loved feeling like they were in a Scorcese movie. They were still closing cases. Just in a different way from when they'd been carrying a badge."

"And neither one of them ever got made for any of it?" Jimmy asks.

"Want to know the truth?" Dick Kelley says. "It took your lawyer lady to take Joe Champi down, probably while Licata just kept laughing his way all the way to some Caymans bank account. Probably didn't even stop long enough to toss dirt on his partner's coffin. Because his own gravy train just kept rolling along."

"So whatever Champi was into, Licata was into?" Jimmy asks.

"We called them brothers from other mothers," Kelley says. "They even looked a little bit alike, the bastards. I saw them one time at a hockey game, both in their Rangers hats. Almost looked like twins."

Jimmy's ribs are starting to ache. He thinks about just one Scotch for medicinal purposes but lets the thought pass right through him. The LIE was no place for even a slight buzz.

"We always heard that there was a third partner," Kelley adds, "but nobody could ever nail that down."

"Any other sugar daddies you might have forgotten to mention?" Jimmy asks him.

"Didn't forget," Kelley says. "Just been saving the best for last. Turns out I got a call right before I showed up here, from an old friend of mine from the 20th, which used to be my shop. He gave up a name I'd never heard but thought might ring a bell with you."

Jimmy waits.

Kelley is still smiling, like he's about to draw to an inside straight.

"You ever hear of an old Yalie hedge-fund guy named Thomas McKenzie?"

SEVENTY

I DECIDE TO GET away for the weekend.

Alone.

It means leaving Rip the dog with Dr. Ben and heading for the city, and my apartment on Christopher Street, for the first time in months.

Despite Rob Jacobson's objections, on Monday I'm going to formally petition Judge Kane to allow me to step away from my client and the case.

I'm aware that it's far from a sure thing that the request will be granted, so soon after she granted my motion to have the trial date moved up.

I'll worry about that on Monday and try to turn off my brain on what Jimmy has told me about Anthony Licata and Joe Champi, and how Licata might have been even better at hiding in plain sight than Champi.

"For the next couple of days," I tell Jimmy, "I'm

going to see if I remember how to show a girl—this one—a good time."

I am treating my trip to the city like a well-earned vacation, the accommodations being an apartment I love, in a neighborhood I love, in a city I still love, even though I no longer spend enough time there.

I drive in on Friday morning, park the car at my old garage up the block, let myself into the apartment, let in some fresh air.

Then I turn off my phone and take the subway uptown to 50th and Eighth, the stop next to the Winter Garden Theater, make my way to Central Park from there. I wander the park aimlessly and happily after that, trying not to get clipped by runaway bicycles. When I get hungry at lunchtime, I walk up to Gray's Papaya on 72nd and Broadway, thrilled that it's still there, and order what is still one of the best hot dogs in town.

Maybe the entire planet.

Ralph Nader, that old priss, once called hot dogs America's most dangerous missile.

What's one more going to do, kill me?

I've always loved walking the city, from the time I was renting my first elevator-car of an apartment in Murray Hill, its one redeeming characteristic being a view out the living room window of the Empire State Building. That was back when I thought, we all thought, we hit the big city not just walking but running: thinking we were all going to live forever, at least until the planes hit our buildings and everything changed.

I have no interest in shopping Columbus Avenue, but then I never really did. So now I go over to the American Museum of Natural History and spend an hour there. Then over to Lincoln Center to stand in front of the fountains, then back over to the park and down to 59th Street before I start to fade, at long last.

When I've taken the subway back downtown to the apartment, I turn on my phone and see several missed calls from Rob Jacobson and some all-caps texts telling me to call him. But no messages from Jimmy, which means no fires we need to put out, at least not today.

I take a shower, pour myself a small white wine, put on a nice dress, one that doesn't hang quite right because of lost weight but I can still carry it off, and take a cab to Sistina, one of my favorite Italian restaurants, in the space it moved into on 81st several years ago.

Henry, the maître d', remembers me, and asks if I'm waiting for someone.

"Mr. Right."

"Still?" he says, formally kissing my hand.

We both laugh before I tell him I'll be happily dining alone.

I decide to enjoy the beautiful evening and walk off the pasta primavera before heading home. No one waiting for me. No one knowing exactly where I am. I feel like I can breathe again. Like the city has taken me back in, told me all is forgiven.

Then I do have one more destination, as much as I hate to admit that to myself.

I make my way over to Third Avenue, the block where the Red Blazer, one of the places where my father had tended bar, once stood.

Right across the street from Elian, the second restaurant my ex-husband had recently opened. I wasn't sure how he could afford that. Maybe he'd found the money for it under his bed.

I know he's there, because they told me so when I first called Café Martin.

Ten o'clock by now, the East Side night just beginning to rise up and even roar.

There I am, standing across the street, hoping to catch a glimpse of him through the window the way I used to stand across the street from Café Martin after we broke up.

I spent the whole day feeling as if I'd been drawn back into the past, *my* past, and now here I am.

Not even knowing why I'm here.

Ashamed that I am.

But here.

Stay or go?

If I make my way across the street and walk into Elian, what will I say to Martin when he sees me? What he said to me after his dinner at Allen Reese's, that I just happen to be in the neighborhood?

Or maybe this: "Buy a girl a drink, for old time's sake?"

Then what?

Play it all the way out, Jane.

Then what?

What do you want to happen with him, as much as you tell yourself you love Ben Kalinsky? And as much as Martin Elian hurt you.

I came to the city to be alone.

Only I ended up here.

Only I could manage to screw up a perfect day with an ending like this.

"Good job, Jane, no shit," I say out loud, feeling once more like a ridiculous teenager.

"What did you say, ma'am?"

A young woman whose dress is too tight and too small, probably about to take the big town by storm, has stopped on the sidewalk.

Long enough to ma'am me.

"Just talking to myself," I say.

"Cute dress," she says, and then swings her impossibly tight butt up Third Avenue.

I'm about to come to my senses and put myself in a cab when a black SUV pulls up in front of Elian.

Less than a minute later, my ex-husband comes walking out of his restaurant, accompanied by a dead man.

SEVENTY-ONE

ON MONDAY MORNING JIMMY is driving me to the courthouse in Mineola for my meeting with Judge Kane. I've told him he doesn't have to do it, that I'm perfectly capable of making the trip on my own. He won't hear of it, says he looked it up in the wingman's manual, and it's one of his responsibilities, no getting around it.

We're talking, not for the first time since I got back from the city, about what I saw in front of my ex-husband's restaurant on Friday night.

"I can understand why you thought you were seeing dead people when you saw a guy who has to be Licata," Jimmy says. "Mickey Dunne used to say there were look-a-likes and reminds-me-ofs. From the pictures I've seen of Licata and Champi, they fall into the second category. Same height, same build, same coloring. Same slouch. Even their Rangers caps. If I didn't know better, I swear I might think the two tough guys were a couple. Like one of those old couples where they start looking like each other the longer they stay together."

"It wasn't long ago that somebody wanted us to think Champi was texting from the other side," I tell Jimmy. "For a second I thought he'd made his way all the way back to the Upper East Side."

I lean back in my seat and close my eyes. "I'd ask my ex about it, but he won't return my calls or my texts."

"Isn't that the one about the more things change the more they stay the same?"

"*Oui.*"

"Dick Kelley mentioned that the tag team of Licata and Champi did some work for restaurant owners along the way," Jimmy says. "So what kinds of problems could old Marty have had that might have brought Licata and Champi into his life?"

"I'll ask him if he ever gets back to me."

So maybe Martin was doing business with Anthony Licata, which meant he could have done business with Joe Champi, too.

Jimmy and I spend a lot of the ride to Mineola speculating if Licata might have been responsible for things we assumed Champi had done, including the disappearance of Gregg McCall, the Nassau DA who hired us to look into the murder of the Carson family in the first place. And maybe drugging Jimmy at McCall's house.

"Could your ex have had money problems you didn't know about?" Jimmy asks.

"Didn't everybody in the restaurant business during COVID?"

"Maybe he found a bad guy to partner up with the way your new friend Allen Reese did with his real estate business."

"Sometimes I get the idea everybody, us included, is in the same repertory company."

We pull up in front of the courthouse. Jimmy says he's going for coffee but will be sitting right here when I come out. I mention that the parking space we're in is reserved for official vehicles.

"What's your point?" he asks.

I get out of the car, leather bag over my shoulder, and head up the same courthouse steps where Jimmy and I stood the day I really decided to take back Rob Jacobson as a client. Feeling the same thrill I've always felt walking up courthouse steps, every single time.

Only now I'm about to do something that in my entire career I've never done once:

Quit.

If Judge Kane goes along with me, in a few minutes I'll walk back down these steps and just walk away.

But as I go through the double doors, I'm suddenly remembering.

"You know when you stop fighting?" my father asked me.

A boy had insulted me at school that day. I might have been twelve. The boy had told me I was more boy than girl, and I'd let him get away with it.

"You stop fighting when you're dead?" I asked, not for the first time.

Dad smiled and shook his head. "Do the time, kid. Even after you're dead, you still gotta be willing to go a few more rounds."

The next day, I waited for that boy after school, told him I needed to show him something, and then gave him a bloody nose. It got me suspended for a week. My father always used to say that winning meant being the last one in the room.

Just not this time.

Sorry, Pop.

I know I'm doing the right thing, for me and Dr. Ben and even Jimmy. Being the last one in the room is no longer worth it, because it's no longer cost-effective, and not just for me.

This time in a courthouse may be the last time, who knows?

Judge Kane's assistant tells me she's inside her chambers waiting for me.

Get it over with.

I'm only in there five minutes. Perhaps not even that. Then I'm passing the assistant's desk again, and on my way down the hall and back through the doors and down the steps to Jimmy's car.

When I'm inside he says, "It go okay?"

"Couldn't have gone any better."

"So, you're out?"

I laugh.

"Oh, hell no," I tell him.

SEVENTY-TWO

Jimmy

JANE SAYS SHE'LL UBER home, where she plans to tell Rob Jacobson to his face that she hasn't quit the case after all. Three or so hours later Jimmy is back in the city, all the way downtown, one of the highest floors underneath the observation deck at One World Trade. The building is in the same footprint where the Twin Towers had been before the planes hit, and where the offices of River View, Thomas McKenzie's hedge fund, are now located, McKenzie having made a big show out of moving back down there.

Jimmy hasn't spent much time in this neighborhood since the planes hit the buildings, too many memories down here, too many people he knew lost that day. With all that, he is knocked out by the kind of panoramic view he remembers from the Twin Towers, just through the windows in McKenzie's waiting area.

There it all is, the same view, even though downtown

Manhattan will never be the same, from the Brooklyn Bridge to New York Harbor, the Statue of Liberty, Jersey, and some of the skyline of Lower Manhattan and, Jimmy is sure, heaven if you knew precisely where to look.

Jimmy has fake-badged his way this far but now runs into McKenzie's assistant, an ice-sculpture with long blond hair and black-framed glasses whose nameplate reads TYLER. No Ms. before her last name. No Mrs. No Miss.

Just TYLER.

"Is that your first name or last?" Jimmy asks.

"It's irrelevant, Detective Cunniff," she says. "Because unless you're here to arrest me, this is the end of the line for you."

"Just trying to make conversation."

"Which now, sadly, is ending," she says, shuffling some papers in front of her and trying to look busy, bored, both.

"You're right," Jimmy says. "My conversation with you *is* ending. But before I go, you need to go inside and tell your boss that I'm here to talk about Anthony Licata, and everything they've always meant to each other. Or I can just talk about it with a friend I have at Page Six."

She considers that for a moment. The gossip page of the *Post* can still sound like the bogeyman to the rich and powerful. Or their assistants. When they aren't reaching for a mention like a junkie reaching for a crack pipe.

Tyler, Miss or Ms. or Mrs., gets up, gives a rap on the door, enters the inner sanctum, and is back in two shakes of a cat's ass, as Mickey Dunne used to say.

"He'll see you," she says. Icily. But then Jimmy expected no less, her being the one who acted like the cat's ass.

"This has *got* to sting," Jimmy says as he passes her.

McKenzie comes around his desk to greet him. Another short rich guy. Jimmy has met a lot of them, from Mayor Bloomberg on down. Or up. No jacket, white shirt, tie knot as big as Jimmy's fist, gray hair buzzed down nearly to his scalp. Small wire-rimmed glasses. He bears little resemblance to his son. But looks a lot trimmer and a lot fitter.

He doesn't shake Jimmy's hand. Fist bumps him instead. One of those. Like the COVID protocols are still in place. Or maybe he's a germophobe.

"What about Anthony Licata?" McKenzie snaps, not wasting any time. "All that name does is get you in the door."

"I was actually surprised to hear that name associated with you," Jimmy says. "But maybe I shouldn't be surprised, since word has it that you used to be besties with a scumbag like Sonny Blum."

McKenzie waves his hand dismissively. "Urban legend," he says. "And total bullshit."

"So, you got hooked up with a cheap goon like Licata instead?"

McKenzie smiles thinly. "Who said he was cheap?"

He gestures to the one chair next to him, walks around a desk the size of a pool table to his own. Somehow the view behind him is even better than the one outside, if that's even possible. McKenzie's money has bought him a view like this, but he somehow bought Anthony Licata on the way up here.

"Mr. Licata and I parted ways some time ago," Thomas Mc-Kenzie says. "He chose to cash out on what he called his 401(k) with me."

"Not what I hear."

"I frankly don't give a shit what you hear," McKenzie says.

"Sure, you do." Jimmy smiles. "Because here we are across the desk from each other, chopping things up like we're boys."

"What exactly do you want to hear from *me*?" McKenzie says. "I have an important call I have to be on in about fifteen minutes."

"Are there any other kind of calls for you?"

McKenzie makes a sound as if Jimmy has just hit him with a body blow.

"Did Licata come to you originally, or did you go to him?"

"You really don't know?"

"More like I'm filling in some blanks."

"I had a friend, from my world, who had availed himself of Anthony's services for a rather delicate situation. When I found myself in a not dissimilar situation, my friend made the recommendation. Sort of like a headhunter in the realm of shit happening."

"And what kind of delicate situation was it, exactly?"

McKenzie's face reddens, just like that. "My son couldn't keep it in his pants, that's what the situation was!" McKenzie is spitting out the words. "And he sure as fuck didn't ever seem to understand the word 'no' as far as I could ever tell."

"He says he didn't rape that girl," Jimmy says. "That Rob Jacobson set him up."

"It no longer matters whether he did rape her or didn't," Mc-Kenzie says. "It eventually went away for everybody involved, once Licata and his friend Joe Champi realized they were essentially pulling on the same rope."

McKenzie leans forward over his desk. "You spoke of Page Six to my assistant. Well, I was going to be good and goddamned if my name was going to be in bold type next to my son's while I was trying to build this fund. So I did what I had to do."

"Robinson Jacobson was the friend who recommended Licata to you?"

McKenzie nods. "Not that their association did Robinson any good in the end, when he was the one who couldn't keep his in *his* pants."

Jimmy watches what looks like a private plane banking toward Jersey, probably coming in for a landing at Teterboro. McKenzie probably keeps his own plane there.

"Did Licata ever mention what he thought might have happened the day Robinson Jacobson Jr. and that young girl died?"

"He didn't offer an opinion and I didn't ask for one," McKenzie says. "He had his own problems with a son who couldn't keep it in *his* pants. And maybe in the end, I didn't want to know what I didn't want to know about my own son."

"You happen to know where I might find your son these days?" Jimmy asks.

Thomas McKenzie stands and offers Jimmy a smile that looks like two razor blades pressed together.

"The gutter is always a good place to start."

SEVENTY-THREE

Jimmy

JIMMY IS OUT OF Thomas McKenzie's office down-town by noon, and out east a little after four o'clock, having stopped to pick up Jane before heading over to Rob Jacobson's rental house.

"I could've handled this myself," Jimmy says as he pulls into Jacobson's driveway.

"Just think of me as being here for quality control," Jane says.

"Heavy on the control, I gather."

"What was your first clue?" Jane asks.

When Jacobson opens the door, he's smiling as if Jimmy and Jane are the first to arrive at the party.

"Look at us!" he says. "The band is back together!"

Jimmy steps past Jane and shoves Jacobson hard, two hands to the chest, knocking him back toward the living room and nearly on his ass.

"Jimmy," Jane says quietly. "You promised."

"I lied."

Jacobson collects himself, but backs away from Jimmy, hands out in front of him, just in case Jimmy charges him again.

"Hey," he says. "Hey, Cunniff. Take a chill pill, okay? What's this all about?"

"Anthony Licata. Joe Champi. Edmund McKenzie. Everything you've held back on them and freaking held back on the day your father and a young girl, who clearly had shit taste in men, died at your fancy digs on Central Park West. That seems to be the day that people maybe started cleaning up for you. From what I can tell, they never stopped until the cleaner-uppers were Jane and me."

Jane puts a hand on Jimmy's arm. He ignores it and keeps moving toward Jacobson, who keeps backing up, seemingly willing in the moment to back all the way to the ocean if it means getting out of Jimmy's reach.

"That pretty much sets the table," Jimmy says to Rob Jacobson. "I think we can throw it open to questions now."

SEVENTY-FOUR

JACOBSON ASKS IF WE can talk while we take the short walk to the beach. Indian Wells Beach, less than a mile away, is outside the range of his ankle monitor, but I make a call and clear it with the court officer.

"He'd be doing us a favor if he tries to swim for it," I say, "all the way to Portugal. Or do the Azores come first?"

"I believe the Azores are a region of Portugal," the officer, Molly Newsome, says.

"Nobody likes a know-it-all," I tell her.

"Look in the mirror," Molly Newsome says.

As we make our way to Indian Wells, Jacobson makes sure to keep me between him and Jimmy, as Jimmy's mood hasn't improved that anyone can tell.

I'm the one to ask Rob Jacobson why he has never once mentioned the partnership between Anthony Licata and Joe Champi, allowing both of us to think that Champi was always acting as a lone wolf, at least where Jacobson was concerned. Like some low-life guardian angel.

"I'm not talking about Licata," Jacobson says. "Not today and not ever. Cunniff can slap me around all he wants. I'll still be alive."

We make our way across the parking lot. Big waves today. Big and beautiful and loud and filling me with a sense of wonder, every time I see them. I think a lot, maybe too much, about all the things the modern world has managed to ruin. Politics and privacy, for example. Civility, you could throw that in, too. But nobody can ever ruin these waves and the scene spread out in front of me. Despite everything happening in my life, the ocean still makes me believe in God.

Even with the way She keeps screwing me around, sometimes on what feels like an hourly basis.

"Where's Licata now?" I ask.

"The guy I'm not talking about? I honestly don't know."

Jimmy snorts. "Honestly. Good one."

"And by the way?" Jacobson continues. "Why does it matter so much? The guy's got nothing to do with my trial, which is supposed to be job one for the two of you."

Jimmy is suddenly on fire again, like Jacobson had pushed the wrong button. "You know what I would discourage you from doing today? Telling *me* what *you* think my job is."

We've made our way onto the beach. Jimmy moves around me, his back to the water, so he's directly in front of Rob Jacobson again. In the moment Jacobson does look as if swimming for it might be a better alternative than having Jimmy back up in his face.

"I now know that Licata and Champi were in this from the beginning, along with your old man and your pal Eddie Mc-Kenzie, and his old man."

Jimmy is pointing a finger at Jacobson, voice rising again, up and over the sound of the water. I know stopping him now, or even slowing him down, would be like trying to stop the waves.

But I have to try.

"Jimmy," I say again.

"Don't Jimmy me!"

He at least puts his hand down. "Are you the one who really shot your father and that girl?" he asks Jacobson.

"No," Jacobson says to Jimmy. "I swear." He tries to back away from Jimmy, nearly slips and falls in the sand. "I've told you before. No matter how much of an asshole you think I am, I'm not a killer."

"But it has to be either Licata or Champi who killed my partner," Jimmy says, his voice eerily low. "You think I'm just going to let bygones be bygones?"

"If it was Joe, what does it matter now?"

"It matters to me," Jimmy says. "So if you know where Licata is, you tell me right here and right now."

"All I ever knew was that he had a place in Montauk somewhere. Or maybe it was Napeague."

Jimmy says, "He's got paper on a place on Elm Lane."

"Not that one," Jacobson says. "I think there was a bigger place somewhere, but neither me nor Eddie ever knew where. I never even had a phone number for the guy. When he had something to tell me, if one of the money transfers was even a day late, he'd call me."

"When's the last time you talked to him?" I ask.

"After Jane shot Joe. Licata wanted me to know that nothing had changed between us even with Joe gone. We met for a drink at the American Hotel. One drink. He told me it was still business as usual until it wasn't. Then they got up and left."

"*They?*" I ask.

"Anthony and his girlfriend. This little Asian woman. He called her Mei, never told me her last name. I got the feeling that she maybe had taken Joe's place in the operation. She didn't say much, but before we finished our drinks, I asked her what she did for Joe. She smiled at me and said, 'Shoot.'"

SEVENTY-FIVE

Jimmy

"YOU'RE NOT GOING TO let this go, are you?" Jane asks when Jimmy drops her off at her house.

"Have you ever known me to let things go?"

Jimmy heads back to his bar after that to make some calls. One of them is to Dick Kelley. Before they left Dorrian's, Kelley mentioned in passing how ten years ago Paul Harrington retired to eastern Long Island. Everybody thought he'd hang around for a deputy inspector job, maybe even at the 24th. But Harrington put in his papers and walked away. Jimmy asks Kelley now if he can find out where Harrington lives.

Kelley calls back in less than five minutes. "Where are you right now?"

Jimmy tells him.

"Well, my friend, you're in luck, because it turns out the Lieu lives over in a town called Water Mill, which even I know is pretty close to you. You want me to find an exact address?"

"I'll find it," Jimmy says. "Sonofabitch, I knew I had to catch a break sooner or later."

He finally comes up with an address on Cobb Road for retired lieutenant Paul Harrington, and a phone number. When Harrington answers the phone, first ring, Jimmy tells him who he is and what he wants to talk about. Harrington says come ahead.

It is, as Jimmy discovers when Harrington shows him in, a very nice house.

"My Sharon had family money she never told me about until she got that headache and never got better," Harrington says, as if answering a question Jimmy hasn't asked. "When she passed, I found out just how much family money. As soon as the check cleared, I found this place and moved out here. I felt like I'd earned it, even if it was my girl's money and not mine."

"Bet your ass you earned it," Jimmy says. "You were a great cop."

"Still am. Don't you feel the same way?"

Jimmy grins. "Until they cover me in dirt."

"Could've waited a little longer to retire, beefed up the pension. But it's like I heard some old baseball manager said when he finally called it quits. It had reached the point where the wins stopped making up for the losses."

They make their way out to the backyard, where Jimmy can see some pretty amazing gardens.

"I could never afford a place like this now," Harrington says. "I could barely afford it at the time. But if I was going to live it out alone, I decided I'd live it out in style." There's a catch in his throat. "I was just supposed to do that with my best girl."

He still has a lot of white hair. About Jimmy's height, maybe a little taller, though he's a little stooped now. Ruddy face. Drinker's nose. Bright blue eyes. Young eyes. Big hands that look arthritic to Jimmy, some of the fingers zigging when they should be zagging.

Jimmy still has the feeling he had when he was just starting out and first ran into Harrington on a case, right after Harrington had been elevated to commander of the detectives at the 24th:

Legend.

Now here they were, breathing the same air, Harrington treating him like they were still members of the same club.

There are a couple of chairs set at a table in the middle of the lawn. They go sit in them. Jimmy goes into more detail about Licata and Champi and why he's still getting after it even though Champi is gone.

"It was me who put Internal Affairs on Licata, when I had him in the 24th," Harrington says. "Before he left the building, I made the prick hand his gun and badge to me. To the end he's telling me I had him all wrong. Still calling me Lieu like we were buddies. Champi must've seen the handwriting on the wall and got his own ass out while the getting was good. Before the two of them began their exciting careers in the private sector."

"Could Champi have staged that crime scene with Jacobson's old man?"

Harrington runs through his white hair a hand gnarled like an old baseball catcher's right hand. "Who better than a detective, especially one who learned the ropes from me? But as hard as we looked—as hard as *I* looked—there just wasn't enough to believe any other doer than the old man."

Harrington offers Jimmy a beer. Jimmy says no thanks. Harrington walks slowly back up the hill to the house, comes back with a can of Corona.

He sits down, takes a sip of beer, and suddenly slams the can down on the table, beer spilling out of the top.

"I fucking hate those bastards," he says. *"I fucking hate dirty cops and they were as dirty as I ever encountered."*

His face is red, and his chest is heaving.

"That badge is supposed to mean something," he says, lowering his voice now.

"I know," Jimmy says, keeping his own voice low, not wanting to set him off again.

It's back to being quiet out here, even as close to the road as the house is. Jimmy wonders if maybe it gets too quiet for retired lieutenant Paul Harrington, his wife gone, after having spent his whole adult life in the barrel.

"I think Licata or Champi shot my old partner," Jimmy says. "And if it was one of them, I can't let that go and still live with myself."

"Mickey Dunne," Harrington says. "Your partner. I heard what happened to him. Crying shame."

Jimmy nods. "And one or both of them made Gregg McCall, that Nassau DA, disappear without a trace along the way. Something else my gut tells me."

"It ever wrong, your gut?"

"Rarely."

Harrington drinks more beer.

"Promise me something," he says now to Jimmy. "If it was Licata, and you do finally put him down, call me when you've finally got him by the balls."

Jimmy salutes. "Yes, sir," he says.

"That badge is supposed to mean something," Harrington says. "And he used it like a goddamn credit card."

SEVENTY-SIX

I AM SITTING WITH Jimmy at one end of Jimmy's bar.

The Mets game starts a little after seven o'clock and Jimmy allows me to watch on the nearby TV.

"You're sweet," I tell him.

"Lower your voice if you're gonna talk shit like that."

It's the day after our walk to the beach with Rob Jacobson. Today has been good.

Brigid phoned me from Meier to say that the treatments are working. The doctors are guardedly optimistic—far from proclaiming her to be back in remission, but recommending she extend her stay.

I can hear gratitude in her voice. My sister seems almost as grateful that her health is stabilizing as she is that Rob Jacobson remains my client.

"I believe you partially did it for me," she says.

"Actually, sis, I did it for me."

Jimmy and I are both drinking draught beer. He's just slid the bowl of peanuts closer to him, explaining that if I don't stop eating them I'm going to spoil my dinner.

Ben Kalinsky, who had a late surgery today, is coming to my house around eight thirty with take-out shrimp po' boy sandwiches from the East Hampton Grill, with a side order of their to-die-for Heavenly Biscuits.

"My body, my choice," I tell him.

"Only if you're a guy, as far as I can tell these days."

It's always difficult to know if Jimmy Cunniff is happy or not. But I know that this bar has always been his happy place, maybe more than ever, now that somebody—we still think Champi, but possibly Licata—tried to burn it down during Rob Jacobson's first trial.

Jimmy keeps one of his laptops here so he can work, from one of the tables facing Main Street. He tells me that today he's been working his ass off looking for an alternative explanation about who killed Hank Carson and his wife and his daughter if our client did not.

The "other dude did it" defense, Jimmy calls it.

The problem is we still don't have another dude, as much as Jimmy wants to make it look as if the late Artie Shore might have done it before he shot himself. If only we had a shred of evidence tying Shore to the Carson house the night they died.

"Maybe the best thing *is* for you to just focus on this case," I tell him.

"The case you were willing to walk away from?"

"I thought it was a woman's prerogative to change her mind."

Jimmy's response is to grab the TV remote and switch the channel to the Yankee game.

"Oops," he says. "Just changed my mind."

We sit in silence then, until I guilt him into switching back to the Mets, just so I can get a score. I am only halfway through my beer, but I tell him I'm going to head home and primp for my dinner date.

"You're not a primper," Jimmy says.

I lean over and kiss him on the cheek. "My face, my hair while I've still got it, my choice."

I reach for my phone, which I've had on silent, just as it begins to vibrate with an incoming call.

NO CALLER ID

"This is Jane."

"Glad I caught the two of you together," a raspy male voice says.

I mouth "Licata" to Jimmy, and motion him closer.

"Saw you with my ex-husband the other night," I say. "How long have the two of you been dating?"

"Ask him, if you can find him."

That stops me.

"What does that mean?"

"Do I have your attention now, smart girl?" Licata says.

There's nobody close to Jimmy and me at our end of the bar, so I put the phone down and put it on speaker.

Jimmy says, "No need to peep through the window. Why don't you come in? I'll buy you a drink before I kick your ass."

There's a pause.

"Shut up and listen," Licata says. "Both of you."

I hold up a finger to my lips, telling Jimmy to let him go.

"Cunniff, you stop asking around about my business. Because I'm telling you straight up: it has nothing to do with your business. Leave me alone, I leave you alone. That's the deal."

Jane says, "Our client's son made me the same offer."

They hear Licata chuckle.

"He's the one you should be worried about," Anthony Licata says. "He's a bigger psycho than his old man ever was."

Then the line goes dead.

SEVENTY-SEVEN

DR. BEN DOES NOT stay the night. His choice, not mine, even though we've resumed sleeping together, sometimes at his place, sometimes at mine.

My choice on that, not his.

"You only live once," Dr. Ben says.

"My line, remember," I tell him.

He has an early flight to Los Angeles to visit his only sister and attend his nephew's graduation from the film school at USC. Even I know the School of Cinematic Arts is a very big deal.

If you live this far out on Long Island, an early flight can mean leaving for the airport as early as four in the morning.

When I kiss him good-bye, I thank him.

"For dinner?"

"For getting out of town for a few days so I don't have to worry about you."

"We've gone over this. You need to stop worrying about me."

"Right," I say. "It must be me who has the hole in her head."

When he's gone, I try to sleep and can't. So I grab the easel that I keep in the guest bedroom, one I set up when I'm working on a trial because sometimes I need to sketch out timelines and facts and even strategies on a great big grease board instead of on my trusty legal pad.

Like bigger print might produce bigger ideas.

The plan, anyway.

I set it up in the living room. Rip the dog, once he realizes all this activity doesn't mean treats for him, flops down next to the easel.

Of course he goes right to sleep.

I start writing down names, Rob Jacobson's at the top of the pyramid, up there next to Anthony Licata and Joe Champi. Then Rob's father and Carey Watson, the dead girl. Then I run through the entire repertory company, including the two murdered families, all the way down to Dave Wolk, the dead surfer dude. Elise Parsons and her daughter.

Once I have them all on the board, I start drawing connecting lines. Eventually I feel as if I'm looking at a homemade map of the New York City subway system.

Most of the lines run all the way up to Rob Jacobson. A lot of them run through his school friend—frenemy?—the guy he calls Eddie McKenzie.

I stare at the board a long time, until it almost starts to make me dizzy with possibilities, before grabbing a rag and wiping it clean.

I go into the kitchen and come back with a small glass of Jameson and replay Anthony Licata's call to Jimmy and me inside my head, and wonder what's changed, and why we are suddenly a bigger threat to him than ever. He wants me to stay out of his business the way Eric Jacobson wants me to stay out of his.

"If Licata wanted us dead," Jimmy said before I left the bar, "we'd be dead already."

"So why aren't we?"

"I'll be sure to ask him next time we chat."

I drain the whiskey and rinse the glass and take Rip out for one last walk, as disinterested as he seems in doing that. When we're back inside the house, I set Jimmy's fancy new alarm, lock the front and back doors, wash up for a second time, brush for a second time, leaving the kitchen light on, the way I always do. Rip takes his usual spot at the end of the bed. Force of habit makes me check the top drawer of the bedside table to make sure that the Glock is there, even knowing that it is.

I'm now ready for sleep, I tell myself.

It's after two in the morning when I hear the ping of the motion detector hooked up to the front of the house. Jimmy has rigged another one for the backyard. It makes a different sound.

They're like early-warning systems before a full-blown alarm is triggered, in case the motion is only a night creature scurrying across the property.

Rip has slept through the ping.

I have not.

I am instantly wide awake, my own inner alarms sounding, breath shallow. I take the Glock out of the drawer, slip out of bed, pad barefoot through the quiet house.

I don't pull back the drapes to look outside, not wanting new light to spill into the yard in case somebody wants to surprise me.

Or worse.

I want to surprise whoever it is.

Maybe Eric Jacobson is enough of a dumb-ass to come looking for a return engagement.

I hear movement then on the porch. Some kind of thud, like something being dropped.

No movement to the doorknob.

I don't shout out a warning. I just hold the Glock in my gun hand. I'm exactly like Jimmy in this moment, tired of letting the game come to me.

I know Jimmy has a key.

So does Ben.

Both know better than to show up unannounced in the middle of the night.

I hear a car engine from out front then, and the screech of tires as I reach for the doorknob and open the door with my left hand.

As I step onto the porch, I nearly trip over the body lying across my doormat.

I look down and see it's my ex-husband, Martin.

SEVENTY-EIGHT

HIS EYES OPEN BEFORE I have a chance to call 911, or Dr. Ben Kalinsky.

It means his eyes open before I kick him awake, which I am briefly and sorely tempted to do.

But one thing between us hasn't changed:

I'm better than he is.

So what I do instead is get him to his feet. Groggy as he is, he realizes it's me, and though I'm not in top shape I'm still strong enough to get him into the living room and finally half lower, half drop him onto the couch.

Rip watches the whole thing, low-growling at him from the kitchen door. Clearly, Rip has a much better sense of my ex than I once did.

"Thank you," Martin manages, his voice thick.

He rubs the back of his neck then, blinks his eyes a few times.

"They drugged me," he says.

It's happened to Jimmy twice. Once at Gregg McCall's house and once at Jimmy's own house.

"*Who* drugged you?"

"Friends of a friend, I guess you could say." He weakly offers a hand shrug.

"Sent by your friend Anthony Licata?"

Martin opens his mouth but then closes it just as quickly, suddenly seeming far more alert at the mention of Licata's name.

"I saw you with him outside your newest restaurant, Martin. I saw you ride off with him. I know who he is and I know what he does. And what I think he's done. Along with a growing sense of what he's capable of."

He shakes his head. "I can't talk about him."

He sounds just like Rob Jacobson.

"Can't or won't?"

"Perhaps a little bit of both."

"Oh, don't be an ass," I snap at him. "You think it's one of those crazy coincidences that they dumped you on my doorstep? Leave a note on your body that says 'Undivided.' Wake the fuck up, Martin."

He seems stunned by the outburst, even though he heard worse language from me in the old days.

"Before we continue, might I have a drink? Whiskey if you have it."

"Sure," I say. "It comes with the turndown service."

I go into the kitchen, get the bottle of Jameson back out, pour a decent amount into a shot glass, and put the glass in front of him on the coffee table.

I don't pour one for myself.

Rip has finally stopped growling. I reserve the right to start growling again myself if Martin Elian tries to feed me a line of bullshit, always one of his specialties.

"Anthony called and said he needed to talk to me, and that he'd send a car. Two men I'd never met before came with the car. They didn't introduce themselves. Or make much conversation. I asked where we were going and the driver said we were going to see the boss. Out east, he said. Then he told me to sit back and enjoy the ride because it was going to take a while. Before long we were on the LIE. Anthony had mentioned a place out here, Montauk maybe, or the town right before it."

"Napeague."

"Yes, I think that's it."

"I don't need a house tour, Martin. What I need to know is what you're doing in business with somebody like Licata in the first place. Or is he just one more poor choice you've made in your life."

"Oh, don't be naïve, Jane," Martin says, a little snap in his own voice. "Unless you're somehow confusing the restaurant business in New York City with church."

In this moment, it is like the old days, and we're

about to start swinging away in the center of the ring. You hang around with Jimmy Cunniff long enough, you end up making a lot of boxing analogies. Just about all of them generally apply.

I smile and shake my head, sadly. "I've always loved it, Martin, when people from out of town think they need to explain the city to me. So you're going to have to be more specific about how you ended up connected enough to Licata that you'd agree to take a ride like that."

"It started when I needed money," he says.

And drinks.

"And all the banks were closed at the time? What are the odds?"

He puts his glass down, leans back, rubs his eyes. "It was during COVID. I had already started the process of opening the sister restaurant when the world slammed shut. I tried to keep everything going by doing takeout at Café Elian. It was my way of furloughing as few people as possible."

I idly notice how faint his French accent sounds. But little need for him to turn on the charm for me.

"Like a lot of other restaurant owners in the city, no matter what I did, I was still drowning."

"And Licata popped out of a bottle like a genie?"

"Sarcasm never suited you."

"Still working on that."

319

"More sarcasm."

"Why didn't you ask one of your rich customers for help?"

"Because, *chérie,* none of those customers *got* rich backing failing restaurants during a pandemic."

Now that he's talking, I think about going back for the bottle and just leaving it on the table, not wanting to slow his roll.

"But," he continues, "one of my rich customers did suggest there might be someone who could throw me a life preserver, at least in the short run. He described him as a broker for people in situations like mine."

"You care to tell me the customer's name?"

"Edmund McKenzie."

And I think: *If my world gets any smaller, I'll be able to fit it inside Martin's empty shot glass.*

"Even though I got my money," Martin Elian says, "I have been paying ever since."

"With interest."

He nods. "He never called himself a silent partner. Referred to himself instead as a member of my board. With what he said were full voting privileges."

"Do you think Licata was the one calling the shots?"

He shakes his head. "I never thought so. It had to be someone doing the actual bankrolling. But the one time I asked, he grinned and said that if he told me, he might have to kill me."

He holds up his empty glass. I go get the bottle and leave it in front of him.

"Everything was fine until the last couple of months, because the new restaurant, after an excellent beginning, began to underproduce. So I reached out to Anthony for more money. Which he gave me."

"Have you paid him back?"

"That's the thing," he says. "I paid him back everything I owed him the night you saw me with him. With all the interest. In cash. So, while I was surprised that he wanted to see me tonight, I never considered saying no."

"Neither borrow nor a lender be, at least not with the First National Bank of Anthony Licata," I say. "Polonius said that, by the way, in *Hamlet*."

He closes his eyes. "Of course he did."

"Sorry, sometimes I can't help myself," I say. "Please continue."

"Thank you so much," Jimmy says. But he grins. "We were just passing through East Hampton when the man sitting next to me in the back seat reached around and I felt the jab. The next thing I know, I'm here."

"They never told you why he wanted to see you?"

"They did not."

It's past two in the morning and I'm tired, more than somewhat. Maybe exhausted suddenly that my ex-husband's problems have become my problems. Or that mine have become his. Either way. And that one of the connecting lines on my grease board now runs right through Martin Elian.

Maybe this is Licata's last warning for me to stay out of his business.

Martin leans forward now. "How much trouble do you think I'm in?"

"How did he leave it with you the other night, when you thought your business with him had concluded?"

"He just told me that I'd hear from him if he was the one who ever needed a favor."

Now I nod.

"He's not after you, Martin. He's after me, for reasons I don't fully understand. At least not yet."

"So what do I do now?"

"Do you still need his money?"

"I no longer *want* his money."

"Then maybe you're done with him."

"And if I'm not?"

"I'm not sure what to tell you. Other than this is what happens when you lie down with dogs."

I turn toward mine. "Sorry, Rip."

Martin says, "You mean dogs like your current client."

I smile quite genuinely now. "Touché," I say. "That's French, by the way."

"What are you going to do about Licata? You obviously know that he's dangerous."

"So am I, Martin. You should know that as well as anyone."

I stand.

"Mind if I take the couch for the night?" Martin asks.

I get out of my chair and walk over to him and lean down, gently kissing his cheek. His scent, even now, is one I remember, vividly.

"I used to love you so much, Martin," I whisper.

He looks up at me, the affection in his eyes quite real.

"I love you, *mon ange*," he says.

My angel. Blast from the past.

He starts to reach up to pull me closer to him.

I back away.

"Call an Uber," I tell him.

SEVENTY-NINE

WHEN HE'S GONE AND I am finally and blessedly asleep, I dream again about my mother.

She is happy, surrounded by a whole flock of her
hummingbirds. And I awaken smiling, a rare occur-
rence these days, the image of her and the birds still
vivid as I make myself a cup of coffee and go down
into my basement, which I keep almost pathetically
neat, and find the box containing the hummingbird
feeder my father once made for her.

The birds keep showing up in my dreams.

When I was little, before she got sick, she taught me
all about her birds, the best way to feed them, the perfect
placement for the feeder in the quietest place on the property. How to make the perfect mixture of water and sugar
that kept bringing the birds back.

"Think about it," she told me. "Refined white sugar

and water. Four parts water, one part sugar. And that's all it takes to make a miracle."

"You think that birds coming back is a real miracle?" I'd asked her.

"Is there any other kind?"

Then she drummed into me how cleaning the feeder often was essential, to prevent mold growth.

"Too much information?" she said one time.

"Never when it comes from you."

Now I felt as if I knew as much about the birds as she once did, remembering without trying, whether I wanted to or not. The miracle wasn't just that they came back, they migrated to Mexico and then returned. How they could chirp and whistle and squeak and buzz, even though I could never get close enough to hear. I just took it on trust, the way I took it on trust that they would keep coming back.

After buying my house, I hung the feeder on a pole in view of my kitchen window, greasing the bottom of the pole with vegetable oil to keep ants from getting at the sugary water I mixed myself. I never bought it premade at the hardware store.

Eventually, my birds found the feeder and then stayed with me for a long time.

I came to love them just as much as my mother had loved her birds.

But then the cancer that had come for my mother came for me. The once happy memories of the birds became associated with death and dying.

Representing Rob Jacobson in court, I kept forgetting to mix the water, letting the feeder go dry for days at a time. I was too sick and too busy to give the process the care it demanded. The birds who once depended on me gave up, probably because they thought I had given up on them.

Finally, reluctantly, I took the feeder down and packed it away, leaving the empty pole in the backyard.

Now I brought the feeder upstairs to my sink, used a small brush to clean the sucker within an inch of its life. A few minutes of honest work made me feel good, cleared my mind of worries about Licata and what he did to Martin, about Eric Jacobson and all those lines pointing to his father, about the pretrial motions I need to file before I start chemo next week.

Mixing fresh sugar water makes me feel just as good. Once I've perfected the proportions, I rehang the feeder in the same quiet place. Through my kitchen window, I stare at it for a long time, still smiling, hoping the birds will find me again.

In a world that keeps getting meaner and more complicated and more dangerous, the feeder looks beautiful to me.

The way the feeder always looks, gleaming and freshly painted, in my dreams about my mother.

I tell myself that if the birds find their way back, it will be a sign.

I could use one.

EIGHTY

WORKING TOO HARD ON Rob Jacobson's case makes the days start to feel longer and longer. I'm exercising too little, not eating as healthy as Dr. Sam Wylie wants me to.

Sam invites me to dinner, just the two of us, midweek, at the Bell & Anchor, on Noyac Road in Sag Harbor.

Good food, good pours, good vibe. On top of that, I'm here tonight with my good friend.

When we've been served our white wines, Sam says, "You look tired."

"What every girl wants to hear," I say. "But I promise: It's a good tired."

Then I raise my glass and she does the same.

"You sound like those people from Arizona who say, well, yeah, but it's a dry heat," Sam says.

"I promise I'm doing all the right things you've told me to do," I tell her. "You'd be proud of me."

We're both wearing blue summer dresses. Sam's navy one fits her much better than mine, in a lighter shade, fits me.

"I'm proud of you," she says softly.

I proceed to catch her up on crazy-town recent events. What most interests her is how Martin showed up like a lump on my doorstep.

"Promise you didn't give him a good kick?" she asks.

"Like I told you. I thought really, *really* hard about it."

She has never liked him, never trusted him. She told me after Martin and I broke up that he was a phony who had probably been cheating on me all along, unless he was incredibly unlucky to have gotten caught the one time that he did.

"I'd like to kick that French bastard," Sam Wylie says. "Right in the bon bons."

I redirect the conversation, asking about her husband, her kids, her annoying dogs.

"They're not annoying. They're adorable."

"You know what they are? They're the dog version of avocados."

"Wait...*what?*"

"Hear me out," I say. "All of a sudden, without anybody noticing, avocados got *way* too popular."

She grins but knows enough to let me go.

"Labradoodles didn't even used to be a thing," I

continue. "Are you aware that they didn't even become an official breed until 1989?"

"You actually researched my *dogs*?"

"You think I'd come out to dinner with you unprepared?" I ask.

I laugh. She laughs. She really does look fabulous tonight. But then she always has, even back in junior high, when every girl we knew seemed to go through an awkward phase except her. Put it another way: nobody has ever accused Samantha Callaghan Wylie of being more boy than girl.

If they had, I would have punched out their lights, too.

I get around to telling her about trying and failing repeatedly, almost spectacularly, to break up with Dr. Ben.

"Well," she says, raising her glass, "I'll drink to that."

"Because I'm still with him?"

"Hell, no," she says. "Because you finally lost a case."

We stretch dinner over a couple of hours. We try to keep the conversation as light as possible, as we've both decided in advance that this evening will be a no-cry zone.

I tell Sam that I'm too full for dessert. She tells me that in her considered medical opinion, I need more food. So she orders us the Bell & Anchor's Dreamy Brownie Sundae.

Two spoons.

"You're too thin," she says.

"Look who's talking."

We laugh again. The waiter brings the dreamy dessert. We both order decaf coffee. It's clear that neither of us wants this night to end. Both of us feeling young. Martin talked about furloughing some of his employees during COVID. Tonight I feel as if I'm on furlough from real life.

Sam finally gets up and heads for the ladies' room. While she's away, I scan a room whose lights have dimmed by now, spot a corner table in the darkest corner of the place, getting a good view of it when the waiter steps away.

And despite my distance from the table, I am quite certain and quite aware that I am looking at Edmund McKenzie and Eric Jacobson, deep in conversation.

When Sam sits back down and sees my face she says, "What?"

"I think I just saw somebody I know. Two somebodies, actually. Or nobodies, depending on your point of view."

I tell her who they are and why it matters to me that they are here together.

"Be right back," I say, and get up from the table.

I've only taken a couple of steps toward them when the main dining room at the Bell & Anchor begins to spin.

I take one more step, and then stop, unable to do

anything now except wait for the world to stop spinning.

Something it refuses to do.

I take a small step to the side, all weight on my right foot, as a way of trying to steady myself, remembering times in the gym when the trainer would make me balance on one foot for thirty seconds.

I bump into a waiter then.

Someone grabs for my arm.

Too late.

I'm falling.

I hear a woman scream.

Last thing I remember.

EIGHTY-ONE

"AT LEAST I DIDN'T consider kicking you to wake you up," Dr. Sam Wylie says.

It's an hour later and I'm hooked up to an IV in a bed in a private room at Southampton Hospital that Sam Wylie has scored for me, mostly because she's not someone to be screwed with, especially not here.

She drove me herself, not wanting to wait for an ambulance. I admitted to her over a couple of bottles of water that for all my chatter about doing the right things, over the past couple of days I've allowed myself to get dehydrated. She tells me it's probably not the only reason I fainted. But likely the biggest one.

I accuse her of being overly dramatic.

"Ending up in the hospital at the end of our girls' night out is what's kind of dramatic," Sam says.

She's in a chair next to my bed.

"You've got to sleep more, you've got to exercise more, you have to hydrate every day and not just when you remember," she says. "All those good things you say you've been doing? You don't get to take a day off, whether you're doing chemo or not."

"I'm trying."

"Try harder. Or you not only won't make it through your trial, you won't make it *to* your trial."

I lift my head slightly and start to speak.

Sam doesn't give me the chance.

"Hush and listen," she says, putting a little snap in her voice. "I'm telling you for the last time that no trial and no client is worth dying for."

"Would you say that if I were defending one of your patients?" I ask.

"We're talking here about the most important patient I've ever had," she says. *"You."*

"I tried to quit the case. I just couldn't make myself do it."

Sam smiles. "Would that have killed you?"

She reaches over and takes my free hand. I think about all the talks we've had in our lives, about everything, in what feels like another life a thousand years before we were doctor and patient.

"For the last time, please answer one question. I promise not to ask you ever again."

"Liar."

She leans forward, squeezes my hand harder. "Is it worth it?"

Ever since I resumed my defense of Rob Jacobson, I've been asking myself the same question.

I squeeze her hand back and remind myself that tonight is a no-cry zone.

In a whisper, I say, "It might not make any sense to you. But it's worth it to me."

She keeps me on the IV for another hour. The nurse comes in and unhooks me, but Sam shakes her head. "Obviously I can't release you. You're still acting lightheaded."

"I'm fine."

"The hell you are," she says. "You can pick up the car in the morning. Besides, your ride is already here."

Dr. Ben Kalinsky pokes his head into the room now.

"We need to stop meeting like this," he says.

He drives me home and gets me into bed, walks Rip. No further conversation, he tells me. He's going to sleep on the couch.

In the morning, Jimmy calls. From the hospital, Sam caught him up on the festivities at the Bell & Anchor.

"I took a ride over to the restaurant after you two

girls left," Jimmy tells me. "I found out some very interesting shit about McKenzie and Eric Jacobson."

"Such as?"

"Such as they go in there a lot," Jimmy says.

There's a brief silence then, from both of us, while I process the information.

"Turns out it's kind of their place," Jimmy adds.

EIGHTY-TWO

Jimmy

THE NEXT AFTERNOON, JIMMY and Jane are drinking iced tea on her back patio. If she's run-down enough to *fall* down, Jimmy tells her, she needs to wake the hell up.

"I'd like you to please cut the shit," Jimmy says.

"Yes, doctor. I slept until nearly noon today."

"I mean it."

"I know."

While Ben was driving Jane home from the hospital, Jimmy made the short drive to the Bell & Anchor, taking a shot that McKenzie and Jacobson were still at the restaurant after watching Jane take a header. They weren't.

But the guy at the host stand was a local who as a college student had bartended for Jimmy. He was an up-and-comer now, the kind restaurants in the Hamptons relied upon to know who wanted to be seen and who didn't.

"According to my guy Jake, McKenzie and Eric Jacobson started showing up together about six months ago. McKenzie shot my guy some money at the time. Rent money, enough to guarantee a table no matter how crowded the place was."

"Makes you proud to be an American."

"They're not at the Bell every week," Jimmy continues. "But Jake says they are there fairly regularly."

"So maybe our friend Eric wasn't riding the wild surf nearly as much as we and his parents thought he was."

"So what we've got here is a guy who hates the father, hanging out with the son," Jimmy says.

"Who hates the father even more."

Jimmy grins at her. "Maybe daddy issues brought them together, like it was destiny."

Jane has finished her iced tea and is now working on the bottle of water next to her cup.

"We're talking here about two guys who basically grew up being called losers by our client," she says.

"Maybe they've got decoder rings for their special losers' club."

Jane picks up a tennis ball and throws it into the yard for Rip.

When he comes back, he drops the ball at Jimmy's feet. Jimmy grins. "Come on, that's funny shit right there."

"Maybe to you."

Jimmy picks up the ball now. Groans as he brings his arm forward, manages to throw the ball about twenty yards.

"I think you might have come off the Injured List too soon," Jane says.

He ignores her.

"I'm thinking that if McKenzie was in town last night, maybe that means he's back living at his South-ampton house," he says.

"Maybe they had a sleepover."

"Wouldn't that be a joy?"

He finishes his iced tea, stands, hands the ball to Jane when Rip brings it back this time.

"You going to head over there?" she asks.

"I am," he says. "It would practically be a sin not to, since talking to losers has always been one of my specialties."

"Maybe we're the ones who should have decoder rings," Jane says.

EIGHTY-THREE

JIMMY SAYS HE'LL CALL only if he finds out anything interesting at McKenzie's house. Nothing unusual about Jimmy Cunniff refusing to treat a cell phone like a pacifier.

After a couple of hours of radio silence, I check his location on my phone, since he's reluctantly given me permission to track him when necessary.

But he's obviously disabled that setting.

I try to get some work in before dinner, knowing he'll call when he does know something, if he does. I spend some time on a Zoom with the two law school students, both women—Estie and Zoe—whom I've hired for research and trial prep.

I continue to hydrate, like a good girl.

Around six I grab my phone and Rip and take a long walk on the beach.

No calls from Jimmy.

No texts.

I check his location again.

Jimmy still has his phone turned off. Or maybe the battery drained and he didn't have a charger with him. I call the bar and tell Kenny Stanton, Jimmy's top bartender, to call me as soon as Jimmy shows up. Or if he hears from him.

For dinner I make myself a fully loaded baked potato, butter and sour cream and crispy bacon chopped up into it, thinking how proud Sam Wylie would be. I even think about texting her a picture of it.

Still no Jimmy when I've finished and cleaned up.

I'm in the living room, watching the Mets game, when I hear my phone.

Not Jimmy.

Danny Esposito, our new friend from the State Police.

He skips the preliminaries.

"Have you heard from Cunniff?"

I tell him that I was supposed to have heard from him by now, that I'd last seen him this morning.

"He called me a few hours ago. Said he had to make it fast, there was something maybe going on with his phone. And to come to his bar. I'm here now."

"He say why he was calling?"

"He said he might need my help on something, but he didn't say what."

I have walked back into the kitchen by now, am staring out the window at my feeder.

No birds.

"But he still hasn't shown up," Danny Esposito says.

EIGHTY-FOUR

Jimmy

EDMUND MCKENZIE'S HOUSE IS on Gin Lane in Southampton, the ultimate old-money address.

McKenzie hasn't been on the premises for weeks. Jimmy knows because he's been checking. But it's still Jimmy's dream that McKenzie and Eric Jacobson are both at the house, so that he can brace them both at the same time.

For now, though, he'd settle for a face-to-face with McKenzie. That way Jimmy can ask him, straight up, about his friendship with Rob Jacobson's son.

Working a case, you can run into something, or something runs into you. Like the night before at the Bell & Anchor, when Jane saw McKenzie and Eric Jacobson together, right before she went down and out and ended up in the hospital.

Jimmy is on his way through Southampton town,

passing Fellingham's, an old neighborhood-type bar he likes almost as much as his own, when his phone pings.

It's not a text alert, he sees when he pulls over, but another device attempting to access his phone.

Or, as far as Jimmy knows, already has accessed it.

No location on the other device.

What the fuck?

If it's not some kind of mistake, somebody has gotten sloppy trying to track his phone. Or hack into his phone remotely. It's not Jane. Jimmy knows she can check his location whenever she wants to. He told her he'd be the one to call her if he found out anything interesting at McKenzie's place, but he's not even there yet.

Jimmy's not enough of a techie to know exactly how they're doing it with his phone, or from where. If he were smarter about phones, maybe he could try to find *out* where. But when he's watching TV and somebody starts speaking cell phone on one of those commercials, he either mutes the set or changes the channel, because he just doesn't give a shit, you could stump him with any question about what 5G even means.

Right now all he knows is that the best thing for him, in real time, is to turn the phone off.

He even considers tossing it.

He hasn't been checking for a tail since he left Jane's. And good luck to anybody who might have been following him in a car. He's taken back roads to South-ampton to stay away from the afternoon westward grind of people who work out here but can't afford to live out here.

Only now he gets this alert.

To him it means somebody is trying to tail him, just not in a car.

Once the phone is turned off, it feels the way it did in the old days when Jimmy was running down a lead with just a gun and badge. Sometimes the only person who knew where he might be headed was Mickey Dunne, and sometimes not even Mickey, when Jimmy needed to be on the move.

He makes the turn onto Gin Lane and is approach-ing Mc-Kenzie's house when he sees the automatic gate at the end of the driveway pull back and a black Tesla spraying gravel in all directions as it ramps up from zero to sixty.

As the car flies past him, he spots Edmund McKen-zie behind the wheel.

Jimmy turns around in the closest driveway and fol-lows the fancy car when it makes its first turn away from the ocean. Something else from the old days.

Follow that car.

Jesus, those really were the days, no matter how old he feels missing them the way he does and thinking about them as often as he does.

But when he looks in the rearview mirror, he's smiling back at himself.

He makes the same turns heading for the village, from a distance, that the Tesla does.

Hell, yeah.

Follow that car.

Old school.

Even if he's chasing an electric car.

EIGHTY-FIVE

DANNY ESPOSITO AND I are at Jimmy's bar.

Still no word from him.

"I can call the boys back at our office and see if they can try to track him off the cell towers out here, when you can find a goddamn tower," Esposito says. "Maybe have them do that triangulation thing they do."

"I just keep telling myself that there must be a reason why he doesn't want to be located," I say, "and why he hasn't reached out."

We're at the end of the bar, my usual seat when it's Jimmy and me. The Yankee game is on the TV closest to us. Esposito tells me that he's not much for baseball, he's more of a hockey guy.

"I knew eventually there had to be something about you I'd find appealing," I tell him.

He drinks some of his beer, licks foam off his upper lip, and grins. "I'm getting this feeling—you must be getting the same one—that there's a bond starting to form here."

"Fight it."

While we sip our beers, I catch him up on Licata, McKenzie, Eric Jacobson. My ex. Even my brief trip to the hospital.

"You lead a very rich and full life," Esposito says.

"Full of what?"

He runs a hand through his wavy hair. "How motivated might McKenzie and the Jacobson kid be to jam up your client if they got the chance?"

"Very."

"Now Cunniff goes off to jam them up if he gets *his* chance."

"Trying to add to his own rich and full life."

"You act like it's no big deal that he's not here," Esposito says. "But being as he's a highly decorated investigator, I can see that you're worried about him."

"Very," I say again.

I have settled into a nice routine. Talking with Danny Esposito, checking the game, checking my phone, watching the front door, waiting for Jimmy to walk through it.

I know how much I love my sister. I have come to love Dr. Ben Kalinsky.

I love my work, more than I should.

I love the holy hell out of my dog.

But Jimmy, in all the important ways, is the true love of my life.

If something ever happened to him, I *would* want to die.

Where is he?

Something happens in the ball game, something that must be good for the Yankees, because the Yankee fans in the place are cheering and clapping.

I check my phone again, the Find My app.

Jimmy's last location was in the middle of Southampton town.

I look back at the door, trying to *will* Jimmy to come walking through it.

"You think McKenzie and Eric Jacobson could take Jimmy down, if it ever came to that?" Esposito asks.

"Not unless McKenzie has a stockpile of automatic weapons at his house."

"Then he'll be here."

"*When?*" I snap and slap the bar with the palm of my hand, loud enough that some of the guys at the other end turn to look at me.

Jimmy finally comes walking through the door about fifteen minutes later. I can see how pissed he is before he gets to the bar, or says a word, because that's how well I know him, he might as well be carrying a sign.

"I got played," he says, and takes the seat next to Esposito.

He makes a motion to Kenny that he wants a drink and wants it right now.

"Beer, boss?" Kenny asks.

"Bourbon. The good stuff."

Kenny brings him a glass of what I know is Pappy Van Winkle. Jimmy throws half of it down in one shot.

"Sometimes," he says, looking past Esposito at me, "I think somebody's been playing us since we took this freaking case, and trying to run us in circles."

"But who?" I ask.

"I thought you were supposed to be the brains of this operation," Jimmy says.

"If you still believe that," I tell him, "then you're right. You have been played."

EIGHTY-SIX

JIMMY GIVES US CHAPTER and profane verse on the wild goose chase all over the South Fork on which he'd been taken by Edmund McKenzie, until they were finally heading back west on 27 from Montauk and McKenzie floored it and passed about a half dozen cars on the double line and lost him like Jimmy's car was riding on its rims.

"Pro tip?" Jimmy says. "If the guy in the Tesla wants to lose the guy in the Jetta, he does."

"Good to know," Danny Esposito says.

One of the stops McKenzie made at the start of their little road trip, Jimmy says, was at the Bell & Anchor. But before Jimmy could follow him inside, McKenzie was back *out*side and heading over the bridge and into Sag Harbor.

"Total head fake, just to screw with me," Jimmy says.

"You think he knew you were coming to the house?" I ask.

"Knew I was coming, knew when I was getting close, wanted me to follow him," Jimmy says. "What I can't figure is why. Which, I might add, joins a whole long list of things I can't figure these days."

He tells Esposito about the alert he got on his phone when he started to get close to McKenzie's house, and how, other than the one quick call he made *to* Danny Esposito, he had shut the phone off.

"What I was going to ask you, is if there's any mechanism to find out who was tracking me, and from where," Jimmy says to Esposito now.

"Not a snowball's chance in Miami," Esposito says. "You could ask the feds, but they're not going to do shit for you. Because here's their dirty little secret: The tracking abilities they do have? They won't even admit they have them."

"Not even a location?"

Esposito grins and shakes his head. "Sorry."

We all drink in silence for a few minutes.

"At least you're safe," I say to Jimmy.

"And a schmuck," he says.

Esposito has a fresh beer. He's mostly listening tonight and not trying to play the part of the cool-dude cop. Another reason, on top of him being a hockey fan, why I am starting to like him a lot more than I did the night I first met him at the Parsonses' house.

"You think Licata is the puppet master?" he asks Jimmy.

"I've got nothing to base this on," Jimmy says, "but I have this feeling somebody else might be calling the shots. Somebody who does keep pointing us in the wrong direction. Look over there, schmuck. Not over here."

Jimmy has already passed on a second drink. He stands.

"I'm going back to Southampton," he says, "to see if the Tesla is back in the mutt's driveway."

"Want some company?" Esposito says.

"Sure."

I tell them to go have their cop fun. I'm heading home, it's getting near my bedtime.

Jimmy leans over and kisses me on top of my head.

"Thanks for worrying about me," he says.

He gives me a long look, his face both somber and curious at the same time.

"What if our guy isn't a murderer?" he says.

"Not to make too fine a point," I say, "but which murders are we talking about?"

"All of them," Jimmy says, then tosses Esposito his keys and tells him he can drive.

EIGHTY-SEVEN

JIMMY AND ESPOSITO'S TRIP back over to McKenzie's house turns out to be another waste of time. No Tesla. No lights on in the house. Nobody home.

"I'll find him," Jimmy tells me when he calls in the morning to give me the update.

"I never doubt you."

"Never too late to start," he says.

An hour later, I'm staring out the kitchen window at the feeder, telling myself that if I just close my eyes for a moment, when I open them at least one hummingbird will have come back.

Instead, the phone rings. Brigid is calling from Switzerland.

"Tell me you're being released with time served and are coming home," I say.

"Not yet."

Her voice sounds small, flat, in a way that has

nothing to do with the distance between us. I know this voice from my sister, have known it my whole life; don't like it and never have.

"It turns out I'm not nearly as good at remission as I thought I was," she says.

"Talk to me, sis."

"I'm coming to the end of one last triple-shot jolt of chemo," she says. "If it doesn't work, they want to discuss a stem-cell transplant."

"I'm coming over there."

"No," she says in her big-sister voice, "you are not."

"Not your call."

"Stop me if you've heard this one before. But my body, my choice."

I remember using the same line on Jimmy the other day, trying to be funny.

This isn't. I don't say anything because I'm afraid I might start crying, that's the last thing I want her to hear, as if I'm feeling sorry for *my*self about my sister's current circumstances. And making this about how I feel. People doing that has pissed me off my whole life. Martin used to do it. He'd be talking about a waitress going through a tough time and before long he'd be complaining how now he had to fire her and how badly he felt about that.

"Don't get crazy until we see how the chemo works. I'm almost done with this cycle."

"Isn't it a little late in the game for you to be telling me not to be crazy?" I ask.

"It must be the drugs talking," she says. "And how about we change the subject, and I get to ask you how *you're* feeling?"

"Nothing to see here. I'm actually feeling pretty great."

"I don't want to break this to you," Brigid says. "But you were never a good liar."

"Wait. Do you really think I got to be one of the top criminal attorneys in the country by being *truthful?*"

We both manage to laugh, even if it doesn't last long.

"I always thought it was you who put the criminal in criminal defense attorney."

"Only when defending one of your old boyfriends."

"Be nice."

"Your old boyfriend makes that extremely difficult sometimes."

I talk about my own upcoming chemo without telling her about my fainting spell at the Bell & Anchor. Brigid knowing about that won't make her feel any better or will only make me feel worse. Basically, I'm still playing the role I've always played in our family:

The strong one.

I was the strong one when Mom got sick, even for our dad, the tough ex-Marine who simply couldn't deal with her illness, or with the prospect of losing her.

Now I had to be the strong one for Brigid. Today, anyway.

"Before I hang up," Brigid says, "I have to tell you something Rob told me on the phone the other night."

I hold the phone at arm's length, stare at it, and sadly shake my head.

"So you're still in contact with him."

"Nothing has changed, Jane. I still love him as a friend."

I can't help myself. "So you're the one."

"Be nice," she says again.

"What did he tell you that you want to tell me?"

"He says that sometimes he thinks about killing himself," she says. "And that scared me."

I don't believe it. Or him.

"I know depression can be as serious a subject as cancer, sis. But he talked about it during the first trial. And as you remember, nobody really bought it then. Sorry, but I'm not buying it now."

"No one fully understands someone's depression except the person experiencing it. Or doesn't understand until it's too late."

"Withdrawn," I say.

"Will you check in on him?"

I tell her I do that frequently and will try to do it today.

There is a fairly lengthy silence now.

I'm the one who ends it.

"Did he happen to mention why he's having these feelings?"

"I asked that question myself. He said it's because of all the terrible things he's done in his life, things that would make me hate him if I knew about them. Right after that, he said he had to go and ended the call."

I make her promise she will call me as soon as she knows about the course of her treatment. I tell her I love her more than she can ever know.

Then I stick my phone in my back pocket and walk out into the backyard.

Still no hummingbirds.

EIGHTY-EIGHT

Jimmy

NO MATTER HOW HARD he tries, Jimmy Cunniff can't get the idea out of his head—or his gut—that Anthony Licata and Joe Champi are the type to take orders and not give them, as slick with their grift as they've always been.

But if he's right about that, it keeps bringing him back to the same place:

Who's been giving them orders all this time?

It's easy to find the original connection between Champi and Licata, they came out of the academy the same year, originally partnered together in Washington Heights, stayed in touch even if they went in different directions the longer they stayed in the department.

Neither one of them ever made detective, what was supposed to be both the goal and the dream for young cops like them. So neither one of them ever showed much interest in working their way up through the ranks, or got anywhere near being a boss.

Nothing for Jimmy to go on here except instinct. But he has thoroughly convinced himself that somebody else was calling the shots when Champi and Licata were moving up into the big leagues of strong-arming and grift, moving in on some of the richest guys in town, creating a business model of high-end custodial work, cleaning up messes for rich daddies, making enough money over the years that they could even get into loan-sharking for somebody like Jane's ex-husband, that phony French prick.

He can't see them as bosses.

Jimmy is back in the city tonight, talking about this with Detective Craig Jackson in the back room at P. J. Clarke's, three fat file folders on the table in front of Jackson.

One for Champi, one for Licata.

One for Bobby Salvatore, who *is* a boss.

"Couple of dirty cops and a much dirtier mob guy from the Island," Jackson says. "You'd think that at some point destiny would have brought them together. But I cross-checked the system like a madman and came up with nada."

"Salvatore never got caught up in a gambling sweep in the city?"

"Jimmy," he says. "I know you want this to be true, that they had to cross paths. But it might not have happened."

"Wouldn't be the first blind alley I ever went down in my life."

Jimmy goes back through one file while Craig Jackson goes through another. Then they switch. They are both taking neat bites of bourbon as they do. Not Pappy. Clarke's doesn't have it. Jimmy asked. Blanton's tonight.

Jimmy is going over Salvatore's file again, the times he was arrested in Nassau County, not for gambling, mostly for assault, from the time he was a kid and collecting for Sonny Blum. An even bigger boss. But somehow he never did serious time. Sonny Blum owned a lot of Long Island for a long time, leaving the big, bad city to the Italians, owned it until dementia got him before another family did. Sonny's business model must have included some judges, too.

Jimmy is running his finger down one of the pages on Salvatore when he stops.

"Arrested as a juvenile offender," he says.

"Who?"

"Salvatore," Jimmy says.

Slides the file back to Craig Jackson, points to the year.

"He would have been, what, about sixteen?" Jimmy says.

"Sounds right."

"What was it for?"

"He was a minor," Jackson says. "Sealed."

"You think maybe you could unseal it?"

It's getting busier in the back room, and noisier, so Craig Jackson goes outside to 55th to make his calls. Jimmy sips Blanton's, remembering when he was young in this place and it was filled with cops and robbers and athletes and actors and even hookers and even way past midnight the night always felt as if it were just getting started.

Jackson is smiling when he comes back to the table.

"Assault," he says. "Shocker, I know. Some buddies of his from Roslyn in a beef with some boys from Hell's Kitchen. Young Bobby put two of theirs in the hospital, one with a fractured skull. Took out an eye on the other."

Jackson had already finished his drink before he went outside. He reaches over and picks up Jimmy's glass now and finishes his.

"How long did Salvatore go away for?"

"He didn't," Detective Craig Jackson says. "And guess who the arresting officer was?"

EIGHTY-NINE

EVERY YEAR, ALLEN REESE waits until everybody else has thrown their Hamptons charity events to throw his own right after Labor Day, mostly just to show that he can. Like his party is the official end to summer.

This one benefits the charter school he started in Harlem.

"We like to wait until a lot of the riffraff has headed back to the city," he told the *East Hampton Star* last week. "Present company excluded, of course."

The party is always held on his back lawn. I've seen pictures, including one aerial view of his tent that looked like one of those domed football stadiums. When I tell Dr. Ben why I want a copy of the guest list, he manages to get his hands on one and passes it along to me. It looks like a convention of A-listers, from as far away as Hollywood. A to Z.

"*A* for assholes?" Jimmy asks.

"You know the deal. I'm just hoping to run into the one in particular."

"And you're confident you'll be able to crash this shindig."

"You make it sound so crass," I tell him. "I prefer to think of it as correcting an invitational oversight on his part."

"You going alone?"

"Now you really are being crass. I'd never even consider crashing a party like this without a date."

Ben Kalinsky and I make it as far as the parking valet at the end of Reese's drive.

The valet checks the list. Tells me there's no Smith on it. I ask if I can see for myself. He hands it over to me.

"There must be some mistake," I tell him.

The young man looks like an extra from the movie *Magic Mike,* the one with the hunky male dancers with no shirts on.

"Trust me," he says. "Mr. Reese doesn't make mistakes like that."

"Do me a favor, before we both make the mistake of you turning me away. Call inside and have somebody find Mr. Reese."

Dr. Ben Kalinsky is staring out the passenger-side window, perhaps toward Connecticut.

"And after they find him, what are they supposed to tell him?" Magic Mike asks.

"That Jane Effing Smith is currently the barbarian at his gate."

I smile. He frowns and walks away, talking into one of those Secret Service mics attached to the collar of his white shirt.

It takes about ten minutes, but he's back.

"Mr. Reese told me that I should tell you to come ahead," Magic Mike says.

"Sorry for the bother."

"I get paid the same whether people bother me or not."

I hand him my keys. As Ben and I head up the drive, he asks, "You're sure you saw Salvatore's name on the list?"

"Right before where mine never effing was."

NINETY

DESPITE A CROWD BEHIND his house that looks more suited for a concert on the Great Lawn in Central Park, Allen Reese manages to spot me before I spot him.

He's wearing a navy linen blazer with a crest that looks like it was lifted from King Charles, white pants, and a pink shirt buttoned a couple of buttons too low, as if he's as proud of his chest hair as anything else belonging to him.

He acts incredibly pleased to see me, but then I know he's required to bullshit people for a living, and at a high level.

"I would have invited you," he says after I introduce him to Ben, "but I could have sworn you didn't like me."

"I heard that anybody who's anybody is here, and tonight suddenly started to feel like a college party with all the cool kids."

He shows me an ungodly amount of teeth as white as his pants.

"Well, I know that's a load of crap."

I flash him some teeth of my own. "Coming from you, that's a huge compliment, Allen."

"I'm assuming you're not here because you want to write a check for my school."

"I will if you promise Bobby Salvatore doesn't get a cut."

He's still smiling. But I know that's bullshit, too.

"You crash my party *and* you give me grief?" Reese asks.

"I apologize. That was out of line."

"Another load of crap. Hell, you're already on a roll."

Over his shoulder I can see John Legend's band starting to move around on a stage set up at the end of the property, the tent open behind them, the Atlantic as the backdrop.

"Has Mr. Salvatore arrived yet?" I ask. "I'm hoping to run into him."

"Might I ask why?"

"Well, sure, you could ask."

He makes a half turn, as a way of taking in the view on his big night, with a star attraction I'm sure is costing him the going rate, in excess of seven figures.

"I haven't seen Bobby yet," Reese says. "But while you wait for him, do me a favor and try not to bother the decent people."

And makes his way into the crowd, in the general direction of Serena Williams.

"Why do you think he even allowed us to come in?" Ben asks.

"He was curious about my real reason for being here."

"Isn't curiosity supposed to kill the cat?"

"Not on your watch, doc."

He grins. "What about fat cats?"

We do our share of mingling under the big top as my eyes keep searching for Salvatore. Ben recognizes more people than I do. I see Steve Cohen, the owner of the Mets, talking to Jerry Seinfeld, an even bigger Mets fan than I am, if such a thing were even possible. Ben begs me not to go over and tell Cohen my thoughts on improving the team for its stretch run.

As I take in the whole scene, I wonder how many parties just like this one there are Out Here every summer, and how many of the same people attend them, summer after summer and year after year.

It must get so exhausting being special.

"So this is how the other half lives," Ben says.

"Well, the half of 1 percent maybe."

We are each carrying around a flute of champagne. Ben turns out to be much better at spotting celebrities than I am, even the B-listers.

I still haven't seen Bobby Salvatore.

We've been under the tent for over an hour, and I've just told Ben it might be time to head back down to the road and get my keys from Magic Mike when my phone buzzes.

JIMMY.

"Hey," I say.

"It sounds like you ended up getting into the party."

I tell him I did but am fixing to leave without getting the opportunity to chat with Bobby Salvatore about being arrested by Anthony Licata when he was a teenager, and how perhaps that forged a lifelong relationship.

"It's why I'm calling," Jimmy says. "Bobby's not coming."

"And you know this how?"

John Legend's warm-up singer is at the microphone now and into his first song, so I can't hear what Jimmy says next. I tell him to hold on while I move behind one of the bars and crouch down.

"I didn't hear the last thing you said."

"Somebody just blew up Salvatore's boat about a mile off Montauk," Jimmy says. "With him on it."

"Any other passengers?"

"Just one."

NINETY-ONE

JIMMY AND DANNY ESPOSITO are waiting for me at the Coast Guard station in Montauk. Chief Larry Calabrese from the East Hampton police is there. The Coast Guard has search-and-rescue boats out in the water already. So does Montauk Marine Patrol.

I see one television truck in the parking lot, from Channel 12, the Long Island station, along with a handful of other reporters, one of whom I recognize from the *East Hampton Star*. They're waiting for Calabrese and Coast Guard senior chief petty officer Robbie MacDonald to hold a briefing.

Jimmy has just finished telling me why he thinks the other passenger on the boat was Anthony Licata.

"We checked with the harbor master over at Watch Hill," Jimmy says.

"Rhode Island," Esposito adds.

"I know where Watch Hill is, hotshot. What you probably don't know is that Taylor Swift has a place over there."

"I keep forgetting the real hotshot is you," Esposito says.

"The harbor master happened to be on the dock when Salvatore was ready to leave," Jimmy continues. "Salvatore has a place over there, too, Rhode Island still being a goombah hotspot. Anyway, Salvatore is with another guy. He introduces him as his buddy Anthony. Big guy, the harbor master says. Older. Kind of a raspy voice, he says." Jimmy grins. "Wearing a Rangers cap."

"Salvatore likes to pilot his own boat," Esposito says. "Forty-five footer. A Hinckley. He must've been on his way to Reese's party. Then *kaboom*. The search-and-rescuers are out there looking to pick up the pieces. Literally."

"No stops between Watch Hill and here?" I ask them.

"There's this thing called AIS ship tracking, for boats," Jimmy says. "Salvatore's boat was hooked up to it, for when he'd make the trip alone, which he'd do sometimes. If you look at a map, it was pretty much a straight shot from Block Island Sound to *kaboom*."

I'm looking out at the water and thinking about the time Nick Morelli's fishing boat was found without him. Salvatore's nephew. Who'd staged his own death on the water. Maybe it ran in the family.

But how could Salvatore and Licata—or just one of them—stage something like this without having to swim for it out on the ocean?

"There must've been a lifeboat attached, right?" I ask.

"Larry Calabrese says one of the first search-and-rescue boats had some engine trouble and came back," Jimmy says. "From Montauk Marine Patrol. Guy said that they found part of the lifeboat still attached to the hull."

Jimmy takes his phone out of his pocket and reads. "Organized crime figure presumed dead in boat explosion off Montauk." He puts the phone away. "Good news travels faster than ever these days."

"And not a wet eye in the place," Danny Esposito adds.

"I really *really* wanted Salvatore to be the big boss of the whole thing," I say.

"And I still want a flat belly," Jimmy says.

"But unless he and Licata turn out to be world-class swimmers…" I grin at Jimmy and Esposito and say, "They're sleeping with the fishes."

I shrug and put up my hands in surrender. "Low-hanging fruit."

We're standing on the dock in front of the station.

All of us looking out at the water now. We can't see the search boats. But they're out there somewhere, presumably with the remains of Bobby Salvatore and Anthony Licata, who first crossed paths when Salvatore was sixteen.

"What did Salvatore say to you that day at the horse show?" Jimmy asks me.

"He said, and I'm quoting here, 'It's not me.'"

"Maybe he was telling the truth for once in his miserable life," Jimmy says.

NINETY-TWO

A COUPLE OF DAYS later, my own next round of chemo staring me in the face, I decide to do something I haven't done in months:

Shoot.

I know I'm not going to feel much like working out once I'm hooked up to the juice again. So I get my air rifle and BBs and head over to the Springs and my running trail near Three Mile Harbor, hoping that my targets are still where I left them on various trees along my old course.

I no longer have the ambitions I once did about competing in no-snow biathlons. I'm not even sure how my stamina will hold up tonight when I'm back on the trail, having had a couple of punk days even before the chemo begins, anticipating the next hit my body is going to take. But I'm hoping that once I'm in motion and the adrenaline kicks in, tonight will start to feel like the old days, if only for an hour or two.

That was back when I didn't know how good I had it, when life's worst, including a bad marriage, wasn't cancer.

In the end, you can only take so many beach walks with your dog, do so much work with weights and stretching in your house, and tell yourself that you're in the best possible shape, whether you've got cancer or not.

Running and stopping and shooting and then running again always made me feel like I was still a real jock.

That's the feeling I'm looking for tonight.

Being the old me for a little while.

It's past seven o'clock and I haven't eaten dinner, but I have leftover pasta to reheat. There are no plans with Dr. Ben Kalinsky because this is his poker night.

All of a sudden, out of nowhere, I decide I need to be in motion. Getting my heart rate up. Getting after it the way I did as the old me, feeling like I'm at the top of my game. What do the announcers always say about starting pitchers with my Mets? I'll go as hard as I can for as long as I can.

Competing only against myself again.

Story of my life.

I start out jogging, telling myself not to push it at the start, I can pick up speed later. The first target is where I left it, right before the first bend in the trail. I stop, get myself into proper shooting position, gun up over my right shoulder, look through the sight, and fire.

I miss.

Then miss again.

Badly.

But the third shot hits the center of the target.

So does the fourth.

I'm back.

I take off again.

Smiling and running free and loose and easy as I head for the third target. My breathing is good, my heart is pumping, probably more with excitement than anything else. I know this feeling, the good adrenaline that sports give you, because it's still part of my DNA, even chemo can't kill it. The only sound out here, when I'm not stopping again to fire, is my sneakers on the trail. It is, all things considered, a very active way of being peaceful.

I'm not timing myself, but can feel myself running free as if it really is the old days.

Not as tired as I ought to be.

And definitely not wanting to stop, at least not yet.

I'm the hummingbird tonight.

By the time I get to the last target and make the

turn for home, I *do* feel as if I'm the one who's flying, head down, almost forgetting the air rifle is in my hands, it feels that light, because of my own sudden and happy lightness of being. I'm running toward the parking lot, faster than I've run all night, like I'm racing the darkness back to where I left my car.

And winning.

I finally stop at the place where I started and drink from the water bottle attached to my belt. Hydrating, like a good girl. Dr. Sam would be even prouder of me than usual.

I'm a good tired tonight.

It's because I really do *feel* good for a change.

When I'm about ten feet from my car, I stop.

I locked the doors before going for my run, the way I always do, especially when I'm alone out here in the night. And I locked one of my Glock 27s in the glove compartment.

Only now I can see the buttons raised through the driver's side window.

I look around.

Nobody else around in the dirt parking lot.

I get a little closer to the car and see what looks like a boot print next to the driver's side door.

Certainly not my own.

And not there when I first got out of the car.

I hear something behind me, wheel around with the

air rifle, and see that it's just a raccoon disappearing into the woods.

I slowly cover the distance to my Prius, not touching the door handle, but looking inside.

There on the front seat is a menu from the Bell & Anchor, big red block letters slashed across it.

One word.

BOOM!

NINETY-THREE

I DON'T GO ANY closer.

Don't even think about touching the door handle.

I don't believe anybody would go out of their way to give me a heads-up that they were about to blow me to kingdom come if I did open the door or start the engine.

But I don't know that for sure.

I back away from the car and stare at it in the gathering darkness and try to assess the current threat level.

Same old, same old.

Not paranoid.

Just alert.

Somebody blew up Bobby Salvatore's boat the other day. Now somebody, maybe the same person, wants me to know they can blow my car if they have the urge to do that, because they've obviously been *inside* my car, unless the sign left itself on the seat.

Or somebody is watching me from a distance right now and has rigged it to blow remotely whether I try to open the car door or not.

Another way of looking at things.

Most likely they just wanted to scare me.

Maybe I am feeling, suddenly, at least a little paranoid.

I get myself back to the start of the trail and take out my phone and call the East Hampton Town Police, tell them who I am and where I am and what my situation is, reminding them that a boat has recently exploded off Montauk, a boat carrying people connected to my current case.

"I'm just being overly cautious," I say. "It's probably not a bomb." I pause. "But it could be."

"We don't have a bomb squad," the officer who answers the phone informs me. "The only thing I can do is hang up and call the County Police in Yaphank."

I give him Danny Esposito's number instead, tell him that I believe the State Police probably do have a bomb squad and dogs and maybe even robots if they think the situation warrants all that. He says fine with him, he'll make the call and send one of their cars over, and to stay as far away from my vehicle as possible.

I tell him if I backed away any farther, I'd be in Connecticut.

I call Jimmy then and follow up with my own call

to Esposito, who tells me that his crew will be there as fast as the sirens and flashing lights can get them from East Farmingdale to East Hampton. The East Hampton cops arrive within twenty minutes, but they tell me that they're going to wait for the staties, they're going to keep their distance from my car, same as I am.

Once the staties do arrive, they do it all by the numbers, taking their time, two of them in the same bomb suits you see in the movies. Danny Esposito stands with Jimmy and me while we all watch them go about their business in painstaking fashion. They use the dog first, and then the robot to open the car door and even pop the hood before it's done. Esposito says that if they wanted to get really fancy, they would have sent up a drone with an infrared camera.

They finally determine that they don't need the drone, because there's no bomb.

"Okay, this is embarrassing," I say to Jimmy and Danny Esposito when the guys from his bomb squad are finished.

"You did the right thing," Esposito says. "This goes a different way if you're not connected to Salvatore and his boat didn't get blown. But you are. Or were. And his boat did get blown. Sending the crew was a no-brainer regardless of whether I like you or not."

"I hope your dudes are getting overtime out of this," I tell Esposito.

He grins, back in character, the cool cop acting as if he's the one in charge, because maybe he has been. "Oh, don't worry, we all are."

I thank everybody on his crew, and the East Hampton cops. I thank Danny Esposito himself. They all leave, and it's just Jimmy and me.

"No bomb doesn't change the fact that somebody followed you here," Jimmy says. "And got inside your car."

By now Jimmy's already informed me he's spending the night on my couch and doesn't want to hear any back talk from me. Time for us to go. But even after the all-clear from the bomb squad, I feel myself hesitating before I open my door.

"Has to be the same people who blew the boat, wanting me to know they could do the same to me if they wanted," I tell Jimmy.

"Boom," he says quietly.

He winks at me.

"Too soon?"

NINETY-FOUR

I SLEEP LATER THAN normal. Jimmy is gone when I finally do get out of bed. He's left a note for me on the kitchen table saying that no bodies have been found off Montauk, but they're still searching. It'll be the Coast Guard calling off the search, when and if it comes to that.

Just not yet.

In the note he also tells me that one of the boats did pick up a blue Rangers cap bobbing in the waves near some of the wreckage from the Hinckley.

By midday, and after a solid morning of trial prep, no one has pointed a gun at me, or tried to abduct me, or threatened to blow me up. But when I make the short drive over to Rob Jacobson's rental house, I do have my Glock in my new leather crossbody bag, from Shinola, a gift from me to me a few days before.

For a change, Rob Jacobson is alone when I get

there, complaining yet again about how bored he is. The two of us have coffee at his kitchen table.

"Brigid's worried about you," I tell him. "She told me the other night on the phone, you were talking about suicide."

His reaction is to laugh, much too heartily.

"Why in the world would I do something like that?"

"Something to do with all the terrible things you've done in your life, she said."

"Good old Brigid. She always did take everything I said to heart."

I lean forward, one elbow on the table, chin in my hand, frowning at him. "You're telling me you made it up about having suicidal thoughts?"

"I was feeling sorry for myself, and I guess I wanted her to feel sorry for me, too."

"Don't take this the wrong way, Rob, but you're starting to give narcissism a bad name."

"And yet, here we still are. Because you and your sister both care about me. Is that why you came over today, to check up on me?"

"It's not," I say, and then proceed to tell him about what happened in the Springs last night.

"You think my son might have had something to do with it?"

"I'll ask him next time I run into him. Any thoughts where he might be, by the way?"

"You're asking me?"

"The witness is instructed to answer the question."

It shouldn't be that difficult a question. He either does know where his son is, or he doesn't. One or the other. But for some reason he takes too long to answer, as if reviewing his options, like somebody reading a dinner menu and trying to decide what to order.

"He actually called me about a week ago to say good-bye, now that I think of it."

"Where's he going?"

"Don't know. Don't care."

"Would your wife know?"

"After he may have tried to drown her in the pool where she taught him to swim? Riiight. He probably asked her to book a flight for him."

It's still like talking to the head of a sitcom family from hell.

"Why would he and McKenzie be friends? Have you given any thought to that?"

"You're full of questions today, aren't you?"

"Humor me. I had a rough night."

"Maybe because they both want me dead," Rob Jacobson says. "Or at the very least want me locked up for the rest of my life so they say they finally beat me at something."

"Any thoughts on why McKenzie and Eric would see me as a threat?"

"Speaking as a narcissist?" he says. "That sounds like more of a Jane thing."

"On that note," I say, and get up and out of my chair.

"Nice of you to stop by. Even when you're giving me shit, it helps break up the monotony."

"Glad to help," I say. "Now I've got one last question before I go: Who really killed your father and that girl that day?"

I don't know what he was expecting from me in the moment. But clearly not that. He rapidly blinks his eyes as if trying to clear them of smoke, something he often does when he's about to lie to my face.

"What brought that up?"

"Humor me again."

"First tell me why we're talking about that again?"

"Because I have the growing sense that everything that's still happening around you and around me started happening that day."

"Problem is, my story has never changed. My father killed her, then killed himself. Took the coward's way out."

"What I keep wondering is if that's the real story."

He stops blinking and his eyes are locked on mine. "I thought I already explained that to you. It's the story that's kept me alive all these years."

"Maybe you're finally ready to elaborate?"

He smiles and slowly shakes his head from side to side, so slowly it's like he's underwater.

"Not if I want to *stay* alive," he says.

Then he tells me to go ahead and show myself out.

NINETY-FIVE

Jimmy

JIMMY CALLS AHEAD TO retired lieutenant Paul Harrington, not wanting to show up unannounced.

"You're in luck," Harrington says over the phone. "I just made up a batch of homemade iced tea flavored with mint I grew myself."

"Lieu," Jimmy says, still using the shorthand for lieutenant. "You're sure you're not too busy for me?"

"I am, just not the way you think. It's the thing about being retired, Jimmy. You can never take a day off."

Now they're sitting on his back patio again, looking out at his gardens. One of the best cops of his time, Jimmy thinks. One of the best of anybody's time in New York City. A cop's cop. Nowadays he tends to his flowers and makes his own iced tea.

That's it, Jimmy thinks. *I'm working till I die.*

"I assume you heard about Salvatore and Licata," Jimmy says.

The iced tea is very good, even though Jimmy has never been one for mint anything.

Jimmy sees the surprise in the old chief's eyes.

"Licata was on that boat? They just said an unidentified passenger. I didn't even think to ask who the passenger might be."

"Pretty sure it was Licata," Jimmy continues. "They haven't found any bodies yet. But sonofabitch if they didn't find one of those Rangers caps Champi and Licata both liked to wear."

Harrington smiles and raises his glass, as if in a toast, and Jimmy does the same. They clink glasses, enthusiastically.

"Mob guy and a dirty cop, both gone," Harrington says. "And another angel gets its wings."

"I feel like I just made your day."

"Gonna be all downhill from here," Paul Harrington says.

He puts his head back, closes his eyes. Still smiling. It's like he's talking to the sky now. "Tell the truth," he says. "Isn't there a part of you that wishes you'd been the one to blow the two of them sky high?"

"But being the cynical bastard I am, I still worry they might just have wanted it to look that way."

"Easier said than done."

"But then I ask myself why they'd want the world to think they were dead."

"I'm gonna assume that they are," Harrington says. "You should, too, and take the win."

"Just speaking to Licata," Jimmy says. "He got away with a lot of shit for a long time."

"Him and that Champi both. Back in the day, when I first got a whiff of what was going on with them, I always wished I could have nailed their balls to the wall and then come back a few hours later and do it all over again."

He reaches for his glass and toasts Jimmy again.

"You come over to tell me the good news about Licata going down with the ship, or is there something else on your mind?"

Jimmy looks out at the gardens again. Harrington has done some job with them, all kinds of bright colors everywhere, almost like a watercolor. Jimmy's never had the urge to be some kind of master gardener. Or any kind of gardener. It's why the good Lord invented landscapers, as much as they cost out here.

"Jane and me, we keep going back to the day Jacobson's old man and that girl bought it at the town house," Jimmy says. "The one thing that's always bothered me is how Champi got there as quickly as he did that day, when he was supposed to be over in Queens. Maybe even arrived before your guys did. Somebody had to give him a heads-up."

"But he didn't arrive before my guys, I'm sure you checked that all out."

"My old partner, the great Mickey Dunne, thought Champi might have, then took a walk to make it look like he *hadn't* already been there, then came back after your guys did arrive on the scene."

Harrington blows out some air. "What difference does it make if it went down that way, even if it did?" he says. "The bare bones of the thing have never changed. The kid heard the shots, found the bodies, called it in. And we could never find a goddamn thing, whenever Champi showed up, that indicated that somebody staged the scene to make it look like murder-suicide."

"Murder book says there was no residue on the kid's hands."

"Nope."

"Doesn't mean it couldn't have been on someone else's, right?"

"You're telling me somebody got into the house without the kid knowing," Paul Harrington says, "did the girl, did the old man, then got out without the kid seeing or hearing? The place was big. But not that big."

"I know," Jimmy says sadly. "It sounds bananas."

"How come you're still so fixed on this, you don't mind me asking?"

"We just keep going back to that day. Both me and Jane. I know I sound like one of those wingnut conspiracy assholes. I started to think that Licata might have been there, too, except Craig Jackson went all the way back and found out Licata had chased some *Miami Vice* drug dealer down to South Beach at the time."

"There's got to be more to this," Paul Harrington says, "or you wouldn't be here."

"There is. The other day Jane asked our client, straight up, who killed those people in his own house. He said he was sticking with his original story."

"End of story then."

"It would've been for Jane," Jimmy says, "if he didn't tell her that the official version of things was what's kept him alive all these years."

Harrington runs his finger around the rim of his glass, frowning, the old cop trying to process new information.

"So what are you asking me, really, Detective Cunniff?"

"For your help."

Harrington smiles. "I'm too old. You know what they say. The legs go first."

"Like hell you're too old," Jimmy says. "If somebody just blew up Salvatore and Licata, it means that somebody else might have been in charge. And is still out there."

"In charge of what, though?"

"Maybe everything."

Harrington looks across his backyard. In the

moment, Jimmy thinks he might be looking all the way back to his cop days. Maybe that's why he's suddenly smiling again, reaching across the table, putting out his hand for Jimmy to shake.

"I'm in," the old chief says.

NINETY-SIX

SOMEHOW, AND AGAINST ALL odds, I'm still a member in good standing of the people who haven't lost their hair in the chemo club.

At least not yet I haven't.

Doesn't mean I won't. Still having my hair isn't some kind of marker that I'm winning my cancer battle. Or that I won't end up back in Switzerland someday, maybe in the next room over from my sister.

Doesn't make me less of a cancer patient than she is.

I just still don't look like one, even when I'm having the worst week of chemotherapy I've had yet. Which I am. By the end of every session, and by the time I leave the Phillips Center in Ben Kalinsky's car, I feel sicker than I did the day before. When I get home every day I lie down on my couch and struggle to get off it until it's time to try to keep food down or try to sleep. Ben keeps offering to stay after he drops me off. I keep telling him that as much as I love him, and I do love him dearly, right now I'm only fit company for Rip the dog.

"Because your dog doesn't keep asking you how you're feeling?"

"Because he doesn't need to ask."

I try to work on the trial in the brief intervals when I'm not feeling sick. But I can't focus for very long on the work that's still ahead of me, the case making my head spin ever more because of the DNA evidence against Rob Jacobson, the neighborhood security video, from more than one house, of my horny client leaving the Carson house on multiple occasions in the middle of the day.

That's the short list.

The rest of the things on the list only make me feel sicker than I already do.

No help at all is that some of the blood that was found on the scene is AB, the rare type that just happens to belong to Rob Jacobson himself.

I've promised myself I won't change my mind again about staying on the case, that I won't go back on my word. But there are times this week when I want to.

As much as I want to live, sometimes I'm so sick right now I feel as if I want to die.

After what has blessedly been my last treatment, at least for the time being, I'm right back on the couch, trying to watch a Mets game, and there is a knock on the door.

I'm too weak and too tired to even stop for the Glock in the front hall on my way to answer it. If McKenzie and Eric Jacobson are here to kill me, I may just let them tonight.

It's Brigid.

She's wearing a blue Duke baseball cap to cover a bald, wigless head. She looks thinner than ever.

But she's smiling like, well, Brigid.

And having her in front of me makes her even more beautiful to me than ever.

"You look like crap," she says.

NINETY-SEVEN

Jimmy

THOMAS MCKENZIE LIVES ON Lily Pond Lane in East Hampton. The father has more ocean frontage than the son. And his place is much, much bigger.

Jimmy decides to just show up, not give him the same courtesy of calling ahead he gave to Chief Paul Harrington.

What's McKenzie going to do, kick him out of his fund?

A tall redhead in a white bikini that covers so little of her that Jimmy wonders what the point is of wearing it answers the door. Jimmy could never guess in a million years what brand the bikini is, or how much that little swatch of material costs. But her body, as Mickey Dunne used to say, is by God.

She's very young. Too young? Jimmy's not sure what that even means anymore.

He flashes the badge he keeps in his glove compartment, one out of his endless collection of badges. Never leave home without at least one.

"Tommy," she calls over her shoulder. "There's a policeman here to see you."

"Don't worry, kid," Jimmy tells her. "If you're carrying a fake ID, I don't want to know where you keep it."

Maybe all these rich old bastards like them young. Rob Jacobson's father did, when he was a lot younger than McKenzie is now.

McKenzie appears a minute later. He's wearing cargo shorts and a faded polo shirt of indeterminate color and is holding what appears to be a five-o'clock-somewhere margarita. He hands his glass to the girl and pats her on the ass as she walks past.

"Relax, Chelsea," McKenzie says. "Not only isn't he a real cop, he doesn't even play one on television."

"Whatever," she says.

"Why don't you go take a dip?"

"I just got out."

"Get back in and I'll be there in time to watch you get back out."

She walks away. McKenzie watches her go. So does Jimmy. And has to admit. It really is some ass.

"Not going to ask me in?" Jimmy asks McKenzie.

"No."

"Curious about why I'm here?"

"Not even a little bit."

Jimmy plows ahead.

"I realized I've got a few more questions about you and the late Anthony Licata. And the late Robinson Jacobson."

"And that, Mr. Cunniff, is your problem. I've already given you more of my time than you deserve. And said more to you than I should have in the first place."

Behind him, Jimmy sees Chelsea dive into the pool. He feels a little sad, knowing he won't get the chance to watch her get out of the pool.

McKenzie starts to shut the door.

Jimmy holds it open with his hand.

"What I'm starting to wonder is just how many clients like you Licata and his partner used to have. And just how big a business it was for them."

McKenzie pushes his sunglasses to the end of his nose, so Jimmy can see his eyes. They're blue, but not much more than the color of spit.

"I told you at my office. My business relationship with Mr. Licata ended a long time ago."

"But what if it didn't?" Jimmy says.

His hand is still on the door.

"What if it just went on and on and on, every time you had a problem with your son you dialed him up? 1-800-ANTHONY. Or maybe it was a problem of your own, maybe with one of your Chelseas?"

McKenzie smiles now. It's not much more than a twitch of his thin lips.

"You really have no clue about what you've gotten yourself into," he says. "Do you?"

"Wouldn't be the first time."

"You're out of your depth, and so is the lawyer lady," McKenzie says. "Do you know what can happen to people like that, whether I once had a business relationship with them or not?"

"Help me out."

"Sometimes they end up at the bottom of the ocean."

McKenzie pushes his sunglasses back up his nose. He could as easily have been talking about getting himself another drink. Or another girl. The threat came out of him that casually.

"One last thing before I go."

"Before I call the real police and tell them you're harassing me?"

"What if your son not keeping it in his pants is an inherited trait?"

Then Jimmy lets McKenzie slam the door.

NINETY-EIGHT

I INVITE BRIGID TO join Dr. Ben and me for dinner at Rowdy Hall, which had just moved to Amagansett from East Hampton and was within walking distance of my house.

"Two patients at dinner are one too many," my sister says. "I looked it up in the cancer rule book."

I'm feeling better now that I've put three or four days between me and the end of chemo. Having Brigid back, even in her own diminished state, makes me feel even better. And as close to her as I've felt in a long time.

Maybe ever.

Something else that's making me feel stronger, and more energized? I'm little more than a week out from jury selection. If this really is going to be my last trial—for a long time and, who knows, maybe forever—I'm determined to go out with a bang.

Figure of speech.

Ben is having a Rowdy Burger. I've gone with the best Fish & Chips on the entire East End. While we eat, we're talking again about Jimmy's visit to Thomas McKenzie, and what McKenzie said about people ending up dead in the water.

"Are you convinced they're both dead," Ben asks, "even though they haven't found the bodies?"

"I don't know how either of them could have survived unless they got into the water before the boat blew and could swim like Michael Phelps."

I tell him what McKenzie said, basically about us being in over our heads.

"You still could walk away, you know," Ben says.

"*You* know better than that."

"We've talked about this before," he says. He has the sweetest eyes, a perfect fit for this sweet, sweet man. "None of this is worth dying over, not when you're fighting this hard to live."

I feel myself squeezing his hand, harder than I meant. *"I need to know."*

It comes out far more fiercely than I had intended, surprising even me.

"Sorry for the outburst," I say.

"Don't be sorry on my account," Ben says, and smiles at me again with those eyes, before I tell him that we're done talking about bad guys tonight, I'm still out on a date with one of the good guys.

More likely the best guy.

We are about to look at the dessert menu when he gets a call. A golden retriever belonging to a tennis pal of his was hit by a car in the Springs. The dog is being rushed to Ben's office. Ben tells the person he's on his way.

I got lazy and drove us here. So I drive him to his office. He calls his nurse on the way.

"We never close," he says.

I remind him that's my line.

I'm on my way home from Ben's office, just turning onto my street, when Brigid calls. "Can you come over?" she asks.

She's not calling from the Meier Clinic this time with chemo news. She's only a few miles away, at the western end of Amagansett. But it's another time when I don't like the sound of her voice, not even a little bit.

"Are you okay?"

There's a pause.

"Just hurry," she says. "Please."

NINETY-NINE

BRIGID'S HOUSE, THE ONE she shared with her husband until she didn't, is an old-fashioned Hamptons saltbox, with a white picket fence around her front lawn. Her new Audi is in the driveway.

The lights are on inside.

I knock on the front door, just to signal that I'm here, before trying the handle.

"It's open."

She's sitting on the couch. No ballcap covering her bald head tonight. Maybe she doesn't bother when she's alone. She told me when I invited her to dinner with Ben and me that she didn't want to put her hair on.

Somehow, as frail as she is, she's still beautiful, at least to me.

Just not alone.

Sitting across from her, cradling what looks like a .22 pistol in his lap, is Nick Morelli.

"Long time, no see," he says.

Then he waves at me with the gun, telling me to shut the door and take a seat next to my sister, there are things we need to discuss.

ONE HUNDRED

"IT'S GOING TO BE okay," I say to Brigid when I'm next to her on the couch.

Morelli is no longer pointing the gun at me. Or us. But it's still in his hand.

"That's entirely up to you," he says to me. "The part about it being okay."

"I don't suppose there's any point in telling you that I'm sorry about your uncle Bobby," I say.

"There's no point, because you're not. And I'm not."

Brigid's living room feels smaller than ever, the air thick with an almost kinetic combination of her fear and my fear for her. And my own anger about Morelli bringing her into this.

Nothing to be done about that now, because nothing ever changes. It's like Jimmy always says: the one with the gun is the tough one.

My own voice is what sounds thick as I ask him, "What do you want?"

"Eric was supposed to deliver a message to you. But you clearly didn't get that message. Or just refused to get it, being the stubborn bitch that you are."

There's no reason for me to reply to that. Mostly because he's pretty much nailed it.

I give Brigid a quick, sidelong glance. She's staring at Morelli in his black T-shirt, black jeans, black boots. Black eyes. Her face is the color of tissue paper. Her hands are clasped on her lap, tightly, the knuckles as white as the rest of her.

"Who sent you here?"

"My boss."

"I thought your uncle was your boss."

"You still just don't get it." He sighs. "You still don't know what you just do not goddamn know."

"Enlighten me then."

"Why I'm here," he says, "is to try to get through to you for the last time." He shrugs and grins. "Do I have your attention *now*?"

The note on Martin that night had said the same thing.

"Undivided."

My sister's breathing is shallow next to me, forced, harsh.

I'm the reason he's in her house.

I brought him into her life.

I did this.

"There's been a change in our business model, I guess you could call it," Morelli says. "At this point, we have no problem with you defending Eric's dad, as long as you leave the rest of it alone. Leave us alone, before we close this thing down for good."

"Close what down, you don't mind me asking?"

He picks up the gun, points at me, squints as if aiming it across the short distance between us.

But puts it back down as quickly as he lifted it.

"Does it really matter at this point?"

"To me it does."

"Yeah," he says, "it would matter to you. Wouldn't it?"

I arch my back, as if stretching it, placing my hands in the small of my back.

Feeling my own gun back there, stuck into the back of my jeans.

How does Jimmy like to put it?

Just in case the ball goes up.

"All you have to do is tell your partner to stop bothering people and stop asking questions about shit that has nothing to do with you defending Eric's sack-of-shit father. Then nobody else has to die, Eric and I ride off into the sunset like the cowboys we are."

"What about your friend McKenzie? Does he ride off with you?"

Morelli gives me a sly look, as if he's got a secret. "I sure do hope nothing happens to him!" he says, his voice suddenly brightening.

He nods at me. "This is a deal you should take, while it's still on the table."

"If I don't?"

"Jane!" my sister says plaintively.

Morelli gets up, walks over to Brigid, and gently lays his gun against her cheek. She seems to shrink inside herself but is too frightened to lean away from him.

He slowly moves the gun up and down, as if he's using it to caress her.

"Then the next one to go is her," he says. "And then maybe all the other people you care about after her. And that dog of yours. For the last time, stop bothering people you shouldn't be bothering, about shit that happened a long time ago and has nothing to do with you."

"Why not just kill me?" I ask. "Joe Champi was ready to."

"Champi was out of control. If you hadn't shot him, I would have had to."

"But you won't shoot me."

"My boss says no, as long as you finally get the message," he says. "He says he owes a guy a favor. And for the time being, you're still the favor."

"Who's the guy?"

"Your father."

I hear the sharp intake of breath from Brigid. Or maybe it was my own.

"What did you just say?"

"All I'm going to say."

Morelli backs toward the door, the gun still in his hand, all the way out of my sister's house, gently closing the door in front of him.

I think about going after him, getting my gun out and firing a couple of shots in the air just to scare the hell out of him tonight the way he scared Brigid. But I don't. My sister has been through enough. We both have.

I try to put my arm around her. But she leans away from me now, as if I'm the one she doesn't want touching her.

"You're going to do exactly what he asked you to do," she says. "You're going to defend Rob and then you're going to let God sort out the rest of it."

"What about what he just said about Dad?"

My fragile sister, my beautiful fragile sister, looks at me.

"Dad's dead," she says. "How about working on keeping us alive?"

ONE HUNDRED ONE

BRIGID AGREES TO COME back to my house and spend the night. I give her my room and take the fold-out bed from the sofa in my office.

In the morning I meet Jimmy at Jack's in Sag Harbor. Jimmy orders a regular coffee. After sleeping only a couple of hours, at most, waiting across the rest of the night to hear my alarm triggered, I've ordered an espresso-and-coffee mix called Mad Max.

"Can you see any possible connection between your father and any of these scum buckets?" Jimmy asks.

"He was a Marine. He was a bartender my whole life until he dropped dead in the bar one day. He grew up in Hell's Kitchen with a lot of kids who could have gone either way. He met a lot of people in his life, on both sides of the line, is what I'm saying."

"Now somebody in this thing of ours owes him a favor, from way back."

"At least according to Morelli."

"Your sister wants you to walk away, which means she wants both of us to walk away."

"And that's exactly what we're going to do," I say. "It's time for us to stop chasing our tails and focus on the trial and let God sort out the rest of it."

I see Jimmy staring across the street as a couple of uniformed cops from the Sag Harbor station wave at him before they get into their cruiser and head up Division Street. By now I'm convinced that Jimmy Cunniff knows the name and rank of every cop on the South Fork, and what they like to order at his bar.

He turns and looks back at me.

"Gotta give you a hard no," he says.

"It wasn't a request, Jimmy."

"I don't care whether it was or not," he says.

He hasn't changed his tone, or raised his voice, doesn't sound angry, or confrontational, or as if he's looking to pick a fight. But I've seen this set to his whole impressive self before, eyes and expression and even body language. The old boxer who once told me he knew everything in the ring except when to stop coming.

"Morelli threatened everybody. You talk all the time about risk and reward in this business. We need to be done taking risks, no matter how hard we want to go at these people. They've already gotten to you more than once. They got to Ben. They got to Brigid. They got to me again. We're out."

"I'm not stopping," he says. He's still staring across Division Street. "Not even if you fire me."

"Come on," I tell him. "Nobody's talking about firing you. Are you kidding? I'd fire myself before I'd fire you."

We both sip coffee. He's back to looking at me. Still completely calm. Sometimes with him that's not necessarily a good thing.

"I'm just telling you how it is," Jimmy says. "One of these people killed my partner. Or knows who killed my partner. They killed the DA who brought us in on the Carson case. I can't let that go."

What comes out of him next comes out in a harsh whisper.

"You should know me well enough by now to know that I don't let shit go."

"Even if it puts us all in danger?"

"What the hell are you talking about, Janie? We're already in danger."

I can't remember the two of us ever having a real argument. We have disagreements all the time, though rarely on the big things. But he never gets genuinely angry with me.

Until now.

"I'm not telling you to let anything go," I say. "I'm asking you, Jimmy."

ONE HUNDRED TWO

Jimmy

HE DOESN'T CALL JANE for a couple of days. She doesn't call him. Longest they've gone since she was in Switzerland.

Jimmy does get a call from Detective Craig Jackson a couple of nights later, almost two in the morning, Jackson knowing how little Jimmy sleeps. He's calling because he's still trying to help Jimmy out. And because Craig Jackson didn't let shit go, either.

"I think I got a lead on who Champi and Licata were answering to," Jackson says.

Jimmy can hear the excitement in his voice, like he's giving off sparks at his end.

"Don't tell me. It was Salvatore."

"Bigger."

The next morning Jimmy is sitting with Lieutenant Paul Harrington, the kind of boss he wished he had with the cops, at the Sip 'N Soda in Southampton, just down from Town Hall. It's a place out of the past, including Jimmy's, 1960s or earlier, with its old-fashioned counter and fountains and homemade ice cream and tiled floor. They're at a small table outside, facing 27A. Harrington has apologized to Jimmy for not meeting him earlier, but one of the perks of retirement is being a late sleeper for the first time in his life.

"You're telling *me* that Jackson told *you* that Sonny Blum himself was running these guys?" Harrington asks.

"Word for word, practically."

Harrington laughs. "Have you seen any of the videos of the poor bastard from a few years ago? One time they found him wandering one of the streets near that fortress he lives in, over there in Garden City, wearing what looked like one of Vincent the Chin's old bathrobes. Remember *that* poor bastard? Mr. Vincent Gigante himself. Brother of a priest. Not that it helped him much when his brain turned to oatmeal."

Harrington is having an honest-to-Christ egg cream because they still serve them at Sip 'N Soda. For the life of him, Jimmy can't remember the last time he saw somebody with an egg cream in front of them.

"My opinion?" Harrington says. "Just thinking out loud here? I think somebody is trying to send you down a rabbit hole."

Jimmy's quiet now, watching the light traffic pass

by in front of them. Maybe he should have gone for an egg cream. He used to love them as a kid, sitting in places like this on the Grand Concourse.

"Maybe you're right," Jimmy says. "Maybe Salvatore and Licata got stupid at the end the way Champi did and pissed off the wrong people."

Harrington takes out the straw and licks the end of it. "You know what they say, detective. The jails aren't full of smart people."

"Maybe I should have looked harder at Blum before this," Jimmy says. "His name did keep popping up."

"Maybe so. We always suspected Sonny had to own cops to stay clear of the cops, even if he was out in Long Island. Maybe he owned some of ours, too."

"You mentioned the Chin before," Jimmy says, as he waves off Harrington's attempt to grab the check. "He only got by with faking he was crazy until they finally nailed his ass on racketeering and conspiracy once and for all."

"Died in prison."

"Maybe I can arrange for Sonny to do the same," Jimmy says.

They're quiet again. Two old cops, a long way from the big city, both of them still not ready to let go. Both of them still wanting to get the bad guys.

"You're really going after him?" Harrington asks.

"Hard."

"Even if it gets you killed?"

"Maybe I'm the crazy one," Jimmy says.

"Whatever you need from me," Harrington says. "You remember that. If Blum was buying cops, I want a piece of that old man, too."

ONE HUNDRED THREE

I FINALLY GIVE IN and call Jimmy, trying to act as if nothing has gone sideways with us. Avoidance isn't one of my greatest skills. But I can do it with the best of them when I'm avoiding a major conflict with my best friend.

I just innocently ask what he's doing.

"You don't want to know."

"Wouldn't I be the best judge of what I want to know?"

"Not today, counselor."

He ends the call. I want to call right back and press him. But I know better. And know enough to give him room, whether I like it or not. Know I have to wait for him to make the next move, or the next call, whether I like *that* or not.

What is this, high school?

From the time I hired him, I've known he's never

been much for chain of command. But it doesn't matter with our partnership, and our friendship. We're equal partners in this, always have been. Whatever he has going on right now, whatever is going on between us, requires patience on my part. Something else not high up in my skill set.

I'm trying to get Brigid to move in with me, just for the time being. She says she's fine where she is and will continue to be fine as long as I do what Nick Morelli told me to do, and back the hell off from him, and Eric Jacobson, and Edmund McKenzie.

"We have a deal on that, right?" she asks.

"Everybody seems to want to be making deals with me these days. Why should my sister be any different?"

"Just do your job," she says, "and focus on defending Rob."

"You know I can multitask with the best of them."

"What I know," my sister says, "is that you have a gift, a genius even, for pissing people off. But now I've seen with my own eyes that these are people you don't want to piss off. And I'm asking you to please not."

"Duly noted."

"So we *do* have a deal, correct?"

"Sure."

"That didn't sound very convincing."

"I try to save my convincing for court, sis."

I don't tell her that what she wants from me

probably doesn't matter in the end if Jimmy Cunniff isn't going to stop pushing. And he's made much more of a career pissing people off, good guys and bad guys, than I ever have.

It's why we make a good team.

We both have always treated taking even one step back like it was some kind of felony.

I keep telling myself to do what Brigid wants me to do and focus on the trial. I know I'm ready for it. My two interns are at full throttle on the kind of trial prep I've always prided myself on doing but simply haven't had the energy for this time, even when I'm not in the chemo chair. And I know what I've always known, anyway, that as much as you need all the information you can bring with you into a courtroom, everything changes when the bell rings. Jimmy Cunniff has always said I'm not one of those people who looks like a million damn dollars in practice. He says I always save it for the game.

One of my law school kids, Estie, asked the other day if I've thought about hiring a jury consultant.

"Already did," I told her. *"Me."*

After I've spoken to Brigid, I sit at the kitchen table for a couple of hours, trying to work, Rip at my feet. But as hard as I try, even into the early evening, I can't get out of my head the image of Nick Morelli pressing his gun against my sister's face. She told me that when she opened the door and saw him pointing the gun at her she was wearing her Duke hat. He made her take it off. He wanted her to be bald and at her most vulnerable. As if walking her back into her own house at gunpoint hadn't made her feel vulnerable enough.

Brigid kept telling me that if she was willing to let that go then I should be, too.

But I'm not her, never have been. She's the one with the same gentle nature that our mother always had, to her dying day. Not me.

I'm more like my father.

Who is owed a posthumous favor, by persons unknown.

He was the one who taught me, from the first time I played hockey, not to let the other girl get the first punch in. He was the one who told me, when I beat up those mean kids, how proud of me he was.

"My girl," he said that night, before going off to work at the bar.

Now somebody has threatened to shoot my sister and has done that with me in the room.

I put down my pen and turn over my yellow legal pad and put my notes back into their manila folder.

Jimmy Cunniff isn't the only one who doesn't let shit go.

I go and get the keys to the car.

And my gun.

ONE HUNDRED FOUR

I STOP BY THE Bell & Anchor first, since the menu scribbled with "Boom" and left in my car came from the restaurant.

If it wasn't Eddie McKenzie or Eric Jacobson or both of them, I'm going to lose a bet with myself.

Jake the host tells me that neither McKenzie nor Eric have been back since the night I was there with Dr. Sam Wylie. I show Jake a picture of Nick Morelli and ask if he's ever seen Morelli with either McKenzie or Eric Jacobson.

He takes a long look at Morelli's face, hands it back.

"With Eric a few times, most definitely."

"Recently?"

"Not sure the last time I saw them together," he says. "But he's been here."

"Call me the next time you see him, too."

He asks how Jimmy is doing. I say, cranky as hell.

Jake grins and says it's been Jimmy's natural state for as long as he's known him.

"Same," I say.

My options from here are limited, and I know that. I have no earthly idea where Morelli is living these days. No idea where Eric Jacobson might be living. I could drive over to the house in Montauk where Jimmy followed Dave Wolk that night. But Jimmy drove past there a few days ago and said the place looked deserted.

I do know, however, where Edmund McKenzie lives.

All I've got.

So I drive to Southampton now. Jimmy has told me the house number on Gin Lane. When I arrive, I see no Tesla parked in the driveway.

But the lights are on inside. A lot of them. I park on the street, so as not to make any noise pulling up the gravel driveway. As I walk up on the grass behind the house, I can hear music, loud, but probably not loud enough to bother Edmund McKenzie's rich neighbors.

I stay close to the side of the house as I make my way around it, finally stopping when I reach the corner.

And there on the back patio are Eric Jacobson and Nick Morelli.

Side by side in lounge chairs. A pitcher of what looks like margaritas on the table between them. Highball glasses in their hands. Jacobson says something.

Morelli laughs, reaches over with his free hand and slaps Eric Jacobson five.

They're facing the far end of the property, acting as if they own the place.

Maybe they used to hang like this when they were jacking these kinds of houses for fun and profit.

Not worrying about getting caught once they disarmed the alarms, which Eric Jacobson tells me is a piece of cake for him.

I don't recognize the song or the band, but that's happening to me more and more.

Now Morelli says something and Eric Jacobson is the one laughing his head off.

I'm very quiet coming from behind them as I make my way across the patio. Neither one of them notices me until I rack the slide of the Glock 27 for effect, the harsh sound making both of them jump.

When Nick Morelli turns, it's the barrel of my gun against the side of *his* face.

"I forgot to mention something the other night," I tell him.

ONE HUNDRED FIVE

MORELLI, STARING STRAIGHT AHEAD, trying to keep his head still, reaches over and carefully puts his glass on the table after I tell him to be extremely careful.

Eric Jacobson, not nearly as cool as he was when he was the one with the gun, is staring wide-eyed at Morelli and me as he reaches over to put down his own glass.

"You be careful, too, junior," I say.

Now they know how it feels to get ambushed.

"You are making a huge mistake," Morelli says in a soft voice.

"Then I'm making progress, tough guy," I say. "I used to marry my mistakes."

"We both know you're not going to shoot me in the head," he says.

"Nope. I'm not. But if you make a single sudden move, or maybe if you even annoy me, it will be one of your kneecaps."

To Eric Jacobson I say, "Turn off the music."

"I have to go into the house to do that."

"The remote is sitting right there. And if you're considering making what would be a huge mistake of your own, you probably know by now what a good shot I am with an air rifle, and from a much greater distance than this. Was it you or Morelli or both of you at the trail the other night, by the way?"

"Keep your mouth shut, Eric," Morelli says.

Jacobson picks up the remote and hits a button and the music stops. Carefully puts it back on the table. We can all hear the ocean now.

Morelli suddenly tries to lean back in his chair and swipe at my gun at the same time, the dumb bastard. I move back just enough to swing the Glock and hit him with it on the side of his head above his ear.

Old habits.

Never let the other guy get the first swing.

"Tough is still the one with the gun, right, Eric?" I ask.

Morelli is bleeding over the ear as I step back from him.

"Where's your buddy McKenzie?" I ask.

Jacobson starts to say something. Morelli looks at him and gives a quick shake to his head.

"Away," Morelli says.

"Permanently, or just temporarily?"

"Away," Morelli repeats.

"Who sent you two after me?"

Again Morelli gives a quick look to Jacobson and shakes his head. The alpha dog. Maybe like Uncle Bobby was.

I raise the Glock and point it at the tip of his nose. Like that's the bullseye in the center of the target. It was my father who first taught me how to shoot in high school, not that I'd need to be much of a shot now if he tries anything else.

"If I tell you that, I'm as good as dead," Morelli says. "We both are."

"She's going to find out eventually," Jacobson says.

"I told you to shut up, Eric!"

The moon above us is as bright as it possibly could be, the sky full of stars. It really is quite beautiful back here, underneath the kind of sky that always seems to get bigger the closer you get to the water. I hear the waves, and the sound of night birds.

"I told you to back off, but you just don't listen," Morelli says.

"I'm actually a terrific listener once you get to know me."

"I left your sister's house assuming we had an understanding."

"Actually, we do," I tell him. "I *am* going to back off, just like you asked. But before I do, I just needed to take this one last big step forward."

"What's that supposed to mean?"

"I've just got a few questions before we all go our separate ways. Starting with this one: What did you mean about my father?"

He puts his hand to his ear and sees the blood on it when he pulls it away. "I need to put something on this."

"When I'm gone. Now what did you mean about somebody owing my father a favor?"

"I don't know."

"Bullshit you don't know."

"Listen to me if you're such a good listener. All I knew was that I was supposed to deliver that message. Tell you that nothing more will happen as long as you backed the hell off. Only now you go and pull something like this."

I have no idea how much either one of them will tell me, even at the other end of my gun. And they both really do know I'm not here to shoot them dead.

What they don't know is whether I'm bluffing about making them walk with limps for the rest of their lives.

Eric Jacobson casually reaches for his glass. No good can possibly come of that.

I turn and fire and shatter the glass, the sound of the gun going off as loud as a thunderclap, not missing his hand by much. But missing it. From close range, I really am a great shot.

I hope I haven't scared the neighbors.

"You crazy bitch!" Jacobson yells.

"Boy," I tell them both, "I wish I had a dollar for every time I've heard that one."

I step back a little more, to make it seem as if the gun is now pointed at both of them.

"Our business is now concluded," I say, "just like Nick here wanted. But now it's the two of you who need to back off."

"That's what you came here to tell us?" Morelli says.

I nod. "And to tell you that if you choose not to back off, and if either one of you, or anybody you work with, or for, goes near my sister or Jimmy Cunniff or my boyfriend, I will find you both again. And the next time I will shoot you dead."

"If you live that long," Morelli says.

Some drops of blood have landed on the shoulder of his white T-shirt.

"I could have done it tonight and told the cops you both attacked me," I say. "So if you think about it, maybe you guys are the ones who owe me a favor now."

"My ass," Morelli says.

"Well put."

I keep the Glock pointed at them as I slowly back my way across the patio. When I get to the corner of the house, I stop.

"Boom," I say.

ONE HUNDRED SIX

Jimmy

SONNY BLUM'S NAME KEEPS coming up, here and there, has from the beginning. Jimmy Cunniff knows why and knows maybe he should have red-flagged it sooner. Bobby Salvatore worked for Blum before going out on his own, if not with Sonny's approval, at least with his consent. Gambling was never a big part of Sonny's operation.

Loan sharking sure was, though, and bad girls, and extortion, and forcing his way into legitimate businesses, and all-around racketeering, and the ever-popular waste management companies. Maybe Sonny didn't view Salvatore as a competitor, or threat, until maybe he did.

Jimmy was so fixed on Champi, and then Licata, the immediate threats, that he never paid enough attention to Blum over there on the edges of this thing, maybe because he bought into the notion that the old man was supposed to be drooling on himself.

None of the mob cops could pinpoint the time when Bobby Salvatore went off on his own. Maybe Salvatore was allowed to go off on his own because Sonny Blum was getting a cut of his profits, was a partner to him the way Salvatore was with somebody like Allen Reese. Maybe they were all in bed together, in one big landfill-type pile.

The last time there were any pictures of Blum, or any video, was when he was seen walking down Seventh Street in Garden City in his bathrobe, mumbling to himself, a few miles from a mansion that the guys from Organized Crime Control said was as well guarded as the White House.

But maybe Detective Craig Jackson's intel was wrong about Sonny Blum being the one behind the curtain. Maybe Blum's mind really has turned to oatmeal, and he isn't capable of masterminding anything these days beyond trips to the bathroom.

But there are still all these connections.

"Lot of pearls," Mickey Dunne used to say when they'd be working a case that threatened to turn their brains to mush. "Our job is to make a necklace out of them."

It's Jimmy's job now, because he isn't going to let

Mickey Dunne's murder stay in Open Unsolved forever. So Jimmy has been working the phones hard the past few days. Gone back to the city for face-to-face time with some of his OCC contacts. Because Sonny Blum is from the Island, Danny Esposito has been working with his Organized Crime task force.

The Jewish Don, they called Sonny Blum in a *Times* piece a few years ago. In the photographs they ran of the old man, he looks like a taller Mel Brooks.

Jimmy has turned the bar into his office tonight, laptop set up under the television set at his corner. He tried to call Jane a few hours ago but got sent straight to voicemail. Probably on a date with Ben Kalinsky.

"How ya doin'?" Jimmy hears now to his left.

He turns. A guy in a dark navy suit, white shirt, no tie, has taken the open stool next to him. Maybe in his forties, maybe a little older. Nice tan. That kind of beard stubble that somehow has been turned into a modern art form. Hair short on the side, a little bit of a fade on top, some gray in it. Small smile for Jimmy, from dark blue eyes that seem to match the suit.

"Do I know you?" Jimmy asks.

"Nah."

"How can I help you then?" He points at the laptop. "Kind of working here."

"I'm actually here to help you."

The guy's still smiling. Lot of teeth. He turns to

Kenny Stanton and orders a Crown Royal, neat. When Kenny sets the glass down in front of him, he takes a small sip of it right away.

"Help me with what?" Jimmy says. "Or maybe I should ask, with who?"

"Sonny."

ONE HUNDRED SEVEN

I SEE A MISSED call from Jimmy when I get home, but his phone is turned off when I try to hit him back.

I call Brigid then, wanting to be honest with her about where I've been and what I've done at Edmund McKenzie's house, and what it might mean for both of us going forward.

I tell it all in a rush after she answers.

When I finish, there's a long silence on her end. I can hear jazz playing softly in the background. One thing she did inherit from Jack Smith is her love of jazz.

"You never change, do you, Jane? You do what you want when you want, and to hell with what anybody else might want."

"Not fair."

"Fair? You told me you were going to leave all of this alone, because *you* told *me* it was the best way to keep

434

me safe. But now I'm probably right back in the line of fire, aren't I? Good work, sis. You've pissed them off and you've pissed me off."

"We were already in the line of fire, both of us."

Another silence, longer than the one before.

"I'm going away," she says finally. "I'm going to get away from here and I'm going to get away from you."

"Go where?" I ask.

"To save my marriage."

Before I can respond she says, "I love you. I hope we both get better. But you really are a selfish bitch."

She ends the call before I can tell her it's the second time I've been called a bitch tonight.

It's late on a Friday night. I try Jimmy again. Phone still off. But what I need to tell him about Nick Morelli and Eric Jacobson can wait until the morning. He'll probably be as angry at me as I've made my sister. Maybe even angrier.

I try to do a little more work, jury selection a few days away. There was a time when this upcoming trial, on the heels of the first one, my client really on trial for another triple homicide, seemed all-consuming to me. But as hideous as these crimes are, more and more I've started to think that they're just one element to a much bigger story.

Maybe Brigid is right. Maybe it was selfish of me to even go looking for those two punks tonight, much less roust them the way I did. But I'm tired of being threatened. I'm tired of being pushed around. I've never let anybody push me around, at least not for very long, all the way back to the mean girls. Martin did it for a while at the end of our marriage.

But I didn't let him get away with it for long.

I've had no choice about cancer, which chose me the way it chooses everybody else, my sister included.

But tonight I made a choice of my own.

My father's daughter.

"My girl," he always called me.

I had a dream about him last night, for the first time in a long time, certainly for the first time since I got sick. He was younger, too, the way my mother is so often younger in my dreams, not the sad old man who dropped dead of a heart attack on the barroom floor, working too hard until the end, drinking too much, doing everything not to go back to the empty apartment after Brigid and I went off to college.

Jack Smith hated being alone, and at least when he was behind the bar, he wasn't. Alone. The tough ex-Marine who never got over losing her, never stopped beating himself up for not doing enough for her, especially once she got sick.

Who owes him a favor, all this time later?

How far back does this story really go?

He always said this about tending bar, my father did:

"You meet all kinds. But their money looks exactly the same once they slide it across to me."

In the dream, he's up in the stands, alone up there, too, watching me play hockey. But when I go up to find him after the game is over, he's gone.

I take my Glock with me when I walk Rip up and down the street in front of my house, come back inside, set the alarm. When I get into bed, I don't put the gun in the drawer of the bedside table, I leave it on top.

Maybe I really do have some kind of death wish, as hard as I'm fighting to live.

I leave a light on outside my bedroom door and open it a crack, so Rip and I aren't entirely in the dark tonight.

It turns out my father wasn't the only one who met all kinds.

So has his little girl.

ONE HUNDRED EIGHT

Jimmy

NO POINT IN ASKING the guy his name again. Jimmy already has a better idea about finding out later, if he needs to.

Just not now.

"Here's how I'd like this to go," the guy says. "Let me help you help me. Think of it that way."

"Win, win, so to speak?"

"Exactly!"

Jimmy sees that the guy is barely making a dent in his whiskey. Maybe he's pacing himself. Or he's already had a few and is worried about driving back to wherever he came from.

"How about we cut to the chase," Jimmy says. "It's getting late and I'm tired."

"Not tired of me, I hope."

"To be determined."

"I like a man who doesn't screw around."

"You might maybe want to hold off on reaching that conclusion."

The guy nods in agreement.

"So here it is," he says. "Sonny, he has good days and bad days. Mostly bad. But out of the sky he just had a couple of good ones, and that's when he found out you've been asking a lot of questions about him. And what he has sent me here to tell you is that he'd like to call a cease-fire. So to speak. Just you and him. A rare opportunity with Sonny, you want to know the truth."

Now Jimmy nods. He's the one smiling back at the guy now.

"You're telling me the guy who's still the head of the mob on Long Island needs a cease-fire with a broken-down ex-cop?" Jimmy says. "Get the hell out of here."

"Just sayin'."

"Does this mean it's Sonny who's been behind all the killing and general bullshit?"

"Not saying that at all," the guy says. "And not here to litigate the past. I am just authorized to tell you that shit got out of hand and now he wants it to stop before anybody else gets killed."

"Not until I find out who killed my old partner."

"Wasn't us," the guy says. "Like I said: shit got out of hand. But now the people who did let it get out of hand are gone."

439

"Who killed Mickey Dunne?"

"Licata."

Just like that, bingo bango, as Mickey used to say.

"Who called it?"

"Licata called it. He was worried that you and the lawyer lady were going to trace too much shit back to him, which you fuckin' ay did anyway, and he did something he never used to do."

"Which is?"

"Panicked."

"I thought it was Champi who did Mickey."

"What Anthony wanted you to think. He wanted you to think Champi did a lot of shit he didn't do."

"And you know all this how?"

He shrugs. "I lead a very interesting life. But all you need to know is that when the boss found out, on one of those good days, he took care of it."

"Why did Salvatore get clipped, too?"

"That's between Sonny and Salvatore. Or was."

Jimmy checks his phone, remembers he turned it off.

"And what do I get if I agree to this truce you're talking about?"

"More of the answers you want to the questions you still got."

"And what if I continue to be the stubborn bastard I've always been, and decide to find those answers on my own?"

The guy has another small taste of the whiskey. Jimmy thinks he drinks like Janie's birds used to.

"Sonny got tired of sending boys to do a man's job when it came to delivering the message he wants delivered."

"So here you are, the man with no name, like Eastwood in those old spaghetti westerns."

"Sure."

It comes out *shoo-wah*. City accent.

"Just so we're clear," Jimmy says, "what is the message, exactly?"

One last smile.

"Jesus," the guy says. "Do we have to draw you a picture? We get our peace accord squared away, or the pause button comes off on the killing, and you all go. Her first."

He stands, drinks up, walks out of the bar without saying another word, or looking back.

Jimmy points at the empty glass sitting there on the bar.

"Bag this," he says to Kenny Stanton, and then calls Danny Esposito and tells him he's got some prints he needs to have run.

Then Jimmy calls Paul Harrington.

"I may have a lead on Sonny," Jimmy says.

ONE HUNDRED NINE

I GO FOR SOMETHING unusual on the weekend:

I go for normal.

I'm still not going anywhere without my gun, I'm not crazy, even taking it into the bathroom with me when I shower. I take it with me when I walk Rip, either on the street or on the beach. I take it with me to the farm stand and the grocery store and Jack's.

Brigid is safe with her maybe-not-soon-to-be ex, at what she calls an undisclosed location in Maine that she promises to me is far from the line of fire.

Rob Jacobson is still calling a couple of times a day to tell me how bored and stir-crazy he is.

"That's where I am with my so-called life," he says. "I might be the only guy in the world to be excited about standing trial for murder again, as long as it gets me out of the house."

Sam Wylie calls to remind me, as if I need reminding,

that my next appointment with her and Dr. Mike Gellis, my oncologist, is scheduled for next Saturday, both of them willing to meet with me on a weekend to accommodate my court schedule. I tell her I'm more likely to forget my birthday than an exciting opportunity like that.

"You know you can drop the tough-guy act with me, right?" she says on the phone.

"What act?"

At least she didn't call me a bitch after telling me she loved me.

Jimmy continues to investigate Sonny Blum, without much success. The only success he's had is with the prints Danny Esposito ran for him off the glass the hard case at the bar left. It turns out they're in the system, and belong to a man named Len Greene, who came up in Blum's organization around the same time as Bobby Salvatore. His service was interrupted by the four years he spent at Green Haven Correctional.

"Ask me what he was in for," Jimmy says.

"I'll bite."

"Blowing up the car of somebody stealing from Sonny."

"Was this somebody in the car at the time?"

"He was not."

"Does Mr. Greene have an address?"

"Yeah. Sonny's house."

"Would it help if I suggested letting sleeping Jewish gangsters lie?"

"No," he says, and ends the call.

His tough-guy act isn't an act, either. But I already knew that.

I work all of Saturday on trial stuff, throwing myself into the grind, knowing the day will end with the dinner I'm preparing for Dr. Ben Kalinsky and myself. For the first time in weeks, I've decided to go fancy with ingredients from Balsam Farms: mushroom Asiago chicken pasta as the main course, preceded by an apple harvest salad.

For dessert I'm reaching for the sky, a chocolate soufflé I've prepped to go into the oven as we start the main course.

"What's the occasion?" Ben says, pouring us more wine.

"It's not really very complicated," I say, leaning across the table, nearly knocking over my wineglass as I do, and then kissing him.

I pull back, smiling at him. "The occasion is that I love you."

"You're right. Not that complicated at all."

"I still am, you know. Complicated as all get-out."

"Just another reason why I love you. And why I'm so happy that you're getting back to work *you* love."

"You mean being a criminal lawyer instead of running around with a gun and behaving like one?"

"Like that."

The soufflé is beyond a guilty pleasure. We clean up the kitchen and share a brandy in the living room and then shut the bedroom door on Rip the dog and make love, after which I experience the best night of sleep I've had in a long time.

I tell myself I'm getting back to my day job, even knowing that my full-time job is cancer.

The next night, alone with Rip, and pizza from Astro's, I'm deep into a dreamless sleep for a change, no visits in the night from either of my parents, when I hear my phone. The clock on my bedside table reads 12:01.

UNKNOWN CALLER.

I instinctively reach for the Glock.

"It's McKenzie," I hear. "You have to help me."

My old friend Edmund McKenzie. He sounds as if calling from the middle of a wind tunnel.

"Why in the world would I do something like that?"

"They're gonna kill me, Cunniff!"

"Where the hell are you?"

"I ran up into Walking Dunes in Montauk after I ditched my car."

A pause.

"They were following me, but my car was faster."

"Why there?"

"I'll explain everything when you get here. Just hurry. I figured they'd come for me eventually."

There's a pause, and now just the sound of the wind.

"I'm tired of looking over my shoulder," he says.

"Why should I trust you?"

"Because I know everything you want to know," he says. "But I can't tell you if I'm dead."

ONE HUNDRED TEN

I WAIT FOR JIMMY.

My house, no traffic, is fifteen minutes, tops, from the Walking Dunes, one of the natural wonders of eastern Long Island, maybe the best before land's end. Four parabolic sand dunes, maybe a hundred years old, that have migrated a mile inland over time from the water at Napeague Harbor.

Open to the public during the day, with a nearly one-mile trail of sand and scrub and even a freshwater bog. Steep, sandy hills accessed by narrow paths with a huge drop-off at the first dune, and a spectacular view of the water and Northwest Harbor up top.

The Walking Dunes is an area where I love to take Rip the dog or do a lot of reading. Back in 1921, a production company based in Astoria filmed some of the desert scenes in Rudolph Valentino's classic silent movie *The Sheik* there.

The wind has risen to a howl. I know from experience the way hard winds, if you encounter them here, can funnel through the dunes, creating the feeling of being caught in a sandstorm.

"How do we know this isn't a trap?" Jimmy asks after we've parked at the end of Napeague Harbor Road.

"He could be anywhere," I say. "A million places to hide. If he's here, that's why he's here."

"Makes it a perfect place to ambush somebody," Jimmy says. "We don't know this isn't a setup."

"We don't," I tell him. "But we're both armed and extremely dangerous."

"He said he knows things?"

"And that he can only tell if we save him from the bogeyman. Or men."

"My new pal Len Greene told me he knows things, too."

"How come everybody knows things except us?"

I lead the way up the narrow trail, past the helpful sign that tells you to enjoy the view before you descend into the wind tunnel. Branches occasionally slap against us, a few catching me in the face and making me curse. The wind seems to have picked up even more since we got out of our car. The moon is very bright and high in the sky.

We both have our guns out as we slowly climb and

stumble our way to the top of the first dune, the approach so steep you can put your hand out and touch the sand. You're supposed to stay on the path when you come here in the daytime. I tell Jimmy I won't tell we're breaking the rules if he won't.

I fall a couple of times. So does he. Now we're both cursing quietly.

We finally make it to the top, staying low when we get there.

I know how steep the drop is in front of us, the distance down to an open area of sand always looking to me like it's the length of a football field.

"McKenzie!" I yell. "I'm here."

Underneath the wind, from down below, I hear a voice now.

"Here."

I look at Jimmy. He nods. We circle back to the trail, staying low until we approach the bigger open area of sand and scrub facing north. Something to behold in the daytime, the whole sweep of this place.

Just not tonight.

We still may be walking into a trap. We both know that. But we've come this far.

And maybe McKenzie was telling the truth about the things he can tell me.

"You wanted to talk," I yell. "Show yourself and we can talk."

"Let's talk," a voice from behind us says. "But first let me see you turn around and toss those guns behind you. It will make our conversation much more relaxing."

Jimmy and I slowly turn, and toss our guns into the sand. When we turn around, we're staring at the long revolver held by Anthony Licata.

He touches the top of his head.

"Had to get a new Rangers cap after I died," he says. "Like it?"

ONE HUNDRED ELEVEN

"AND IF YOU'RE THINKING about getting cute and going for your guns," Licata says, "take a look behind you."

A small woman has come up out of the dunes to our left, maybe fifty yards away, maybe closer, pointing her own gun at us. She has to be the one whose voice I heard, unless there's more than just the two of them.

"That's Mei," Licata says.

"I believe we've met," Jimmy says, looking over his shoulder.

"Where's McKenzie?" I ask.

"Probably in a bar someplace by now."

"I thought we were all going to live together in peace," I say.

"We were," Licata says. "But the two of you just would not stop, no matter how many times you got warned."

"I hear somebody still owes my father a favor."

"Unfortunately, that deal is now off the table. I got my orders to end this."

"From Sonny?" Jimmy says.

"That old fool?" Licata sadly shakes his head. "You two still don't know what you don't know."

I'm reviewing our options, limited as they are. Maybe nonexistent. I'm sure Jimmy is doing the same. The clock is running, and it's clear Anthony Licata and the woman didn't just bring us here to talk. But Licata is dragging things out now, maybe just for the fun of it, as if he needs us to know that he's gotten the better of us, and that we both could choke on it.

Ours guns are behind us in the sand. Theirs are pointed at us.

"How'd you survive your boat trip?"

"I never took the boat trip," he says. "Well, my hat did. Does that count? Bobby didn't even notice I left it in the cabin before I wished him bon voyage."

"Who wanted Bobby dead?" Jimmy asks.

"Who didn't?"

Then, just like that, he's tired of talking.

"Enough," he says.

"One more dying request," I say. "You'd grant a girl a dying request, wouldn't you?"

"You never fucking stop talking, do you?"

"I need to know who killed those two families."

He hesitates. I see him nodding, as if ending a conversation with himself.

"Aw, why the hell not," he says. "What does it matter if you know which one of them did it?"

We hear the first shot then, from our right, maybe from the second dune, even if that would be some shot.

The bullet thuds into the sand wall behind Licata.

As Licata tries to find cover, another bullet hits the dune behind him. Out of the corner of my eye I see Mei running toward the second dune, firing in the direction of the shooter.

The next shot from the second dune puts Mei down in the sand, face first.

"Mei!" Licata screams, as if the bullet had hit him and not her.

Then there's another shot fired out of the night, and another. Jimmy and I are flat on the ground then, reaching for our guns. As I roll to my side I make out the figure of someone scrambling into the sand at the bottom of the second dune, stopping just long enough to raise a long gun and fire another shot at Anthony Licata.

Who the hell is that?

I look the other way and see Licata running for cover, sliding down the dune in the direction of the ocean.

Jimmy and I drop to the ground.

"Who's that?" Jimmy asks.

"Dunno — is he on our side?"

"Or wants to take everybody out," Jimmy says, "one by one."

Then he adds "Fuck it" and tells me to go after the shooter.

Then he's on the move in the night, going after Licata to end this once and for all.

ONE HUNDRED TWELVE

TOO MUCH SAND AND slope and distance between the shooter and me. I wait for him to turn and fire at me, but he doesn't, and I can almost make him out as he runs into the woods, heading south, in the general direction of the parking lot.

A man, tall and slender, wearing dark clothes. Maybe black clothes.

Eric Jacobson was dressed in black when he came to my house.

I'm the one sprinting back to where I left Jimmy.

I slide down the dune. I spot Licata moving in a crouch of his own along the thickest woods over there, as if he's after Jimmy now, and not the other way around.

In the light of the moon, I see the blue cap and the glint of Licata's gun.

The only shooter I can worry about in the moment is him.

Licata isn't looking in my direction as I crawl, gun in hand, slowly through the sand in his direction.

Where is Jimmy?

I know I'm finally close enough to take the shot if I want it.

No time to wait for Jimmy, or for Licata to take the first shot if he spots me.

Just Anthony Licata and me now at the bottom of the dunes.

"Drop it, Licata," I shout at him now. "Or I will shoot you dead."

He freezes.

"Okay," he shouts back. "Okay."

I see him turn, slowly raising his hands, until he's facing me.

But as I move toward him, the world begins to spin.

I'm dizzy again, the way chemo makes me dizzy sometimes, the way I was dizzy that night at the restaurant before I fainted.

As I struggle to maintain my balance, I lower my gun to my side.

As my arm drops, Licata raises his and fires.

But I'm already falling as he does.

Going down again.

Just not down and out this time.

I may be dying, but not tonight.

Licata's bullet sails over my head as I hit the ground.

His second shot misses, too, but not by much, the bullet spraying sand against my leg. Then I'm rolling away from that spot, expecting another wave of dizziness as I keep rolling in the sand.

It doesn't come.

I won't let it.

I'm Jane Effing Smith.

I pull out of the roll and am already running for cover, through the scrub, as soon as I have my legs back underneath me.

I'm waiting for Licata to take his next shot when I hear Jimmy.

"Licata!" he yells as he comes out of the trees to my left, from the water side of the dunes.

Licata turns and fires at Jimmy now, sending Jimmy diving for cover.

Licata's the one caught in a crossfire now and he has to make a decision.

Jimmy or me.

He turns back to me.

Too late.

I've stopped running, squared up, and raised my Glock.

Just me and the target now.

Like all those nights on the trail.

Stop, aim, shoot.

I hit Licata high up on his chest and spin him half-way around. He turns back to face me once more and raises his gun for the last time. I hit him again in the chest and he goes down and stays down as Jimmy comes running out of the woods.

Jimmy takes off his own windbreaker as he kneels down next to Licata and tries to stop the bleeding. When I get there and see how much blood there is, I know Jimmy's too late to contain the wound, or the blood. He has to know, too.

So does Anthony Licata.

But he's still looking to deal, all the way to the end.

"Help…" he croaks.

A bubble of blood comes out of his mouth.

"Trying here," Jimmy says grimly, pressing down harder with his windbreaker, now soaked in blood.

"I…can help you…"

"How?" Jimmy asks.

"Proof…"

"What kind of proof, Licata?" I can hear the urgency in Jimmy's voice, both of us knowing Licata is running out of time.

"Insurance…case he ever tried to screw me…"

Licata's eyes are rolling back.

Jimmy leans down closer to him and speaks so softly I can barely make out what he's saying under the wind roaring louder and harder than ever through the Walking Dunes.

"Proof on who?" Jimmy says.

I hear Licata say "The..." His voice trails off. Everything nearly gone now, like his life is spilling out into the dunes along with all the blood.

Then all I can hear Licata saying back to Jimmy is this:

"Who."

Jimmy leans down close to Licata now and I can see Licata trying to say something more, but nothing comes out, and then his head falls back and his eyes close and he's still.

"Shit," Jimmy says.

He sits down next to Licata, still holding his gun. I step away and make the call to 911 on my phone. Maybe ten minutes later, we hear the first sirens in the distance.

We're still sitting there when we hear Licata's phone.

While Jimmy goes into the side pocket of Licata's down vest for the phone, I walk back to where the woman, Mei, was shot.

But she's disappeared.

ONE HUNDRED THIRTEEN

Jimmy

THEY DON'T FINISH WITH the town police and the county police until it's past four in the morning. Jane and Jimmy drive into East Hampton after that to formally give their statements. Chief Larry Calabrese is waiting for them. Jimmy tells Calabrese what he needs when he and Jane are finished.

Calabrese says he'll do his best.

Jimmy doesn't tell him about the phone but promises Jane he'll hand it over to the police later.

Jane drives Jimmy back to her house. Jimmy gets into his car and heads back home to Sag Harbor and wakes up Detective Craig Jackson. Craig Jackson: who has turned into the kind of wingman that Mickey Dunne was. Another old dog with a bone.

Jackson and Jimmy commence working the phones, starting with Anthony Licata's burner. Jackson says he's going to wake some people up, screw 'em, this shit matters to him now, too, and get as many phone logs as he can, both numbers, at this time of the morning.

At seven thirty, time to put a bow on this before word of the shootings gets out, so Jimmy drives over there.

He's clearly shocked to see Jimmy standing there when he opens the front door, looking as if Jimmy woke him up. But then he told Jimmy he likes to sleep late.

Jimmy uses the same raspy voice he'd used when he answered Licata's phone at the Walking Dunes, and had done a damn good impression of Anthony Licata, if he did say so himself, his voice muffled just enough by the wind and bad cell service out there.

"You asked me over the phone if it was done," Jimmy says to retired lieutenant Paul Harrington. "Well, you are."

Harrington opens his mouth and closes it.

It's a caught look that Jimmy knows well. A look that all cops know. Harrington has just never been behind it, until now.

"You probably wondered why he had the call on speaker," Jimmy says. "But when I saw it was you calling him to ask if Janie and me were dead, I wanted her to hear it too, her being an officer of the court and all."

"I have no idea what you're talking about," Harrington says.

Harrington's not moving. Neither is Jimmy. Harrington's wearing sweatpants and a T-shirt. Nowhere to put a gun. But Jimmy's is handy if he needs it.

"Funny thing," Jimmy says. "Before Licata died, Jane thought he said 'Who,' when I asked who sent him. But that's not what I heard. I heard him say 'Lieu.' Rhymes with you. What you said he used to call you. And probably still did, since he was still working for you, you sonofabitch."

Harrington tries to shut the door now. Jimmy is already through it, shoving Harrington back into the foyer with both hands, knocking him sideways into a small antique table against the wall, as pretty as his flowers. Then Jimmy has his gun on him, just in case.

The guy was a cop once, if maybe the dirtiest one of all.

Jimmy uses his free hand to take out Licata's burner phone.

"You've been out of the game too long," Jimmy says to him. "Phones like this have memories, too."

"I'm not saying another word," Harrington says. "You only have what you think you have."

"I have a call that we'll prove came from your phone and that I answered," Jimmy says. "One that Jane Smith heard. The aforementioned officer of the court. 'Is it done?' you say. And I say, 'You mean, did I kill them?' And you say, 'Of course that's what I mean, what the hell did you think I sent you there to do?' She figures we got your ass. Accessory to attempted murder, conspiracy. The state cops have probably already gotten a judge to sign off on an arrest warrant."

"Good luck with that," Harrington says. "You need to tie a rock to this shit before it floats away."

Jimmy watches Harrington give a little shrug to his shoulders now, straightening, like a boxer Jimmy has hit with a straight right hand in the old days, trying to gather himself even after his bell has been rung.

"Licata could barely talk at the end," Jimmy says. "But he said he had proof. And you know what the cops found on his laptop, not even password protected? Some of the phone calls he taped with you over the years. The insurance policy he talked about before he closed his eyes for good. No honor among thieves, am I right, Lieu?"

Harrington doesn't acknowledge what Jimmy just said. He's smiling to himself now, nodding, as if there's no problem here, he's still in charge.

"You know what I think?" Harrington says.

"That you're screwed about twelve ways to Sunday?"

"I think that if you're not going to use that gun, get the hell out of my house," Harrington says.

"Have it your way."

"You're not a cop anymore, Cunniff," Harrington says. "You can't arrest me."

The door opens then and Danny Esposito comes walking in, warrant in one hand, handcuffs in the other.

"I can," he says, and then starts reading the former commander of detectives, 24th Precinct, his rights.

ONE HUNDRED FOURTEEN

"WE'VE ALREADY GOT PEOPLE doing one of those deep dive things into his phone records," Danny Esposito says. "His dead wife didn't pay for that house. But I got this funny feeling Sonny Blum might have."

"Lot of calls on Harrington's phone to Sonny's house," Jimmy says. "Turns out that Sonny isn't just old. He's old school. Still uses a landline."

The three of us are at a table at Jimmy's bar on Tuesday night, the night before jury selection begins. Lieutenant Paul Harrington is in custody at the same jail in Riverhead that once housed Rob Jacobson.

"The way I see it laying out," Jimmy says, "is that Sonny had Harrington in his pocket, all the way back. He worked for Sonny, and Licata and Champi worked for him. The rich guys called Harrington first, not them."

Jimmy goes quiet now. I see him staring at the

Yankee game on the TV set over the bar, but don't think he's looking at baseball.

"What?"

"There's still too much we don't know," he says.

He turns to face me. Even in his bar, I imagine a shadow having fallen across his face.

"I gotta ask again: Who *was* the shooter in the dunes?"

"Maybe somebody who didn't want Licata to tell us who killed those two families. Maybe McKenzie hung around. Maybe it was Eric Jacobson or Morelli."

"I need to know," Jimmy says to me.

"And where's our friend Mei?"

"Out there," Jimmy says. "We gotta find her, too."

"We've got time."

He turns to me and smiles. It's as if the shadow leaves his face, that quickly. In that moment, I remember just how much I love him.

Jimmy reaches across the table and covers my hand with one of his old, crooked boxer's hands.

"All the time in the world," he says.

We all leave early. I get to bed early for a change, feeling as if tomorrow is my equivalent of the first day of school.

When I'm up and showered and I've done my face and hair—still hanging in there, God bless it—I get into the new sincerity suit I've purchased for today's appearance in court.

And before I even make myself a cup of coffee, I stand in the middle of my kitchen, ridiculously excited. Feel the thrill of it all, all over again, even if all I will be doing today is interviewing prospective jurors. Asking them questions before Kevin Ahearn and I get to all the questions the trial will answer, the ones I need to answer for myself, and about my client, about who murdered the Carsons of Garden City if he didn't.

And if he didn't, who wanted it to look like he did.

Murder, I think, and can't help myself from smiling.

Still the main event.

And I'm going to be in the middle of it, again, in the middle of the effing action. Nobody killed me in the dunes. Now here I am, feeling this alive again, because I am on my way to court. I'm always talking and thinking about the juice being pumped into me while I do chemo, the juice that's trying to keep me alive.

But what I'm feeling now, as I stand in my kitchen, *this* is the juice making me *feel* alive.

When I finally do make myself the one cup of coffee I'm allowing myself before I get into the car, I walk over to the kitchen window and take a look outside.

I see the hummingbird then.

About the Authors

JAMES PATTERSON is the most popular storyteller of our time. He is the creator of unforgettable characters and series, including Alex Cross, the Women's Murder Club, Jane Smith, and Maximum Ride, and of breathtaking true stories about the Kennedys, John Lennon, and Tiger Woods, as well as our military heroes, police officers, and ER nurses. Patterson has coauthored #1 bestselling novels with Bill Clinton and Dolly Parton, and collaborated most recently with Michael Crichton on the blockbuster *Eruption*. He has told the story of his own life in *James Patterson by James Patterson* and received an Edgar Award, ten Emmy Awards, the Literarian Award from the National Book Foundation, and the National Humanities Medal.

MIKE LUPICA is a veteran sports columnist—spending most of his career with the *New York Daily News*—who is now a member of the National Sports

Media Association Hall of Fame. For three decades, he was a panelist on ESPN's *The Sports Reporters*. As a novelist, he has written seventeen *New York Times* best-sellers, the most recent of which is *The Horsewoman,* his first collaboration with James Patterson.

For a complete list of books by

JAMES PATTERSON

VISIT
JamesPatterson.com

 Follow James Patterson on Facebook
@JamesPatterson

 Follow James Patterson on X
𝕏 **@JP_Books**

 Follow James Patterson on Instagram
@jamespattersonbooks